For Doodies and Fifi

I still think you were crazy for trading California sun for Toronto snow and taking me with you... but I'm glad you did. Becoming a temporary Canadian was pretty awesome.

Head over Skates

GIGI BLUME

SODASAC PRESS
PUBLISHING HOUSE

SODASAC
PRESS

FIRST EDITION

Library of Congress Cataloging-in-Publication Data has been applied for.

ISBN: 979-8-9861828-8-9

Cover design and illustrations by Once Upon a Cover

Head over Skates

"Half the game is mental;
the other half is being mental."
– Jim McKenny

MPONI

CHAPTER ONE

Owen

There's nothing like the sound of the first few strides as my blades hit the ice. The smell of early morning, freshly smoothed sheet. The crisp, crunchy sound of my skates running across the glassy surface, echoing throughout the rink. The otherwise quiet solitude, alone in the arena long before my teammates arrive for morning skate.

This is what I need on game days. To erase the tension in my life outside this arena. To breathe in the silence. To be blessedly alone on the ice, even if only for a short while.

Except... I'm not alone. Mine aren't the first tracks on the ice. I know these tracks aren't from last night, because I was one of the last to leave. Other than the junior Zamboni driver. That tiny woman with honey-blonde hair, who reminds me more of a stray kitten than an ice technician. When she's not wearing a beanie low on her head, hair pokes out of her high bun in all directions. And those whiskey-colored eyes, big and round. Just like that sad yellow kitty I found behind the dumpster when I was a kid. My parents didn't let me keep it, though.

I've spoken to the Zamboni driver once, only once. Okay, it was more of a passing grunt when the other guys were giving her post-game high-fives. She took one look at my hand, hanging aloof at my side, gave me a cursory once-over, and popped her ear-buds in—shutting me out. To clarify, I was having a rotten day and just needed to get away from people before my chest caved in on me. Sometimes, just a little space will keep me from feeling out of control. Hence—my early morning solo skate.

Ever since that day, I hardly glance her way when she whirls onto the ice—that unruly bun barely visible over the massive snow tank of the resurfacer machine. I try not to stare at those pink cheeks and that slight upturned nose when the fans cheer for her just as much as they do the players. The way her little lips curl at the corners right before she dips her chin down to feign embarrassment.

Sometimes I wonder why she wears beanie caps or covers half her face with a scarf. Sometimes she hides under a baseball hat. But she always, *always* wears skin-tight black leggings, clinging to her fit, freakishly small form.

Last night, I could hear her cheerily saying good-night to the arena manager and security team right after she'd cut the ice for the evening. Lights clanked off, and no one crossed past the boards after that.

That's how I know I'm not the first on the ice this morning. The trails are light—barely visible. But they're there.

I close my eyes and take a deep, cool breath.

It's fine. Whoever it was is gone now, and I can still clear my head. If I don't get in this time alone on the ice, tonight's game will suffer. Focus. Mindset is key.

I unclench my fists and continue my ritual. Crossovers. Edge work. Pivots and turns. At this moment, right now... the ice is mine and mine alone.

But then I see movement from the corner of my eye. A streak of powder blue darting behind the player benches. And when I turn, it's gone. Moments later, a heavy door clangs in the bowels of the building. I come to an abrupt stop, spraying ice shavings everywhere.

What the heck? Who else would be here this early in

the morning? Only the day security manager who let me in. But he always stays at his post, guarding the rear entrance.

Again, I try to ignore the distraction. I don't own this arena. I'm not entitled to my privacy. I'm just a little—ya know—prickly when I don't get it, that's all.

After about fifteen minutes of too many thoughts cluttering up my head, I decide to hit the gym. I lift for over an hour, then steam off in the sauna before the rest of the team starts to trickle in. The heat is a calming contrast to the chill of the ice from earlier. By this time, I'm back at baseline, ready to go. It wasn't an ideal morning, but I made due.

Sawyer, one of my wingers and best friend, wanders into the video room with that look about him. I can tell by the slight tinge under his eyes that he went out last night. Probably hooked up with some chick, drank too much, and didn't get all the sleep he needed. He's a stand-up guy, he really is. But he makes crappy choices. If we lose tonight, I'm gonna have strong words for him.

"You look like crap," I say, half serious. "Pull yourself together before Coach sees you."

He flops into the plush leather theater seat next to me. "I'm fine," he grumbles, and pulls his cap further over his eyes, lazily sliding his butt to the edge of the seat.

The Toronto Titans are killing it this season. Mostly due to the extreme discipline Coach Knight expects of us on and off the ice.

So game day prep? It's a whole ritual, starting a day or even a couple before, depending on how big the showdown is gonna be. We hit the ice for practices and drills, get in those workouts, all that jazz. Gotta load up on veggies, loads of protein, and slow carbs the day before - that's like the magic formula. Helps us bounce back from all the body-busting stuff and keeps our immune game strong.

Some guys hit the books or the screen after dinner, to try to clear their minds. Me? I'm into strategizing, sizing up the competition, getting in that headspace.

Everyone's got their thing on pre-game day. But sleep? That's not up for debate. It's the MVP of recovery and performance. Gotta nail that shut-eye, no excuses. Make sure that rest is on point!

But Sawyer. He thinks he's invincible. One day, that devil-may-care attitude is gonna come back to bite him where the sun don't shine.

"Just make sure you get some sleep this afternoon, okay? And drink some water."

He gives me the side-eye, about to say something snarky. But then his lip curls and he slaps my knee. "I got this, Jablonski. I even brushed and flossed this morning, too."

"Yeah, well you forgot deodorant. And get your paw off me before we show up in the gossip column."

"Too late," says a voice behind me. Griffin, the best goaltender I've ever known, slides over and takes the seat on my other side, nudging me with his elbow. He's too bright-eyed and bushy-tailed for his own good, and smiles so much, it gives me a headache.

"Turn it down a few notches, bro," I say to him. "You've got all day."

Taking out his phone, he clicks through to a social media post, showing a photo of me, Sawyer, and my other winger, Hendrix walking into the arena together in our game day suits. The caption reads:

Toronto Titans' Preening Pucks

I snort. "Click-bait."

But Griffin chuckles deep in his throat, clicking through to the article. It's a blog with lots of hockey-related ads littered among the main text.

And there we are. Sawyer, Hendrix, and me. Not just the one picture. But several.

Griffin reads an excerpt from the article using an over-the-top newscaster's voice.

"The ice in Toronto isn't the only thing heating up this season as the city's beloved hockey heroes, the Toronto Titans, find themselves making headlines for more than just their on-ice prowess. While the team boasts an impressive roster, it's the trio of star players—Owen 'Juggernaut' Jablonski, Sawyer 'Bonecrusher' O'Malley, and Hendrix 'Enforcer' Ellis—that have tongues wagging for all the wrong reasons."

Griffin pauses to glance at me, wiggling his brows, then continues to read.

"While their skills on the ice have never been in

question, recent rumors suggest that their off-ice antics might be affecting their game. The trio, often seen frequenting the city's hottest spots, have been drawing attention for their extravagant peacocking in front of the fairer sex."

"Peacocking?" Sawyer snorts.

Griffin clears his throat. "One die-hard Titans fan, who wished to remain anonymous, expressed concern, stating, 'I love watching them play, but sometimes it feels like they're more focused on scoring dates than scoring goals.' As the hockey season progresses, all eyes will be on Jablonski, O'Malley, and Ellis to see if their off-ice distractions impact their on-ice performance. Will these preening pucks redirect their focus to the game, or will their extracurricular activities continue to steal the spotlight?"

"What, nothing about you?" I say to Griffin. "The Titans' golden boy?"

He just shrugs. "I'm not interesting enough, I guess."

"That's because sex sells," growls Sawyer, provoking Griffin to steal his hat. "Hey!"

As if summoned by the fertility fairies, Hendrix pops in out of nowhere, taking the seat next to Sawyer.

"Are we talking about my favorite subject?" he chirps, smacking Sawyer in the back of the head.

"It's just a stupid blog," I say, poking Griffin's armpit, giving Sawyer the chance to steal back his hat. This turns into a ridiculous game of tug of war over my head, the two of them pulling on the hat, Sawyer kicking his leg over my lap to gain an advantage. I curl my knees up and try to shield myself from the two of them, squeezing my eyes shut. It's all in good fun, but these guys can act like pre-teen boys sometimes.

"Do I need to separate you three or do you need the room?"

I open my eyes to find Coach Knight looming before us, crossing his arms with that look on his face. The look of a fed-up dad who can't wait to send his kids back to school after being stuck inside with them all winter break.

He's shaking his head at us now. "Save the energy for the ice, boys."

Hendrix is laughing his face off. "What did I miss?"

"Nothing, according to this," I say, plucking Griffin's phone from his fingers and passing it to Hendrix. Of course, the phone screen had blacked out by now, leaving Hendrix even more confused.

"Some blogger trying to get clicks," Sawyer says, finally getting his hat back. He slides the bill over his eyes and slumps back into his previous lazy position.

"Nobody reads those things," I say dismissively. "It's not like it's CSBN."

Griffin takes back his phone to unlock it, finding his way back to the original social media post.

"This post alone got over six-hundred thousand likes," he says, showing us the screen. "And it's only a few hours old."

I scoff, reading the account name. "Blades After Dark? Is this a joke?"

Coach chuckles, nodding knowingly. "Hah. That one."

"You've seen this?" Griffin asks incredulously.

Coach shrugs. "Yeah. The writer always posts after midnight. It's kind of his trademark."

Hendrix steals the phone to read the article he missed out on.

"It's complete BS," I say.

Coach gives me a dry look. "Yeah. So?"

"So?" I practically stutter. "I haven't so much as eaten out in months. That's defamation of character."

I work hard, keep to myself, and stay out of trouble... well at least off the ice. My reputation as a serious athlete means a lot to me.

He half laughs. "Don't pay the press any mind. Come on, now. It's time to start."

He turns toward the front of the room and claps his hands as loud as thunder. By this time, the whole team is assembled, facing the smart screen where Coach will go over strategy for tonight's game and play videos to highlight tendencies of our opponent and how we can exploit them.

Cue evil laugh.

But I can't shake the feeling I've had since I arrived this morning. I just feel... off today. Like my skin is a little too tight, or as though I put my shirt on backwards.

The feeling follows me all day. During my off-ice

stick handling and shooting drills, after lunch, when I go home for my pre-game nap, and especially when I get back to the arena wearing my game day suit.

My eyes are everywhere, searching for fans with cameras, or looking up at the security installments. That blog had images from all sorts of angles. When did they get those pictures?

And I don't know why it bothers me so much, but I can't shake it. I've never cared about the press. But for some reason, that blog post hit differently. Because it wasn't about hockey. It painted me as something I'm not. And I guess, after how hard I've worked to get where I am, someone can just come along and write whatever the heck they want, even though they know they're full of it.

The thought of it stews in me all night. So much that I get thrown into the sin bin more than once.

I'm just not in the zone tonight, which is good news for the Seattle Sea Lions.

Sawyer and Hendrix are on the first line with me. The power players. Fans and press fondly nicknamed our trio *The Killers* because we're so shrewd on the ice. A game against a low-ranking team like the Sea Lions usually ends in complete slaughter. But tonight, even the fourth line plays a better game than us.

Oh, we'll still win, but barely.

When the Sea Lions score their one and only goal, they're so stunned and overly excited, they stop and stare at each other for a full ten seconds. And although sound doesn't carry well from beyond the boards, I swear I hear a little *whoop whoop* behind the Zamboni door. And when I chance a glance, I spot a certain little kitty cat with a powder blue beanie, pumping her fists in the air.

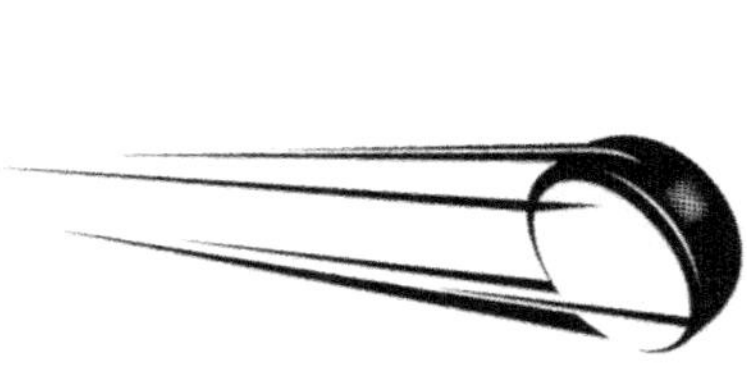

"To be the world's best,
you have to beat the world's best."
- Dorothy Hamill

MPONI

CHAPTER TWO

Emily

His head whirls over his shoulder and those icicle eyes burn into me with a fury. Did Owen Jablonski actually acknowledge my presence? Not that I want his attention. Especially after I just cheered for the other team. But I can't help it. I love rooting for the underdogs. They were over the moon to score a goal. It was so cute.

And who does Owen think he is, anyway? Star

center. Team captain. Nice butt. Blah blah blah. He might be a fine drink of water, but his grouchy temperament isn't doing him any favors.

So I lift my chin and hold his stare, narrowing my eyes with a wicked smirk.

Yes, sir. I did hoot for the Sea Lions.

My eyebrows lift in challenge and he spins a quarter turn to face me fully.

But then something glorious happens.

For the one-point-five seconds he takes his focus from the game, a streak of pink flies over the plexiglass and smacks him squarely on the side of his face, sliding onto his collar. It takes him a second to realize, but when he does, there's a furrow in his brow as he lifts the tiny, lacy garment. But with those bulky gloves on, he loses grip, and the garment falls flatly to the ice, landing in a tiny, hot pink triangle.

I. Can't. Even.

This is just too good. I only wish I had my camera. Two young women are plastered against the glass, screaming like they're at a rock concert. They are one hundred percent focused on the players and not the sport. The kind of puck bunnies that arrive early just to watch the guys do their on-ice stretches. I'd bet they wouldn't even be able to tell you the rules of the game if pressured under pain of death.

Personally, I don't condone objectifying any person. And let's be honest, if a man were to throw his tighty whities at a professional female athlete, we'd be all up in arms about it. So why is it cute or silly when the genders are reversed? It's not. But I laugh anyway...

Because Owen "Juggernaut" (or as I like to call him —"Junk-for-nuts") Jablonski deserves it. I am so going to have fun writing about this in my blog tonight.

When I started *Blades After Dark,* I never thought anyone would read it, but now that it's taken off like wildfire, I have an obligation to come up with good content. Not to mention the few sponsors who pay to run their ads on the sidebar.

A whistle sounds and a ref picks up the panties, just being casual about it. Owen heads back to the bench as the second line takes the ice. These guys are good, and the Titans will win tonight thanks to them. The first line forwards, the trio who some call *The Killers,* have been off lately. There's Sawyer "Bonecrusher" O'Malley, who's the playboyest player that ever played. And I'm not talking about hockey, here. To put it plainly, he's a party animal. I'm still trying to track down some of his one-night stands for interviews. No luck so far.

Then there's Hendrix "Enforcer" Ellis. He's the least controversial of the three, but I'm pretty sure it's only because he covers his tracks well, and I don't care to dig too much.

But Owen, he's a slippery one. He'd like to come off as Canada's golden boy, but I know his true colors.

What he did to my friend Jaime, for starters. And while I respect her privacy too much to tell her story publicly, I can use my platform to at least prevent other women from falling into Owen's den of lies.

I take my little notebook from my pocket to scribble down a few lines for tonight's blog post. If I don't write it down now, I'll forget later when I'm staring at a blank screen. I can't live without this thing. The best dollar store purchase I ever made. Bonus love for my fuzzy pen. Also a dollar store deal.

At the end of my shift, I'm so distracted writing notes for the blog that I don't realize the arena is silent (the way I like it) until I'm relatively alone. I jot some ideas in my notebook. Then, after inspecting the ice, I stick around a little longer to make sure everything is ready for tomorrow's game. The crowd is long gone, and the players' dressing rooms have gone quiet. It's just me, my manager, Joe, and the security team. It's late and I'm tired, but I'm not about to go outside without my beanie hat. I took it off before I cleaned the augers, and now it's not where I put it.

"Hey Joe," I say. "Have you seen my hat?"

"No, but Emily," he says, holding out my notebook and fuzzy pen. "Found this on the resurfacer seat. Try not to leave personal items on the equipment."

Oh, snap. I only hope he didn't see what's inside. If he did, I'm toast. And probably fired.

"Uh, thanks. I promise it won't happen again."

He must notice the sheer embarrassment on my face because he said, "I didn't read your diary, if that's what you're worried about. We're allowed to bring something to do for breaks and downtime. It's a safety issue to leave it on the Zamboni, that's all."

"Got it, boss." I salute him and sling my skates over my shoulder by the laces, heading out to do one more sweep for my beanie. I'm looking in all the little crevices where it might have fallen, even in the bathroom. But it's nowhere to be found. If only the souvenir shop were open, I could buy a beanie with the team logo on it. Not really my style, but who cares in the freezing Toronto night? The cold air burns after a mile or two walking home. I guess I'm going to have to rough it.

I head to the service exit, digging in my bag for my earbuds, when I crash into a brick wall.

A nice smelling brick wall.

I'm basically face to face with the broadest chest I've ever seen this close up. Okay, as a former figure skater, I've gotten up close and personal with my partner's chest (among other body parts), but he had a dancer's body. All lean muscle and lithe form. Not to mention, looking at Pierre did nothing for me. This man... this hockey player. He's almost another species. This proximity to him triggers a complex reaction in my body, like all my muscles are on fire but also loose and floppy at the same time.

When I look up, Owen's icy blue eyes are fixed on me like he's about to slash me to bits and hide my body in Lake Ontario. But his mouth. Oh, lawdy. That teasing mouth is curled into a devilish grin.

"Looking for this?" he says, holding my beanie with his forefinger.

I gulp. By the way he's holding it, one would think it's just as scandalous as those pink undies from earlier. And then a thought slams into me. What if he's trying to get with me? What if this is one of his womanizing tricks? Cornering me in an empty hallway like I'm low-hanging fruit.

Not today, mister. Not any day, actually. Sisters before misters.

But I lift my chin, not giving him the slightest satisfaction, and hold the high ground in this situation.

"Yes," I say, voice barely wobbling. "As a matter of fact, I was. Thank you for finding it for me."

This, folks, is the longest conversation I've had with the man in the six months I've worked here. The only conversation, really. And it's also the only time I've been so close I can smell his soap. It's lemony and herby, with a hint of pine. How does a man who sweats for a living smell so good? Then I remember there are showers here. THERE ARE SHOWERS HERE. I will myself not to visualize this man showering under the same roof as me while I do my work.

Yes, I am possibly insane. I blame the soap.

I reach for my beanie, but he lifts it higher, out of reach. I hop from my tippy toes, which is easy for me with these figure skater calves, but he's so tall, I can't get at my hat.

"Can I please have my hat now?" I say, lacing my tone with an edge of irritation.

He doesn't merit my request with an answer. He only smirks and lets his gaze drift to the skates hanging over my shoulder.

He hooks the finger of his free hand through the blade. "It was you, wasn't it?"

"What are you talking about?"

"This morning. There were tracks on the ice. It was you."

"Yeah. So? We're allowed to free skate during off hours."

Something twinkles in his eyes, like frost is crystalizing in them even more. All the warm fuzzies I was getting from his soap smell is gone, replaced by a shiver up my spine.

Then, as if he suddenly realizes how close he's standing, he takes a step back with a jerk. He's still holding my beanie, but it's close to that broad chest now.

"What's your name?"

"Emily."

"I heard you cheering for Seattle... Emily. Why?"

"Is it a crime to cheer for the other team?"

"No. Just curious."

"Well, I'm curious about when you'll hand over my hat so I can go home and..."

I almost said write. As in writing my blog post.

"Go home and what?"

"Sleep." And seeing something shift in his features, I add. "Alone. I s-s-s-sleep alone."

Gah! Why am I this way? If I was smart, I'd tell him I had a seven-foot-four boyfriend who could whoop him six ways from Sunday without even trying. Said imaginary boyfriend is waiting for me outside. Said boyfriend gets really jealous. Said boyfriend *knows* what Owen did to my gal, Jaime. How Jaime cried for days. Unconsolable.

But, alas, there is no such boyfriend. And I'm a terrible fibber, anyway.

Owen tilts his head to study me. It's like he's trying to figure me out. Or maybe he's wondering if I'm from another planet.

"Are you planning on using the rink tomorrow morning?"

Why does he even care? I know he comes in earlier than the rest of the team to use the rink. I made sure to get off the ice before he arrived this morning. Does he seriously expect to have a fresh sheet all to himself?

So typical for a guy like him. It makes me want to scream and skate all over his ruggedly handsome face. UGH.

Instead, I bat my eyes and lay on the sugary sweet voice I had to use for the press back in my Olympic days. Times when I was so tired and emotionally spent, but still had to put on a happy face for the camera.

"Hmm, I don't know," I say. "I *might* want to skate in the morning. I'll have to see how I feel."

His nostrils flare and I know I've got him.

"But if I don't get my hat back in three seconds, I can't be responsible if I lose track of time on the ice."

He holds my gaze, face frozen solid, like an ice sculpture. Then, pressing his lips together, he shoves the beanie at me and tromps away. I should feel proud of the way I stood up to him. But instead, that muscle-floppy-fire is making me acutely aware of my giant boyfriend-less existence.

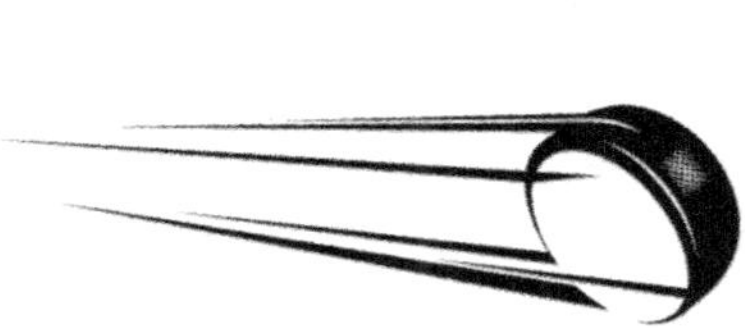

"Great moments are born
from great opportunities."
– Herb Brooks

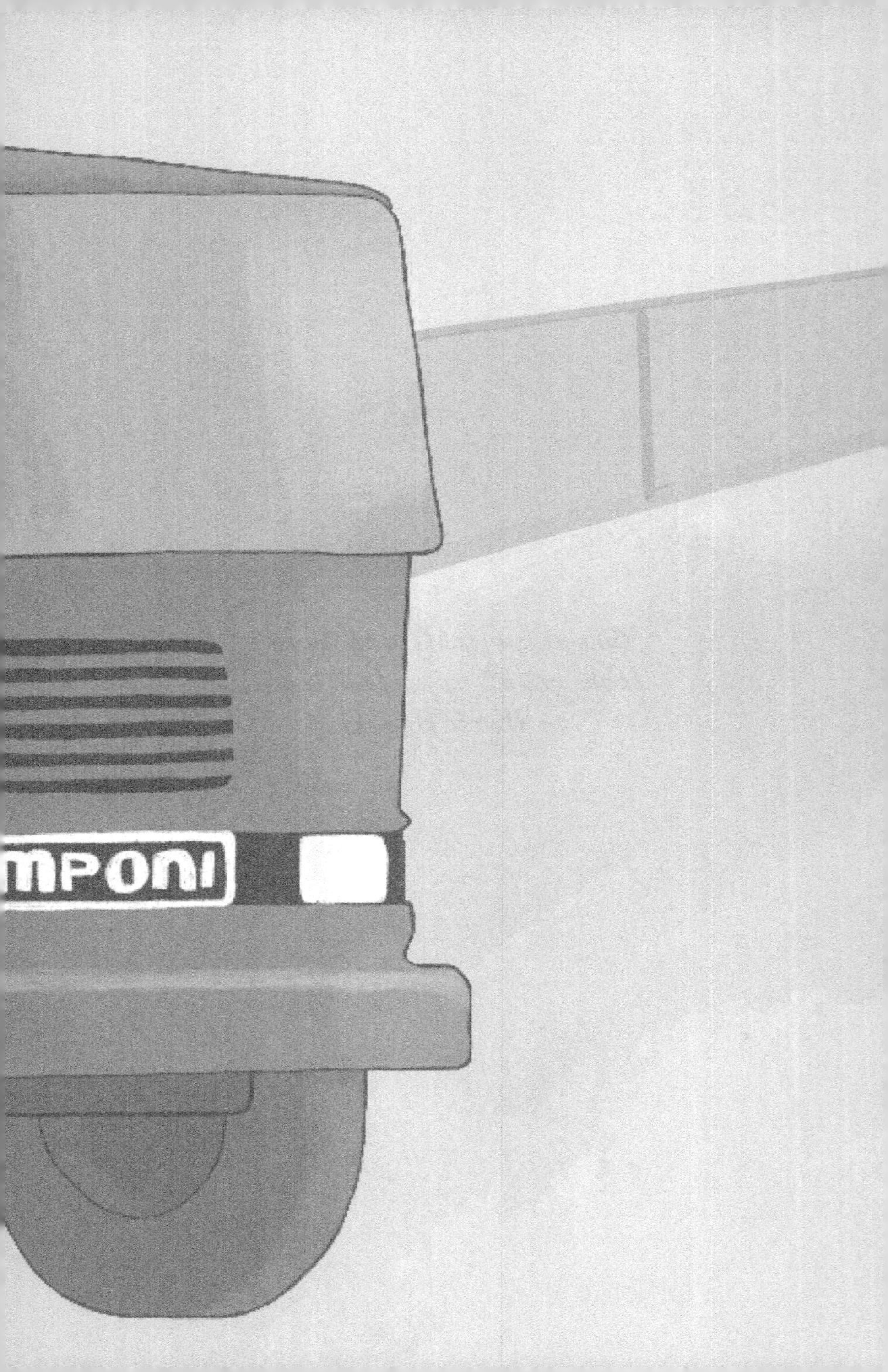
mPOnI

CHAPTER THREE

Owen

The principal at John G. Simcoe Elementary is talking—scratch that—*lecturing*, but I don't hear a word she says. Whatever trouble my little brother, Cyrus, got into, I'll get the whole story from him later. Currently, the other nine-year-old boy in question, some punk-faced bully, no doubt, sits next to his snooty mom, shooting Cyrus a nasty look that says, "I'll get out of this unscathed, unlike you, dork."

I've been in Cyrus' seat. Years ago in an office much like this one. But I deserved it. I was an angry kid. But Cyrus isn't like me—although I sometimes wonder if he's trying too hard to remedy that.

"I'm concerned about the influences Cyrus is getting at home, Mr. Jablonski," says the principal.

Her desk plaque says her name is Ms. Burk. Not Miss. Not Mrs. She's middle-aged, dressed in a sensible business ensemble, and has twin wrinkles between the eyebrows—presumably from scowling at children all day.

"Your... profession," she continues. "And the media..."

I look at Cyrus, hunched over, staring at his shoes. Laces dangling in sad, droopy lines. The hem of his jeans is a little muddied. He's kind of a ragamuffin. But I love every inch of that kid. Even if he has a different mother than me.

"This is the second fight he's gotten into this year, Mr. Jablonski. And his teachers report he's uncooperative in class."

I don't want to be one of those guardians who think their kid can do no wrong and assume the teachers just don't *"understand"* his genius. But in this case, I'm certain Cyrus is being labeled the lost cause, and he's not getting the education he deserves. He's smart and shy and really sensitive. Also, a little disorganized. Yes, the inside of his backpack is scary. One time I found Cheeto dust, an old stick of gum oozing out of the wrapper, a banana peel, and a dirty sock. I will never put my hand in there again without nylon gloves. But he's a good kid. And whatever he did to that brat sitting at the other end of Ms. Burk's desk, I'm sure he was provoked.

"Where is Mrs. Jablonski anyway?" says the kid's mom. She scans her eyes down my body, then back up again to meet my glare.

"There is no Mrs. Jablonski," I say.

But she already knows this. She knows Cyrus is my brother, not my kid. And that his single mother, who never took my father's name, works two jobs.

"My brother's mom couldn't get away from work," I continue. "You're going to have to settle for me."

She twitches a perfectly sculpted eyebrow and turns to address Ms. Burk. "Clearly, the boy has issues. I'm just glad this has been brought to my attention."

"Maybe you should turn your attention to teaching your kid to pick on someone his own size," I snap.

She gasps and practically jumps on Ms. Burk's desk. "See? This is what I'm talking about. No manners. What do you expect from someone that beats up grown men for a living?"

I stand up from my chair, letting it screech on the hardwood floor. "What I do for a living is none of your concern."

She cowers as if I'd do anything to actually hurt her. Cyrus, still hunched in his seat, lifts his chin, eyes wide.

"Mr. Jablonski, please sit down," cries Ms. Burk. "We have an issue on our hands and this is not helping."

I point a finger at her. "You know what's not helping? This meeting. Come on, Cyrus. We're leaving."

"Mr. Jablonski, I must insist—"

"No," I say, towering over both women with my full six-foot-three height. "You don't get to gang up on me and my brother, placing all the blame on him for what clearly was an unfair fight."

The mom is absolutely scandalized now, and hangs her mouth open like a fish. She makes this scoffing sound at the back of her throat. If she were wearing pearls, she'd be clutching them. Meanwhile, Ms. Burk's eyebrow wrinkles are forming a trench, and if she pressed her lips together any tighter, they'd crack.

"Let's go, Cyrus." I reach out to help him with his backpack. It's surprisingly heavy. He slides off the chair and shuffles along with me as we get the heck out of that horrible office. One more minute in there and I would have hyperventilated.

I hear Ms. Burk call after me even as I stride down the hallway. "I will have to schedule another meeting before Cyrus is allowed back in classes, Mr. Jablonski."

Once we turn a corner, I slow down and stop to check on Cyrus. His cheeks are stained with tear tracks, and he's got a bruise on his jaw. I crouch down to tie his shoes.

"You okay, little man?

He nods. Sniffing.

"Want to go get some ice cream?"

A small laugh escapes his lips. "It's two degrees outside."

"How about one of those killer donuts at Tim Hortons?"

"Am I... am I expelled?"

I finish the double knot and tap on his shoe. "Nah. We're just taking a little break. We'll gorge ourselves on donuts and maybe pick up a pizza on the way home."

"Can I stay with you tonight?"

"I'll have to talk to your mom about that, okay?"

I take his hand and lead him down the street to the Tim Hortons, that's blessedly not too busy for this time of day. Just after the lunch rush, and just before the afternoon coffee crowd.

I don't eat sweets during game season, but I order myself a coffee and treat Cyrus to two donuts. One for now and one for later.

He digs in, getting icing on his cheeks and milk on his upper lip. After a long while, he seems better than earlier. I hand him a napkin before he wipes his sleeve across his face.

"If you don't want to talk about it, that's okay," I say tentatively. "But at some point, I'd like to hear your side of the story. And I'm sure your mom will, too."

My heart breaks for the kid. I was sixteen when we found out my dad had another family. Shannon, Cyrus' mom, knocked on my mother's door, visibly pregnant, looking for my old man one night. I'll never forget it, partly because it was a few days before my sixteenth birthday and Dad said he couldn't celebrate with me since he had business in Calgary. Turns out, there were two other women there, unaware of Shannon. Unaware of me and Mom. One of those women has a daughter who might be my sister, but doesn't want anything to do with us. I'm not even sure the little girl knows we exist.

Cyrus shifts his eyes side to side, maybe embarrassed to talk about getting into a fight today. But if there's anyone he can talk to, it's me. I'm the only one who won't judge him or lecture him.

"Seth and two other guys cornered me in the bathroom," he says with a sigh. "I thought they were gonna beat me up."

"Did they?"

"I was just trying to wash my hands. But they kept coming at me, like they were trying to back me up into one of the stalls. And I panicked."

"That kid in the office. Was that Seth?"

"Yeah."

"I saw a cut on his forehead. Did you do that?"

I love my brother, but he's a little scrawny. If he took a swing at that brawny kid and gave him a cut like that, I don't want to admit I'd be proud, but I am. A little. But I dare not let Cyrus know that.

"I… I swung my backpack at him. And he fell and hit his head on the hand dryer."

"Did you know hand dryers blow fecal bacteria onto your hands? You're better off letting them drip dry."

His mouth curls sideways, like he's trying not to laugh.

"I call them poop blowers."

"Ewww!" he says, sticking out his tongue.

"So this Seth guy hit his head on the poop blower. Then what happened? How'd you get that shiner?"

I gesture to the bruise on his jaw.

"One of the kids punched me and ran off. Then the other guy went and tattled to the teacher."

"Let me guess. Poop-head Seth played the victim."

"Pretty much, yeah."

I nod my head, understanding all too well how mean kids can be, especially when they find someone smaller than them to pick on.

"Ms. Burk said this is the second time you've been in a fight this school year?"

How did I not know about this sooner?

Cyrus twists his lips. "I got into it with a boy on the playground a while ago."

"And who started that fight?"

He shrugs. "No one. It just happened."

I sigh. "Okay. Thanks for telling me."

I start to clean up the sugary mess on the table.

"Are you mad?" he asks sorrowfully.

"Am I mad? Yes. But not at you."

I'm mad at that Seth kid. I'm mad at his clueless mom, who lets him get away with crap. I'm mad at the school. But mostly, I'm mad at Dad. As much as I try, I can't step into that role for Cyrus. His mom is too proud and a little distant, and only recently let me spend more time with him. I've offered countless times to help financially, but she shuts me out.

"Your mom might be pissed, though. She'll probably blame it on me for being a bad influence or something." I take a sip from my cup. It's already cold.

"Because you're a preening puck?"

I almost choke on my coffee. "*WHAT* did you just say?"

"I read about it on a website. Mom didn't stop me."

"What are you doing on that side of the internet?" He had to have gotten that from that terrible blog. "You should be watching Pokemon or playing Minecraft or something. Not reading some crap gossip online."

"I googled you."

"You don't need to google me. I'm right here. You shouldn't believe everything you read on the internet, anyway."

Unfortunately, I'm not Shannon's favorite person, simply because, to her, I represent Dad's other life. And if she's reading fake news about me over Cyrus's shoulder, it's just going to strain our relationship further.

"I only get to see you once or twice a week. Take me to one of your games, at least."

He's got a point. I'm either on the road or hyper-focused on the home games when I'm here. That doesn't leave a lot of time for family. One of the many reasons I don't date.

"If your mom says it's okay, I'll get you and your friends box seats."

He deflates a little. "I don't have any friends."

I hate this for him. All my money, fame, influence. And my little brother doesn't have anyone to invite to a game. It sucks that I can't do anything about it.

"Hey, I got the new Mario vs Donkey Kong. If you're extra nice, I'll let you win. Once."

It will be a distraction for him, at least until I have to take him home tonight, where I'll attempt to talk to Shannon.

"Oh yeah? Maybe I'll let *you* win once," he teases.

"Not likely, little man. Just stay off the internet, okay?"

And if I ever find out who runs the Blades After Dark blog, I'll make them wish they never learned to write.

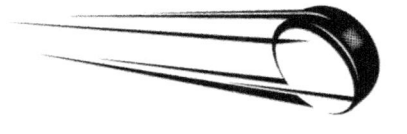

“All hockey players are bilingual.
They know English and profanity.”
– Gordie Howe

MPONI

CHAPTER FOUR

Owen

It's the first home game in a week and we're ready to kick some Chicago butt. The visiting team is one of our toughest rivals, but Coach Knight took us through some sly strategies during today's video briefing. With the energy of the crowd of Toronto fans, Chicago doesn't stand a chance. Although we still need to be on our best game tonight. No distractions.

Sawyer hit all the drills today and seems to be in

good form. Hendrix has his head in the right place, too. Things are looking good.

We're in the dressing room, about to change into our gear, when I slip my phone out of my suit pocket to tuck it away for the night. But something tugs in me, and I find myself looking up that *Blades After Dark* blog. It's been weighing on me ever since I found out Cyrus had been reading it. I've felt itchy about it since last week. Not to mention how Shannon didn't even let me walk him into her house when I dropped him off that day. She'd said the school called her and that she'd work with them on the problem *without* my help.

As if Cyrus is a problem at all.

Clicking through to the blog, I find the latest post with more fake gossip. There are pictures of Sawyer with two women on either arm. He's at The Crowned Loon, the Team's usual watering hole, where we go to blow off some steam. Die-hard fans like to find us there after big wins, but during the season, we don't drink or stay late. It's not surprising to see some of the photos were taken there. But then I scroll to see a picture of me on the ice. Alone. It had to be taken during one of my morning skates. During the time I need to help me focus the rest of the day. Early morning, when the doors are *not* open to the public.

The *Blades After Dark* blogger works at the arena.

I rack my brain to remember all the people who work here. Other team members, management, security, cleaning staff....

Zamboni drivers.

There are two regular drivers here. Joe, who's been here forever, and the new girl. Emily. I hadn't seen her before six months ago.

I click around the blog, looking for the earliest post. Five months ago. Just after Emily started.

Coincidence? Possibly.

But who else is in the arena that early? Only a handful of people.

"You okay, bro?" Griffin nudges my shoulder. "You look a little pale."

"Yeah, I'm fine. I shouldn't have gone online, that's all."

He looks at my phone screen. "You still worked up over that blog? I just thought it was funny. If I'd known you'd get bent out of shape, I wouldn't have shown it to you."

"Nah, you're right. It's just a dumb thing. Hey, do you know that girl Zamboni driver?"

Smooth transition, Owen.

"Emily? Yeah, she's hot, but kind of keeps to herself. I see her at The Crowned Loon sometimes."

"You do? Does she take a camera? Takes pictures of the team?"

"Uh, not that I'm aware of. But everyone takes pictures of the players on their phones. Why?"

"Oh nothing. As team captain, I want to make sure Sawyer watches himself."

"Yeah, he's a wild card lately. But take it easy on him. He's going through some stuff."

He pats my back and leaves to wrap his stick.

I make a mental note to talk to Sawyer someday soon. Find out what's happening with him. He's not the bleeding heart, talk it out kind of guy, but if I can meet him where he's at... See where he's coming from. It's not just about the game or the championship title. He's my friend. At least I hope he is enough to let me help him before he spirals out of control.

I take five minutes to myself before the game to meditate in silence. It's not easy to find a quiet spot, but there's a supply closet near the equipment manager's office I discovered a while ago. It's my little refuge.

I'm feeling pretty good by the time I get out onto the ice. Sawyer, Hendrix, and I are the starting forwards. The crowd always goes wild when we take the ice before the puck drop. *The Killers*. Fans love to shout it.

Kil-lers. Kil-lers!

But I hear something else tonight. I can't make it out at first. But when I look up into the stands, I see a big banner held up by some female fans.

And what they're chanting is the same as what is written in bold letters on the banner.

PREENING PUCKS.

Big, red lipstick imprints are painted all around the lettering. Sawyer is eating this up, skating in a big circle, blowing kisses at the fans. The cheering gets louder. I don't know if this is a good thing or a bad thing. I'm thinking bad. That little blogger has single-handedly made a mockery of us. I glance over to Coach Knight to gauge his reaction, but something else catches my notice.

From the corner of my eye, that powder blue beanie snags my attention, and I turn to it as if I'm drawn in like a magnet. Or rather, the woman wearing it is drawing me in. That dark blonde hair feathering out on the side of her face. That tiny little form, sitting on top of the Zamboni. That devilish curl of her lips as she takes in the chaos of her handiwork. And a camera with a lens bigger than her whole arm pressed against her eye.

That witchy little alley cat. I suspected it all night, but now I know, beyond a shadow of a doubt. Blue beanie girl is the *Blades After Dark* blogger.

I am going to Take. Her. Down.

Phase one of my plan is to find incriminating evidence. I'm not sure how, but just knowing the truth allows my mind to focus on the game.

During the first intermission, she's resurfacing the ice. The perfect time to go through her camera to see if any of the images match the ones on the blog. But Coach Knight has us in the locker room almost the entire eighteen minutes, going over an emergency strategy. We're down by a goal. Priorities.

But during the second intermission, Joe's running the resurfacer. He's got this cute kid riding along with him while the song *I Wanna Drive a Zamboni* plays over the speakers. The kid is beaming. Waving at the crowd like he just won the Stanley Cup. He reminds me of Cyrus a little bit. I wonder if my brother would like a ride whenever he gets to come to a game. *If* Shannon allows it.

I follow along as the rest of the team heads back to the locker room, but keep to the back so I can take a turn towards the Zamboni gate. I don't exactly know what my plan is here, but I have to take a chance Emily might not be back here right now.

Making my way around the building, I take the final turn into the area where Joe has his office. To my extreme disappointment, Emily is there, sitting with her back to me on a swivel chair, her ankles crossed on top of Joe's desk. On her lap is a notebook, and she's furiously writing something in it with a pen that looks like it got stuck in a fur ball. On the desk, her camera sits next to a pile of papers and a big Thermos. If I could get her to leave the office...

I take another step and she stops writing. Does she know I'm here?

"Well, well, well," I say, deciding to lean into the advantage of surprise. She stiffens and snaps the notebook shut. "What are you doing, little cat?"

Her head spins around and she levels me with a hard stare. "I beg your pardon?"

I raise my arms to take hold of the wood frame above

me, my body taking up the entire doorway. Her lips part ever so slightly.

"I asked what you're doing," I say, super casually.

"No. Did you just call me... a cat?"

I shrug. "You remind me of a little stray cat... on top of that big machine you drive."

Her eyes narrow on me. "What are you doing here?"

I glance down at the camera. "I saw you taking pictures."

A long pause while she thinks of a paltry excuse. Then she uncrosses her ankles, spins to face me, and stands up. Taking a few steps toward me, she crosses her arms, and my palms start to sweat at the notion she might invade my personal space. After that night I confronted her with her beanie, I need to remind myself to keep my distance.

"Why are you suddenly taking an interest in things I do?"

I scoff. "I'm not."

"Then what are you doing here?"

My eyes shift to the notebook under her arm, and when she sees me noticing it, she tucks it behind her back.

Curious.

"Do you like to write?" I pry.

"No."

"Then what's that for?"

She glowers at me, those lush, thick eyebrows

lurching down over her bright hazel eyes. "Maybe I like to make lists."

"Oh? What kinds of lists?"

"One hundred and one ways to slay my enemies. World domination in ten easy steps. That sort of thing."

I'm willing to wager that's not far from the truth.

"And how is that going so far?" I say, venturing into the room against my better judgment.

She lifts her little chin in defiance. "Better than expected."

She seems quite pleased with herself. This little waif of a woman that smells like watermelon and some other fruity scent I can't put a finger on. No, no no. I will not be putting my fingers on *anything*.

And although I'm one hundred percent ready to call her out, something in me pauses. Like I need to make it count. And so I find myself drawing closer to her. Crowding her. Towering over her.

I'd like to think it's to intimidate, but that would be a lie. She's my black hole, and my stupid body keeps moving her way. Getting sucked into her orbit.

I tilt my head, my face inches from hers. And the way her breath hitches, and those pretty pink lips part, I almost want to kiss her. Almost. It's just a chemical reaction.

The whirring of the Zamboni coming in through the gate reaches my ears, signaling intermission is almost over.

Emily cocks her head to the side, and I think for one

split second, my heart pounds, thinking she *wants* me to kiss her. But her eyes are giving off murdery vibes, and she lifts one dubious brow. "Well, I'd like to say it's been fun but..."

Yeah, go ahead and dismiss me, little alley cat.

With a derisive sniff, I rake my eyes over her in one slow swoop, and much like my earlier attempt to intimidate, my body reacts just the opposite, because after all... I'm still a guy. And it strikes me here that she's more beautiful up close now that I can make out the sunburst of color in her eyes, her delicate nose... the long, elegant column of her neck...

It freaks me the heck out. And in one of the most uncool moments in my life, I turn and run away. Well, I run as well as one can in skates.

I don't talk to her again the rest of the night.

But all is not lost, because after the game, when I'm trying to slip out of the locker room, Nancy, the executive assistant to the Titan's president, stops me to personally congratulate me on a good game. I really don't think I deserve her praise tonight, but any time one of the execs takes notice, I let them say whatever they want, as long as it's positive.

I thank her and say, "I'm a proud Titan, ma'am. Just promise never to trade me and I'll play my best for Toronto."

"Oh, I can assure you," she says. "We have no intention of letting you go."

"I appreciate that. I really do."

I shake her hand and bow my head a little. I've come to learn it's prudent to use my best manners whenever possible. A talent I never learned from my parents. But I picked up a few things along the way and learned quickly how far you can get with honey instead of vinegar.

Except when it comes to *some* people—like Ms. Burk and that repulsive mom at the school. Or a certain Zamboni driver, who incidentally catches my eye just as I'm shaking Nancy's hand.

Nancy turns to see where my attention wandered to, and when she sees Emily in the distance, her whole face smiles.

"Oh! I heard we had Emily Brooks in our employ, but I could hardly believe it. I understand she's trying to keep a low profile these days."

Utterly confused, I say, "What do you mean? Why would she need to keep a low profile?"

Other than her height, which I can't imagine getting much lower.

"Well, ever since she left the Olympic team, that is."

I blink. Emily the Zamboni driver is… an Olympian?

Noticing my furrowed brow, Nancy asks, "You didn't recognize her? Her face was on cereal boxes."

Not wishing to look like a complete dolt, I say, "Oh… yeah. She was a… skater, right?"

As good a guess as any.

Nancy sighs. "Would have won gold, too. Oh well."

She shrugs it off and changes the subject, telling me

she's looking forward to the game against the Quebec City Nordiques and fully expects us to win the Canadian championship again this year.

"You can count on it, ma'am."

She offers me a wink and is swept away by her entourage of executives and management staff, leaving me determined to step it up from here on out. Les Nordiques are a tough team to beat, and I know they have their sights set on that championship trophy. It's not uncommon for the Canadian champions to go on to win the Stanley Cup, but even if they don't, having that silver trophy on display here at the Blizzard Dome gives us bragging rights for a whole year. I have no intention of letting it go to Quebec City.

If we're going to beat their asses next week, there's no way in H-E-double hockey sticks I'll sit through another game of panty-throwing women calling us preening pucks. Now that I know Emily's secret, a plan is already forming in my head and I'm looking forward to the next opportunity to confront her.

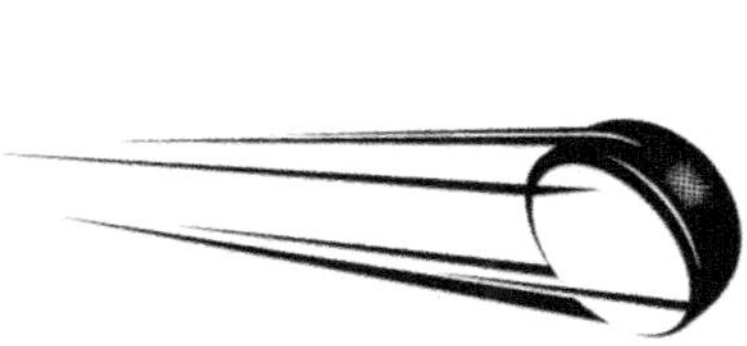

"I don't know the secret to success,
but I'm pretty sure
the closest thing is preparation."
- Michelle Kwan

MPONI

CHAPTER FIVE

Emily

The ice beneath my skates is crisp and smooth, and as I push off, I feel the satisfying whoosh as I leave a trail of sparkly ice in my wake.

I have the rink all to myself this morning, since I decided I have just as much right to be here at this time of day as Owen does. In any case, I don't expect him for another forty minutes, so I'm safe. But even if he does find me here using the rink before him, so what? I don't see *him* here late at night resurfacing the ice after forty burly men carve into it for an hour and a half. And Owen certainly is burly, with broad shoulders and thick, strong legs. He's basically a tree.

No no no. I can't let him invade my thoughts. It's just me, myself, and I this morning. The only audience I have are the frosted breath clouds that follow me around. The blades cutting through the ice, making a delicate shushing noise, like a librarian gently quieting a room full of unruly books. The subtle whispers of my steel blades, cutting through the surface, whispering secrets to the ice.

Shoosh, swoosh, swoosh.

I find solace in the cold embrace of the ice, my little escape from life, if only for a moment.

The solitude is liberating, a chance to leave reality behind, (which is less than stellar ever since my Olympic dream was swept out from under me) and just breathe in the cool air of the arena, even though the lingering smell of propane from the Zamboni hangs around. It's a peculiar mix of circulated air and the mechanical scent of a fresh resurfacing. Yet, it adds to the charm, like the backstage smell of a theater just before the curtain rises.

There's a magical romance that unfolds every time I lace up my skates and take to the ice. It's my home, where I've spent my entire childhood and adolescence preparing for two defining weeks of my life. The Winter Olympics. Only to have it taken away in one devastating swoop.

It’s still strange to skate without a partner, even though it’s been a few years. My coach urged me to change disciplines and train for the singles competition for the future. Ekaterina Gordeeva did it, after all.

But I can’t bring myself to do that.

I’m so immersed in my loops, I don’t even notice Owen has been watching me from afar until his steel scrapes the glass. I turn around, only to see him coming at me. With each powerful stride, he effortlessly slices through the ice, his body moving with an innate elegance as he carves a determined line into the frozen surface to corral me against the boards.

I push off and pick up speed, gliding across the ice as fast as my blades will carry me. But Owen is right on my tail. I veer left, and he mirrors me. I zigzag right and he's there again, matching my every move.

There's no shaking this guy. He's relentless.

I pour everything I've got into my crossovers, praying my little legs can out-power his massive thighs. But it's no use. He's gaining on me.

In a last ditch effort, I stop short and pivot a perfect three-turn, darting back the way I came. Owen over-shoots just enough for me to slip past him.

"Not so fast, Kitty Cat," he calls out.

I feel Owen's presence filling up the space behind me, back on my tail.

I'm running out of ice. The boards loom large ahead. If I want to escape, I'll have to think fast.

At the last second, I veer along the boards. But he's too quick, angling his body to block my path.

I slam on the brakes, ice chips spraying as my blades scrape to a halt. Owen stops mere inches from me, his hulking frame towering over me. I'm trapped.

"You've got some moves," he says with a cocky grin. "But not good enough to shake me."

My heart races, only partly from the chase. His gaze sears into mine with an intensity that makes me shiver despite the heat on my skin.

I force myself to hold his gaze. "Are you done having fun? Because some of us have work to do."

He places one hand on the boards beside my shoulder, leaning in close. "I just want to talk."

His breath caresses my cheek, sending a tingling rush over my skin. I swallow hard, willing my nerves to settle. I can handle Owen Jablonski.

I duck under his arm and back away a few feet to a safer distance. "About what?"

He pushes off and closes the gap between us again. "You."

He's so fast, I don't even have a chance to escape him. He is a mountain rising before me.

Hot, blue eyes drill into mine with the intense ferocity of a tiger, yet there's a hint of a smile on his mouth.

He leans in close, trapping me, his powerful presence a great big wall of man.

"I know it's you," he says, with a voice low and husky. "You're the one behind that damn hockey blog."

My heart races as his words hang in the frigid air. How did he find out? I took great care to keep my identity concealed, to protect myself from the repercussions of revealing the truth. But now, standing before Owen, all of my carefully constructed walls begin to crumble.

I swallow hard, trying to steady my trembling breath.

“I don’t know what you’re talking about,” I manage to muster the courage to reply.

He slowly shakes his head. “Don’t play games, little cat. You know exactly what I’m talking about. I’m curious, though. Preening Pucks? With your sharp tongue, you could have come up with something better than that.”

I force a laugh. "What makes you think it's me?"

A sly smile curves at the corner of his lips, putting my female bits on alert. "Oh, Emily," he drawls, his voice laced with amusement. "You underestimate me."

With a deep breath, I muster all the strength within me and meet his smoldering gaze head-on.

“You’re delusional.”

“Am I though? It all makes sense now. That enormous camera. Your little notebook. The guilty look you have in your eyes even now.” He tilts his head, and I swear he’s the devil himself as he bends down to growl a dark, heated whisper in my ear.

“You’re. Busted.”

I can feel the depths of his voice crawl down into my belly button. Down through my legs. My knees. My wobbly ankles. If I look down, surely I'll find the ice has melted into a puddle at my feet.

I must not look down at any cost, because he can't win this. I won't let him even think he has me, not for a second.

"Awww," I croon like I'm talking to the big baby he is. "Did somebowy get his feewings hurt?"

His face is so, so close to me. One more inch and our noses would touch. Yet I stand my ground, even under his hot stare and accusing grin.

"You think you're funny, don't you?"

"I think... no. I *KNOW* I have the right to post anything I want on my blog."

He laughs hard and snaps his fingers. "Aha! So you admit it."

"I, uh..."

"I wasn't one hundred percent sure. I was ninety-nine point nine percent sure, but now... ha ha! I got you."

He can't possibly have been bluffing this whole time. The snake. I roll my eyes and make to slide away from him, but he scoops around me with those big, black skates and blocks my exit. I sigh, tired of this game of his. So what if he found me out? It's not like I can get fired over it. Joe loves me.

I give him a sarcastic slow clap. "Congratulations. You just proved you're a certifiable stalker. It's not going to stop me from writing what I want."

Owen's smile widens, his eyes gleaming with mischief.

"Au contraire, mon petit chaton. I know your secret. Who you are. Wouldn't that make a fun social media post?" He fans his fingers out like he's throwing a headline out into the ether. "Emily Brooks trades Olympic gold for Zamboni."

"You wouldn't."

"Oh I would. Unless..."

"What do you want?" I say through my teeth.

"So glad you asked. I want you to write a new blog post," he says, his voice dripping with arrogance. "A post that speaks only of my greatness on the ice."

I snort. "Your greatness? Somebody has an oversized ego."

I'd laugh at his audacity if I wasn't so angry. How dare he!

"In addition to your post covering the highlights of the game and our athletic discipline, you are going to mention my charity work, and the many generous donations I've made to transitional housing and underprivileged children's sports teams."

"If you think I'll blow your horn, mister..."

His eyes darken as they dip down to rake over my lips. Ugh. He's such a pig.

I hate him. I really do. Not just for Jaime's sake. The way he treated her. But because he's simply horrible. I would have come to that conclusion myself even without all those tears Jaime wasted on him.

Yet, as I weigh the consequences in my mind, I realize that I have no choice but to comply. In order to protect myself and the life I have built, I will have to sacrifice my integrity. I'll write that blog post. But that doesn't mean I can't have a little fun with it.

"Fine," I spit out. "But remember this, *Owen*. Manipulating others may get you what you want in the short term, but it will never fulfill you in the long run."

His eyes flicker with a mix of surprise and curiosity, but he quickly masks it with an impish grin.

"We'll see about that, Emily," he replies cryptically before turning on his heel and gliding away across the ice.

We'll see indeed.

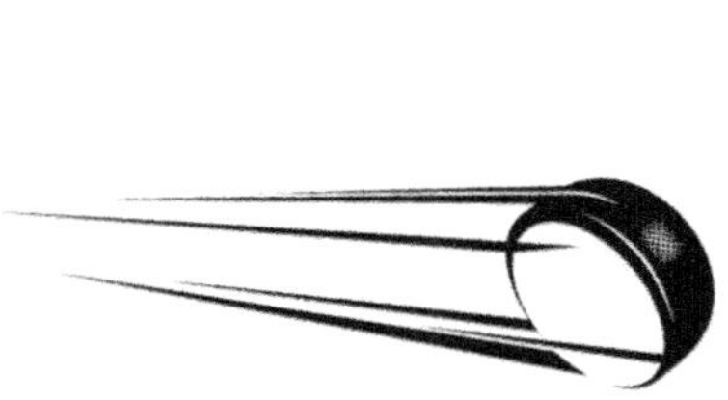

"I went to a fight the other night
and a hockey game broke out."
– Rodney Dangerfield

MPONI

CHAPTER SIX

Owen

There are not a lot of people in this world I despise. True, the things my dad did screwed me up for life, not to mention Cyrus and all the other people he's messed with. I don't hate him, though. I'd rather forget he exists, but what I feel is not hate.

The handful of people I've crossed paths with over the years who'd really pissed me off are out of my life now. I hardly remember any of their names.

Then there's Emily.

She gets under my skin in a way I can't explain. Thoughts of her pop up in the most inconvenient moments. When I'm having an innocent sandwich, there she is, taunting me with those whiskey eyes and sparkling wit. The other day as I passed Nathan Phillips Square, the reflecting pool, a smooth sheet of ice in the winter months, I imagined her there and it provoked something so heated in me. So I decided to take the long way home from the arena from now on. Even during this morning's drills, I got irrationally livid and cussed so loudly, even Coach Knight raised an eyebrow. And believe me, nothing surprises him.

Emily kept her promise to write "good" things about me in last night's blog post. But she worded it in such a way, all the praise read more like back-handed compliments.

All I could think of was, "Well played, Brooks. Well played." And something inside me swelled at how freaking clever she is, as though she's become my worthy rival in a video game. However, as much as she stirs something in me that makes me want to jack-hammer walls, this thing between us is far from hate. The way my body reacts whenever she's near—I'd say it's definitely not hate.

Hate, if I can use such a strong word, is reserved for a special class of person. And if a genie appeared to me right now and granted me a wish to exile anyone to a desert island with no way off, I can only think of one guy. And that would be Quebec City's defenseman, Georges Lemieux. Okay, not just him. I'd send the whole damn team away, including the head coach, because he's a weasel. As a matter of fact, I happen to know Coach Knight has his own personal vendetta against Quebec's coach, Claude Rousseau.

The pre-game rituals are in full swing as we gear up to face Quebec tonight. I go through my usual groove, like how I always lace my left skate before my right, or tape my stick with the same precise technique I've used since high school. The familiar routine helps to steady my racing thoughts, and I take a deep breath, trying to push away all distractions.

We all have our own superstitions and rituals, from lucky socks to pre-game mantras. But one thing's for sure, we're all focused on one goal: winning.

Tonight's game is crucial. We're only two points behind Quebec in the standings, and a win tonight could put us in a prime position for the playoffs. But it won't be easy. Quebec has been dominating the competition, but I am fueled by a fierce determination to destroy them, and especially Georges Lemieux.

As I imagine kicking his ass, my muscles flex and my adrenaline pumps through me. Sure, he might be able to intimidate other teams, but I'm about to turn his winning streak into a losing streak so bad, he'll be begging for mercy and a plastic participation trophy.

The dressing room is buzzing with excitement as my teammates and I get ready to hit the ice. Coach Knight calls us together for a final pep talk. His voice booms with authority, but there's an underlying fire in his eyes that speaks of something more personal. He knows what this game means to all of us, especially to him.

"Listen up, boys," he begins, his gravelly voice cutting through the silence. "Tonight, we're not just playing hockey. We're going to war, and our battlefield is the ice. You all know who's waiting on the other side—those damn Nordiques. I don't care about the history, the stats, or the records. What matters is what's happening tonight, right here, right now. This is our time. Our ice. Our game. I want to see heart out there, the kind of heart that beats red and black. You've been through hell and back together, and tonight, you're going to leave everything on that rink. You'll fight for every inch, every puck, and every goal."

The whole team grunts and nods their heads in agreement. We're all eager to get out there and take down Quebec.

Coach Knight continues, "We know they like to play dirty. Well, they've got another thing coming. We're the Toronto Titans, and we don't back down. We hit hard, we skate fast, and we leave it all on the ice."

He looks around at each of us before adding, "And remember, tonight is personal for me, too. That son of a cow Rousseau wants my head for his trophy room. So go out there and play for the name on the front of your jersey, not the one on the back."

I glance at Sawyer, who nods silently beside me, that

goofy look on his face triggering a memory of when we first met—young and stupid. We've come a long way since then, and tonight is our chance to show everyone what we're made of.

And then, for some reason, it got me thinking about Emily. Like, out of nowhere, and I feel this urge to prove myself to her. Can't explain it, so I shove it way, way down. She pretty much messed up the assignment in every way possible, but instead of confronting her about it, I've been avoiding her all day. Oh, I mean to make her fix it, but talking to her before the game does nothing but distract me. She's like an itch... the kind you just want to get rid of. But the more you scratch, the worse the burn on your skin. I'm already hot and bothered just thinking about it.

Coach ends his pep talk with his usual chant. "Titans on three! One, two, three, TITANS!"

With a resounding hoot, we all hit our sticks against the ground in unison. It's time.

As we step onto the ice amidst a roar of cheers from the crowd, I sense a shift in the atmosphere. The rivalry is palpable, charging the air with an intensity like nothing else. The puck drops, and chaos ensues as bodies collide and sticks clash.

Lemieux taunts me from across the rink, his smirk infuriatingly arrogant. Damn, he's ugly—with one tooth missing, and that thin, pasty face, he looks like a *Canada's Most Wanted* poster. I'd say it's a face only a mother could love, but I'm pretty sure he was dropped off at a zoo as a baby and raised by baboons. The mean kind with red butts.

The game starts off intense, with both teams playing aggressively. But we hold our own.

Late into the second period, I manage to steal the puck from one of Quebec's players and quickly pass it off to Hendrix, who takes off towards their goal with lightning speed.

But just as he's about to shoot, Lemieux comes out of nowhere and body checks Hendrix into the boards.

I race over towards Lemieux and shove him with all my might. He stumbles back but doesn't fall.

"Tu veux jouer dur?" he sneers at me. "Jouons dur!"

Play rough? Bring it.

He digs his stick into my ribs, provoking me like the baboon he is. In an instant, I lose control of myself and retaliate with a force I didn't know I possessed. It's like all the frustration from the past few weeks pours out of me. Gloves drop, and fists start flying as the entire arena erupts into chaos. Players from both teams join in the brawl, a blur of motion and fury.

In the midst of the chaos, I manage to land a punch to Lemieux's face. He stumbles back, surprise flashing in his eyes as he touches his lip and finds blood. The crowd roars in approval, and I feel my adrenaline surge. But then, out of nowhere, a fist connects with my jaw. It sends me reeling backwards onto the ice.

I barely have time to process what's happening when Lemieux is on top of me, his fists raining down. I manage to duck and roll away, tackling him off balance. His legs splay out from under him, and we crash onto the ice together.

Through the melee, I can see Sawyer trading blows with another Quebec player while Coach Knight shouts from the bench.

Suddenly Emily flashes in my mind again. What would she think of this? Probably that it was dumb testosterone-fueled idiocy. She'd be right. And she'd put it in her freaking blog.

Maybe it wasn't the smartest decision to get involved in a fight with a guy nicknamed for how much damage he can do to another human being's face.

The referee blows his whistle, but no one seems to hear it over the cacophony of cheers and jeers from the crowd. It takes several tense moments before he and two more refs manage to pull us apart and call for a break.

"Jablonski! Lemieux!" He shouts at us both in equally angry French and English, probably cursing at us in both languages at once. "Penalty box! Now!"

Lemieux grins at me as blood trickles down his split lip. "A plus card, Juggernaut," he says, laughing, as though this is all just a game to him.

"As if, Lemieux," I grit out, shooting him a glare.

I resist the urge to punch him one more time as I follow the ref's orders, skating my way over to the penalty box with a chorus of boos and cheers ringing in my ears. As I settle onto the hard bench, I ignore the watchful eyes of the crowd and instead let my gaze drift across the rink to where Emily sits atop her Zamboni. Her expressive brows arch, and she's got a wicked curl on her pretty little mouth.

She meets my gaze, and for a second everything else falls away—the noise of the crowd, the chill of the air, even Lemieux's goading laughter. It's just us. Her delicate face scrunches up as she shakes her head at me, a triumphant smile playing on her lips. As I watch her fold her arms underneath that hideously oversized parka she always wears and toss back her head in laughter, I can't help but grin back. I can almost hear her say, "This is *SO* going in the blog. Deal with it, Jablonski."

The rest of the game is a blur - a mixture of blocked shots, hard checks and missed opportunities. The final score isn't in our favor, and Les Nordiques gloat in our faces during the post-game handshake.

Making my way back into the locker room after bidding adieu to our disappointed fans, I find myself actually looking forward to my planned visit to the Zam Queen and tell her exactly what I think about her little stunt. Those passive aggressive veiled insults in her latest blog post, as if I wouldn't notice. How I'll make her squirm when she realizes I won't stand for it. And she'll have to write a new post. This time, under my watchful eye.

She'll get all worked up because she hates me so much (although I still have no idea why). And then her claws will come out as she bickers. Those witty comebacks... the way her eyes light up when she's sparring with me. How I want to wipe that witchy smirk off her face—the many, *many* ways I can think of to do just that.

"And what are *you* grinning at, Juggernaut?" Lemieux's voice shatters my thoughts. "You lost."

"Oh, just thinking how we're going to destroy you in a few weeks in Quebec," I reply quickly.

He glares at me with a smug sneer. "A little advice. Enjoy the championship trophy while you can."

"You're still sore we took it from you last year?"

He throws me a conceited snicker. "Mark my words, *glandu*. It will be like stealing candy from a baby."

"Hosier," I scoff as he saunters away.

The last thing I want to do after a tough loss is sit through another interview rehashing everything that goes wrong. But that's the job. So I put on a polite face and give the usual platitudes about regrouping and staying focused. My mother taught me manners.

But I'm exhausted after trying to give conciliatory, boring answers to their lame questions.

As soon as it's over, I make a beeline for the showers. The hot water rinses away some of the frustration as I mentally prepare for the conversation ahead with Emily.

After toweling off and getting dressed in comfortable clothes, I find her in the hallway. She's carrying her purse and looks like she's just finishing up for the night. Her wavy blonde hair is pulled back in a messy bun, face scrubbed clean of makeup. Even in jeans and a hoodie, she looks cute, though I'd never admit it.

A slow smile spreads across my face as I remember the "compliments" she paid me in that sassy blog post last night. It's time for a little payback.

"Going somewhere, Kitty Cat?" I ask, leaning against the wall to block her exit.

Those whiskey eyes widen in surprise. "Jablonski? What are you still doing here?"

"I could ask you the same question. But I think we both know the answer."

She blinks those big hazel eyes innocently. "What are you talking about?"

"You know what." I cross my arms. "That blog post you wrote last night."

"Oh, that." She waves a hand. "I said lots of nice things about you, too. The donations you make, how you're the team's leading scorer..."

"You also called me 'cocky,' 'hot-headed,' and 'unable to take criticism.'"

She shrugs. "I mean, it's not untrue."

I clench my jaw. She's infuriating. "It's completely uncalled for. You're supposed to be writing fluff pieces, not critiquing my personality."

"I'm a journalist, Owen. I call it like I see it."

“Journalist? I think you’re using that term a little too freely.” I take a step toward her. She stands her ground, chin lifted defiantly. "So here's the deal. You're not leaving my sight until you write another post—a positive one that I approve of. And I'm going to watch you write... Every. Single. Word."

She lets out a sharp laugh. "Yeah, that's not happening."

"Well, I'm not taking my eyes off you until you do. So either we go to your place, or you come to mine." I let my gaze travel down her body.

She shudders. "Ugh, I don't trust you alone at my place, and no way am I going to your sex lair."

I roll my eyes. "It's just a nice bachelor pad."

"Uh-huh. Well, we can stay here if you want me to write a new post tonight. But we are not going anywhere alone together."

I look around the empty hallway and grin. "The Zamboni office it is."

I grab her hand before she can protest and lead her down the hall. I am not prepared for the shot of electricity straight to my chest from the feel of her skin. But I'm committed to it, so I hold on tight. She grumbles but doesn't resist. This might actually be fun.

We settle in the tiny office, knees bumping under the cramped desk. With every touch, my stomach coils with a feeling that's been dormant in me for a long time. But I'm here to play it cool, so I lean back and clasp my hands behind my head, watching as she pulls up the blog on her laptop.

"Go on then, compliment away," I say with a smug grin.

She types a few words, then pauses, nibbling her lip

in concentration. I find myself staring at her mouth and have to drag my eyes away. Focus, Jablonski. This is about revenge, not about how hot she looks right now.

I watch her bite her lip in concentration, leg bouncing with nervous energy. Man, she's cute. And fiery. I can't remember the last time someone stood up to me like that. It's kind of hot.

Stay focused, Jablonski.

"So what are you writing about me?" I prod. "My charity work? Hockey skills? Chiseled abs?"

She lets out an exaggerated sigh. "Yes, Owen, I'm writing all about your perfect abs and how you score goals left and right and donate millions to orphaned baby pandas."

"Now you're getting it," I laugh.

She shakes her head, suppressing a smile. "I can't concentrate with you looming over me."

"Oops, my bad." I make a show of leaning away to give her space, but keep my eyes glued to the screen.

She resumes typing, fingers flying over the keys. I catch a few phrases like "sculpted physique" and "dazzling smile" before she angles the laptop away.

"Ah ah, let me see."

With a huff, she turns the screen back toward me. I scan the paragraph, nodding.

"Not bad," I tease. "But I think you can do better than 'sculpted physique.' How about 'god-like body chiseled from granite'?"

Her eyes flash with irritation, but she changes it. The

more she writes, the more creative her descriptions become. And the more amused I am, even though there's no way I'm going to let her publish any of that.

"'Eyes like shards of ice that pierce your soul.' A bit over the top, don't you think?" I ask with a chuckle.

"You wanted nice, I'm giving you nice," she snaps.

I shut the laptop lid and slide it aside. She inhales sharply as I lean in, bracing one hand on the arm of her chair.

"You're not as subtle as you think, little cat," I murmur, brushing a strand of golden hair from her face. "I'm not some guy in a romance novel. I'm a serious athlete. Now delete all that crap and start over."

She huffs and makes a cute growly sound in her throat. "This isn't as easy as it looks. All that work I just did."

"Delete it. Except the part about the baby pandas. You can keep that."

"Unbelievable."

I can practically see the steam coming out of her ears. It's adorable.

No, no, no. Not adorable. I like kitty cats as much as the next guy, but it's all fun and games until their claws come out. And by the look in Emily's eyes, she's getting ready to sharpen hers.

"A little less snark. A little more clickety clack," I say with a teasing grin.

"Clickety clack? Really? You know... Junk-for-nuts Jablonski, I might regret telling you this, but I—"

Suddenly, the lights go out, plunging us into darkness. For a second, I just stand there in silence as my eyes adjust.

"That can't be good," Emily says dryly. Before I can respond, there's a loud clanking noise, and the AC shuts off.

"Well, ain't this cozy," I mutter.

"Yup, definitely a power failure," she concludes. I hear her moving around, probably feeling her way along the wall.

“The ice!” I say in panic.

"No problem, the backup generator will kick in any —" She starts to say when a crashing sound echoes down the hallway. Emily and I both freeze.

"What was that?" she whispers. The words are barely out of her mouth when the lights flash back on. We blink and exchange a look, then take off running down the hall toward the sound.

As we round the corner to the trophy case, I feel my stomach drop. The glass is shattered, shards everywhere, and the Hart Memorial Cup is gone.

"The trophy!" Emily gasps. We hear footsteps pounding away from us. Without thinking, I bolt after the thief, Emily on my heels.

We careen around another corner and almost slam right into Hal, the elderly night guard. He's wheezing and out of breath.

"Someone just ran past... with the trophy..." he pants, pointing down the hallway that leads outside.

"Wearing all black. Too far away. I couldn't get a good look at the getaway car."

Emily and I look at each other in dismay.

"Who would dare steal from the Blizzard Dome?"

But even as the words leave my mouth, I already know who did it.

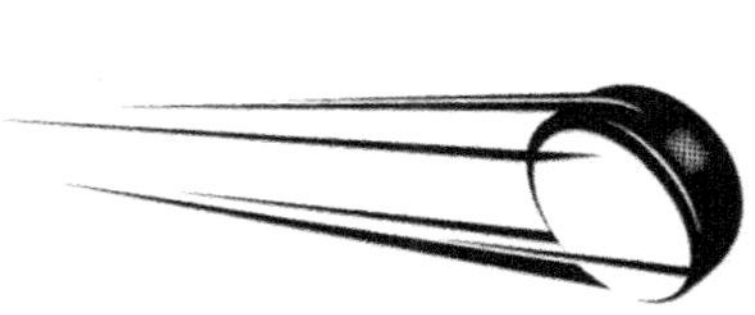

"Every day, someone realizes a dream.
I believe dreams help light our darkness
and give us the push we need
to move across the rink of life."
- Kristi Yamaguchi

mPONI

CHAPTER SEVEN

Emily

The heavenly aroma of hot pizza fills my cozy living room as I fluff the throw pillows on the couch in preparation for girl's night. I've got the string lights glowing softly overhead and a bottle of pinot grigio chilling in the fridge. Now all I need is for Jaime and Maggie to arrive with the popcorn and chocolate, and we'll be ready for a night of gossip, pizza, and binge-watching reality TV.

As if on cue, there's a knock at the door. I hurry over and swing it open to reveal my two best friends standing there with arms full of goodies.

"Special delivery!" announces Maggie, holding up two bags overflowing with every flavor of chocolate imaginable.

Jaime sniffs the air appreciatively. "Mmm, something smells amazing, Em! Is that the goat cheese and fig pizza from Enzo's?"

"You know it!" I say with a grin. Nothing beats their wood-fired gourmet pies.

The girls kick off their shoes and make themselves at home, Jaime settling onto the couch while Maggie raids my wine glasses.

"So, how's life? Any new guys on the horizon?" asks Maggie. Straight to the point, Mags is always snooping into my love life.

I roll my eyes good-naturedly. "You know I don't have time for dating right now. I've got my job at the arena and my blog to keep me entertained."

Jaime nods understandingly. "The blog is so good, Em. It's only a matter of time before it takes off."

Then her expression shifts to one of concern. "But you can't let it take over your whole life. Don't forget to have a little fun, too!"

Leave it to Jaime to play therapist and get straight to the heart of things. She's right though, I have been kind of single-minded lately.

"I know, I know," I sigh. "It's just... for fun, and I

think, in a way, I've finally found something I like almost as much as skating."

Both Jaime and Maggie are quiet for a moment. They know how devastating it was when my partner disqualified us from competing in the Olympics. I had dedicated over a decade of my life to the sport, only to have it ripped from under me in the eleventh hour.

Maggie hugs me, reaching around to pinch my butt, and I scream in surprise.

"Girl, tonight, we are going to stuff our faces with pizza, drink lots of wine, and veg out to trashy TV!"

She punctuates this declaration by sauntering over to my tiny kitchen, popping the cork on the wine and filling our glasses. I have to laugh. Trust Maggie to know exactly how to lift my spirits.

"Cheers to that!" I say, raising my glass. The crisp white wine is cool and tart on my tongue.

Jaime lifts a slice of pizza from the box, the melted cheese stretching deliciously. "Mmm... Enzo's really outdid themselves with this one."

The combination of flavors is absolute perfection—the sweet fig jam contrasting with the salty tang of the goat cheese and the chewy, blistered crust. The three of us lapse into contented silence as we devour slice after slice.

"Alright ladies, time to queue up the latest episode of 'Love at First Swipe'!" announces Maggie.

"Ugh, I can't wait to see if Amanda chooses Liam or Tyler this week," Jaime says, before taking a huge bite of pizza. Strings of mozzarella stretch deliciously from her mouth.

"My money's on Liam. He's way more her type," I reply. Though truthfully, I don't care that much about the outcome.

"Nothing like crap TV, junk food and girl time," declares Maggie.

During a commercial break, Maggie refills our wine glasses and Jaime brings over a tray of chocolate truffles. The dark chocolate shells crack under our teeth, revealing smooth, velvety ganache centers.

"So...I have a confession to make," I say hesitantly, keeping my eyes glued to the pizza crust remnants on my plate.

Jaime and Maggie stop chatting and turn to look at me curiously.

"I, um, I may have gone back on my word a tiny bit," I continue, feeling my cheeks flush.

"What do you mean?" asks Jaime, her brow furrowing.

I take a big gulp of wine, steeling my nerves. "Well, you know how I promised that my next blog post would totally drag Owen's name through the mud, after everything he put you through."

Jaime nods slowly, her expression unreadable.

"The thing is," I rush on quickly, "Owen kind of figured out I'm the one behind the blog and, well, he insisted I write a favorable post about him."

I chance a look up at Jaime. Her eyes have gone

steely and her mouth is pressed in a thin line. Uh oh, she does not look happy.

"He threatened to reveal my identity if I didn't comply. I tried to get out of it, but he wouldn't budge," I say pleadingly.

"So you just... gave in?" asks Jaime, her voice tight.

I've failed as a friend. Jaime is the most sensitive person I've ever known. She's still not over Owen. The other night, she ran to the bathroom and cried for twenty minutes when a Toronto Titans commercial came on. We only watch streaming shows after that.

I hang my head, feeling ashamed under her hurt gaze. "I'm so sorry, Jaime. I know I should have stood my ground, but I panicked."

Maggie glances between us worriedly. "Come on, Jaime, cut her some slack. It was a tough position to be in."

"I guess," mutters Jaime, though she still looks upset. An uncomfortable silence settles over the room.

"Let me make it up to you," I beg. "Just say the word and I'll write the most scathing, brutal takedown of Owen ever. I'll dig up every nasty rumor and embarrassing story about him that exists."

A slight smile tugs at Jaime's mouth. "As tempting as that sounds, getting back at Owen won't change anything. I appreciate you wanting to defend me, but it's not worth compromising yourself."

I feel a rush of relief at her words. Dear, sweet, forgiving Jaime.

Maggie claps her hands decisively. "This calls for more wine! Here's to friends who have each other's backs."

She tops up our glasses and raises hers in a toast. After a beat, Jaime lifts her glass too and clinks it against ours.

The knot in my chest loosens. Jaime's forgiveness means everything to me. I know now more than ever that I need to stand up to Owen. My blog and my principles are too important to cave again.

Maggie breaks the residual tension by turning up the TV volume. "Enough of this heavy stuff. We've got a rose ceremony to watch!"

I glance between Jaime and Maggie, uncertainty gnawing at me. I want to make this right, but I also don't want to make things worse.

"I know that look," Jaime says, pointing her pizza crust at me. "You're second guessing yourself. Don't. Owen is the one in the wrong here."

"Exactly!" Maggie chimes in. "He can't just go around bullying people into getting what he wants.

"You know what?" Jaime says, sitting up straighter. "I'm done moping over that jerk. He doesn't deserve one more tear from me."

"Thatta girl!" cheers Maggie, pumping her fist.

My eyes widen at her bold words. Sweet, gentle Jaime, who cried for two weeks straight after she found out he cheated on her. She still hasn't gotten over it. Sometimes I catch her staring into space with a sad look in her eyes. When that happens, I have to snap my fingers in front of her face and tell her a funny joke. After six months, I'm running out of jokes.

A wicked grin spreads across Maggie's face. "Ladies, it sounds like this calls for some expert level pranking. And lucky for you gals, I just happen to be a pranking mastermind."

"Should I be worried right now?" I ask nervously. When it comes to mischief, Maggie has zero limits.

"Relax, it'll be harmless fun," Maggie assures me breezily. "Now, we could start small—like loosening the tops on his Gatorade bottles before a game so he ends up drenched."

Despite myself, I have to laugh. The mental image of smug Owen covered in sticky blue liquid is pretty great.

She holds out her hand, palm down. "Let Operation Take Down Owen commence."

Jaime immediately places hers on top. They both look at me expectantly.

"Oh, um, alright then." I add my hand to the stack. "I'm in."

Maggie nods, looking satisfied. "First things first, we need to do our research. Find out everything we can about Owen's habits and schedule. Look for weaknesses or anything potentially embarrassing we can use against him."

I frown slightly. "We can't do anything that can be traced back to me."

Maggie waves her hand. "Of course, of course! We'll

keep it light and humorous. Just enough to ruffle his feathers."

I have to laugh at Maggie's sheer enthusiasm for humiliating Owen. Her schemes start out relatively tame, like printing out photos of his face and plastering them all over the arena. But it doesn't take long before she's suggesting full-on breaking and entering into his house to pull pranks.

"As hilarious as that would be, maybe we should start with something a little more legal," I say gently. The last thing we need is to get arrested over this jerk. My thoughts fly to sitting in the cramped office with Owen. How he'd purposefully nudge my knee with his. If he was trying to get a reaction out of me, he succeeded. I think I did a pretty good job at hiding it, though. And then the whole fiasco with the trophy. Yeah, I think we should keep our payback against Owen on the right side of the law.

"Good point," sighs Maggie. "We'll keep the B&E plans on the back burner for now."

The three of us start eagerly tossing around concepts, building on each other's ideas. Soon we've got plans ranging from childish, like filling his locker with packing peanuts, to more clever schemes meant to unsettle him, like swapping out his branded water bottles with ones that have insulting labels.

I can't remember the last time I saw Jaime so fired up and determined. A tidal wave of affection for my friends swells inside me.

“Oooh, I know!" Maggie says, sitting up straighter. "Let's mess with his superstitions. All hockey players have them."

Jaime taps her chin thoughtfully. "We could switch out his lucky mouth guard for one that's slightly off."

Uh oh, I think we may have awakened the vengeful beast within her.

"Or mix up the order of his gear in his locker?" I suggest lamely, warming up to the idea.

"Love it!" says Maggie. "Subtle things to throw him off his game."

The ideas start flowing faster. Maggie wants to put baby powder in his lucky socks. Soon we're all giggling at the image of Owen's confusion and annoyance over these minor torments.

"Okay, okay, what else?" I ask between fits of laughter.

Maggie’s eyes light up impishly. "I've got it. Let's make him think his teammates are messing with him instead of us."

"Genius!" I exclaim. "We can pit him against them in some silly feud."

Maggie nods. "I'm envisioning locker room pranks taken to the next level. Honey in his shoes, swapping out his shampoo, jock straps on the ceiling..."

"Ew gross!" Jaime and I shriek in unison, dissolving into renewed laughter.

"We'll have to be sneaky," I say once I catch my breath. "But I think we can pull it off."

Jaime lifts her wine glass again. "To Operation Take Down Owen. Let the games begin!"

I'm surprised by the sudden steel in her voice. Her earlier hurt seems to have vanished, replaced by a look of cool determination.

We clink glasses, scheming smiles on all our faces. A warm feeling rises in my chest. Let him try to threaten me again. I'll be ready. Owen better watch his back—he has no idea what's coming for him.

A knock at the door interrupts our scheming session. I reluctantly set down my wine glass and make my way over, peering through the peephole. Ugh. It's Cody, the obnoxious guy from down the hall. Just my luck.

I plaster a polite smile on my face and open the door a crack. "Oh, hey Cody. What's up?"

He leans against the door frame, giving me an obvious once-over. "Hey there, Emily. I was just on my way out and thought I'd stop by to say hi to my favorite neighbor."

His eyes linger on my bare legs, and I resist the urge to grab a blanket to cover up.

"That's nice of you," I say briskly. "Well, I've got company over so..."

I start to close the door, but Cody wedges his foot in the gap. "Company, huh? Don't be rude, why don't you introduce me?"

Before I can protest, he pushes past me into the apartment. I clench my jaw in irritation. So much for girls' night.

"Jaime, Maggie, this is my neighbor, Cody," I say tightly.

Jaime gives him a thin smile while Maggie just lifts her chin in cool acknowledgement. They can sense my discomfort.

"Wow, look at you lovely ladies," says Cody, his gaze bouncing between them. "How is it that I didn't know Emily had such hot friends?"

I resist the urge to gag. Could he be any more of a sleazeball?

"We were just having a girls' night in," I hint pointedly. "So like I said, now's not really a good time..."

But Cody is already strolling around the living room, making himself at home. "Nonsense! There's always time for pretty girls and cold beer. Got anything to drink?"

He winks at me before flopping down on the couch next to Jaime. She immediately scoots away, shooting me a pleading look.

I cross my arms, gearing up to insist he leave, when Maggie pipes up.

"Actually, Cody, we were just discussing our book club." She holds up the empty wine bottle. "This pinot grigio paired perfectly with our latest read."

I have to suppress a smile. Clever Mags.

Cody's face falls slightly. "Oh, a book club? Not really my scene. What are you reading?"

"'Infinite Jest' by David Foster Wallace," Maggie replies smoothly.

Cody looks lost. "Is that some cheesy romance novel?"

"Oh no, it's an extremely dense, complex work of postmodernist fiction," Maggie says. "With over a thousand pages of allegorical themes and allusions. But I'm sure a smart guy like you would appreciate it."

She bats her eyes at him innocently. I nearly choke trying to hold back my laughter.

Cody tugs at his collar, suddenly looking ready to flee. "Uh, yeah, maybe I'll check it out."

He stands abruptly. "Anyway, I should probably head out. Have fun with your book talk, ladies."

"Are you sure you can't stay?" Maggie asks sweetly. "We were just about to discuss the existential philosophy underlying the characters' development."

Cody is already halfway to the door. "Yeah, uh, sounds fascinating, but I just remembered I have this...thing. Gotta run!"

The door slams behind him. As soon as he's gone, the three of us burst into laughter.

"Oh my god, that was amazing!" I say, collapsing onto the couch. "The look on his face when you brought up postmodernism!"

Maggie takes a mock bow. "Why thank you, thank you. Just doing my part to scare off scummy men."

"Ugh, what a creep," says Jaime, shaking her head. "How do you put up with him as a neighbor, Em?"

I sigh, the laughter fading. "I try to avoid him as

much as possible. But he's always finding excuses to drop by uninvited."

Maggie squeezes my shoulder. "That's not okay. Let us know if you ever need back up. We've got no problem helping fend off harassment from entitled jerks."

Like Owen.

I smile, feeling a rush of gratitude. I really lucked out with these two.

"Thanks, I appreciate that. Hopefully he got the message tonight."

Maggie lifts the empty wine bottle, waving it enticingly. "This calls for a refill! Here's to girls supporting girls."

She returns from the kitchen with a freshly opened bottle of Sauvignon Blanc. As she tops off our glasses, I notice her sly smile.

"You know, after the Cody incident, I think we deserve some laughs," she says. "Let's roast the pathetic excuses for men we've had to deal with."

Jaime giggles and nods eagerly. "Ooh yes! Story time."

I have to grin. Only Maggie would turn creep encounters into a comedy roast.

"Alright, I'll start," Maggie declares. "Get ready for the saga of how I catfished my slimeball ex."

Jaime and I exchange amused glances as Maggie launches into her tale.

"So remember Brad?"

I nod. “The guy so in love with himself he used your credit card for botox?”

Maggie rings an imaginary bell. “Ding ding ding! Five points for Gryffindor. Anyway, I was determined to get revenge on that narcissistic pig. So, I created a fake dating profile using pics of a cute brunette I found online. Of course, hornball Brad took the bait and started messaging her."

I shake my head, already chuckling. Maggie has zero filter when it comes to calling out crappy guy behavior.

"We start chatting, me pretending to be the brunette, and he asks her out to dinner. So I pick this super fancy steakhouse and tell him to dress nice. Meanwhile, I sent the restaurant an anonymous tip that he was a notorious dine-and-dasher."

Maggie pauses for dramatic effect, clearly relishing the story.

"So Brad shows up in a suit, thinking he's hot stuff waiting for his Tinderella. And the maître d' tells him politely that he needs to pre-pay for the meal."

"No way!" Jaime exclaims, eyes wide.

"Yup!" says Maggie gleefully. "And it gets better. I sent a local modeling agency to the restaurant too. They pretended to scout him, saying he had the perfect 'before' look for their weight loss transformation ads."

By now, Jaime and I are doubled over laughing. Trust Maggie to deliver peak petty revenge.

"Genius!" I say. "The ultimate blow to his ego."

Maggie takes an exaggerated bow. "It was my finest work. Your turn, Jaime! I know you've got stories."

Jaime blushes. "Oh gosh, I don't really have any fun ones..."

"Come on, there must be at least one loser ex you can tell us about besides *he who shall not be named*," Maggie coaxes. “And by ‘he’ I mean Owen.”

“I think we caught that,” I say.

"Well..." Jaime hedges. We gaze at her expectantly until she relents.

"Okay, there was one guy I dated who was just the worst. Total mama's boy."

Maggie nudges her encouragingly. "This is gonna be good, I can tell!"

"Alright, alright!" Jaime laughs. "So Kyle still lived at home with his parents, which was strike one. And he kept calling me by his ex's name, Kaitlyn."

I shake my head in disbelief. "Sounds like a real winner."

"Oh, just wait. The best part is how I got back at him," says Jaime, clearly getting into the story now. Her eyes light up with mischief as she leans in. "I signed him up to audition for that show 'Five Dates and a Wedding.'"

Maggie's jaw drops open. She holds her wine glass in mid-air, frozen in disbelief. "No freaking way!" she exclaims after a moment, before taking a long sip.

"I wish I could say I was making this up, but it's 100% true," Jaime says, struggling to contain her grin.

"Not only did I sign him up, but I may have also written his audition letter posing as his mom."

At this, Maggie does a genuine spit take, spraying wine all over herself. "You did not!" she gasps, doubling over with laughter.

"Oh I did," Jaime nods, looking mighty pleased with herself. "I went on and on about what an amazing catch her little Kyle was. How he was such a gentleman who still lived at home to spend time with his parents. Just really talked him up as the most eligible bachelor ever."

Maggie is laughing so hard there are tears in her eyes. "That is epic! Did he actually go through with the audition?"

"He did!" Jaime confirms. "I never heard if he made it on the show, but just knowing I sent him on that journey is satisfaction enough."

"Remind me not to get on your bad side," Maggie jokes, wiping her eyes. “And here I thought you were all sugar, no spice.”

Jaime shrugs and takes a sip of her own wine, still smiling. "All is fair in love and war."

"That is iconic!" I proclaim.

We all dissolve into laughter again. My cheeks hurt from grinning so hard. It feels amazing to be silly and bond over tales of ridiculous men.

Maggie tops off our glasses one last time. "To sisters from other misters!"

I clink glasses with my friends and add, “To Operation Take Down Owen!”

"Life is just a place
where we spend time between games."
- Fred Shero

MPONI

CHAPTER EIGHT

Owen

Ugh, what time is it? I blindly slap at my nightstand until I find my phone. 10:32 am. Crap. I've got seventeen missed calls and twice as many angry texts. Lovely. Nothing like waking up to an avalanche of rage from your agent and coach first thing in the morning.

I flop back against my pillows and rub my eyes, trying to shake the cobwebs from my brain. Last night was a gong show. That whole mess with the stolen trophy, staying late to file a police report, not to mention working on that stupid blog post with Emily. Okay, that part wasn't so bad. Right now, my head is throbbing like a jackhammer.

Reluctantly, I call my agent, Isaiah, back. He picks up on the first ring, yelling before I can even say hello. "Where the hell have you been? I've been calling all morning!"

"Sorry, I overslept," I mumble, stifling a yawn.

"This is unacceptable, Owen. That robbery is all over the news and we need to control the story. I need you in front of the cameras ASAP."

The thought of facing the rabid media horde right now makes me shudder. "Can't we push it to this afternoon? I'm exhausted."

Isaiah scoffs. "Don't be such a prima donna. Shower, get downtown, and spin this properly. We can't have people thinking you're somehow involved."

"Involved? You think I had something to do with the trophy being stolen?"

"I don't know what to think! Get your ass in gear and fix this." He hangs up abruptly. Charming as always.

I stare up at the ceiling, tempted to pull the covers back over my head and hide from the world for a few more hours. But I know Isaiah will just keep harassing me if I don't face the music.

With a groan, I drag myself out of bed and into the shower, hoping the hot water will help me feel slightly less like death warmed over. I've got a raging tension headache building behind my eyes and my muscles ache from being tossed around the ice by those Quebec goons last night. The last thing I want to do is slap on a happy face and make nice with the reporters. I can deal with them after games. This is bringing on a pain in my chest I haven't acknowledged since I was a teenager.

Ten minutes of yoga followed by my morning meditation calms me down. Then, after getting dressed, I make a smoothie with extra protein powder and check the 20 increasingly impatient texts from Coach Knight. He wants me downtown at the arena ASAP. Ugh, fine. Apparently, the execs are breathing down his neck. I chug the smoothie as I head out the door, its chalky sweetness coating my throat.

The bright winter sunlight pierces my eyeballs like shards of glass as I drive downtown. I slip on my aviators, but they only provide minor relief. By the time I pull into the underground parking garage, it feels like my brain is throbbing against my skull. Maybe I've got a concussion from that fight with Lemieux. Would serve Isaiah right if I puked on his fancy Italian loafers during the press conference.

I meet Coach and Isaiah in the media room. Coach's gray mustache is quivering like an angry caterpillar as he lectures me about responsibility. Isaiah shoves a cup of coffee into my hands, telling me to drink up. I choke down the bitter sludge and try to pretend I'm paying attention to whatever Coach is droning on about.

After what feels like an eternity, the reporters start filtering in. Isaiah ushers me to the table at the front of the room, the bright camera lights shining directly into my already throbbing eyeballs. The Titans' owner, Malcolm Chase, sits at the end of the table so he can get up and address the room from the official team podium for his opening statement before going back behind the table. He's all composure and poise in his three-piece suit and stoic expression. The tone of his voice soothing —almost lulling. Like flu medicine.

Then the floor opens up for the Q&A. I paste on my best media-ready grin as the first question comes flying at me.

"Owen, what can you tell us about the robbery?"

I repeat the same story I told the cops last night about hearing a noise and finding the smashed case. They keep peppering me with questions, but I stick to the script, feigning shock and outrage. After twenty tedious minutes, Isaiah finally ends the torture session and I make a beeline for the exit.

I'm almost to the parking garage when my phone rings again. Please don't let it be Isaiah demanding round two with the reporters. But it's not him—it's Nancy from the exec office.

"Owen, I just wanted to check in after the madness this morning. How are you holding up?" Her voice is warm with concern.

"Oh, hey, Nancy. I'm alright, just a long night and a painful presser."

"You poor thing. Tell you what, why don't you come up to my office for a bit and put your feet up?"

I hesitate. Hanging out in Nancy's office doesn't sound much more appealing than being accosted by reporters. But she's being nice and I'm too exhausted to argue.

"Yeah, okay. Be there in five."

Nancy bustles around, fussing over me as soon as I step into her office, bringing me a bottle of water and some Advil. I sink into the plush couch with relief. The cool leather feeling soothing against my tense muscles.

"Oh honey, you look absolutely wiped," Nancy clucks, perching on the edge of her desk across from me. Her office is bright and airy, with large windows overlooking Lake Ontario. I pop two of the pills and chug half the water bottle in one go.

"That press conference was a nightmare," I confess, leaning my head back and closing my eyes. The image of the mob of reporters shouting and cameras flashing burns behind my eyelids.

Nancy makes a sympathetic noise. "I can't even imagine. You handled it so well, though, staying calm and collected up there."

I give a half-hearted chuckle. Calm and collected is far from how I felt, pulse racing and hands shaking the whole time. But I managed to choke out the team's official statement without completely losing it, at least.

"I only wish I'd been fast enough to catch the bastard."

"Don't be so hard on yourself. When I spoke to Mark, he said he didn't even realize the car speeding past him in the parking lot was a robber until the next day."

"Wait. Mark was there? Mark, the equipment manager?"

"Yeah. He was warming up his engine when the getaway car wizzed right by him."

"Well... did he give any details? Make, model, license plate?"

Nancy shakes her head, her blonde curls bouncing around her shoulders. "No, unfortunately not. He wasn't paying that close attention to the car. He just wrote it off as some hot-rodder speeding through the parking lot."

I nod, considering this new information. Huh. So Mark was there, and I didn't even know it. What was he doing at the arena so late at night? He's always been a little strange, not gonna lie. I make a mental note to ask him about it later.

I thank Nancy for the mini spa treatment and head out, my headache fading slightly. The early February air still has a bite to it, but the sun is bright, melting the snowbanks lining the streets.

I swing through the McDonald's drive-thru to grab Cyrus a Happy Meal. I know the egg salad sandwich or whatever warmed over concoction Shannon packed will be straight in the trash the minute he opens his Baby Yoda lunchbox. The kid deserves a treat.

I pull up outside his school just as the bell rings, unleashing a stampede of wildlings onto the playground.

Kids are already swarming the playground equipment and grassy fields. I scan the chaos, looking for Cyrus' mop of unruly brown hair. Finally, I spot him sitting by himself under a big oak tree, picking at a sandwich. My heart twists. He looks so small and vulnerable. I weave through the mob, trying not to attract attention.

"Hey, buddy!" I say.

Cyrus's head snaps up, his eyes going wide with surprise and delight. "Owen!"

He leaps up and wraps his arms around me, grinning up at me, gap-toothed.

I hand him the Happy Meal bag discreetly.

"I thought we could have lunch together. But let's keep this on the down low." I wink.

Cyrus peeks in the bag, his face lighting up. "Whoa, a cheeseburger! And fries! You're the best."

I ruffle his hair. "Anything for you, kid."

We sit together under the tree, chatting about his day while he eagerly devours the forbidden fast food. In between bites, he tells me about the cool dragon story he's writing in his notebook. His shirt and face are soon smeared with ketchup and grease. The pure happiness radiating from him makes my crappy morning fade away. I sip my coffee and soak up this time together, knowing these moments are fleeting. Cyrus will be a moody, monosyllabic teen before I know it. But right now, with this little kid's excitement over a Happy Meal and his goofy grin, I'm savoring every second.

Before I realize, the bell rings, and Cyrus saves his leftover fries for later.

“Here,” I say, adding my untouched fries into his bag, “Take mine, too.”

Cyrus beams up at me, smiling with ketchup on his chin. I chuckle and turn to sneak off campus before I get busted.

I'm sprawled out on the couch at home, trying to unwind after the insanity of this morning. Some nature show is playing in the background while I scroll through my phone. I'm just starting to relax when an incoming call from Shannon pops up on my screen.

My shoulders tense reflexively. Conversations with Cyrus's mom are about as fun as a root canal. I debate letting it go to voicemail, but with a sigh, I swipe to answer.

"Hey, Shannon, what's up?" I say, aiming for a casual tone.

"Don't you 'what's up' me, Owen!" Shannon snaps. "I know you took Cyrus fast food today."

Crap. Busted.

"It was just a burger, no big deal," I say casually, trying to downplay it.

"It IS a big deal. I've told you a million times not to undermine my rules like that."

"Come on, Shannon, the kid was thrilled. Didn't you see how happy he was?"

"That's not the point! You can't just swoop in with treats whenever you feel like it. I'm his mother. I make the rules."

I run a hand through my hair in frustration. "Look, I was just trying to do something nice for my brother..." I start, but Shannon cuts me off.

"Well, your 'nice' gesture caused a huge problem. Cyrus got into a fight today because the other kids were jealous and tried to take his fries."

Aw crap. I sit up, guilt hitting me square in the gut.

"A fight? Is he okay?" I ask urgently.

"He'll be fine. But this is exactly why you can't pull crap like that, Owen," Shannon lectures.

I slump back against the couch, worry swirling in my chest. I was just trying to do a good thing for the kid.

Shannon's still railing at me through the phone. "I can't have you confusing him like this. It's too disruptive."

"I'm his brother. I'm just trying to be there for him," I protest.

"Well, maybe he'd be better off if you weren't," Shannon snaps, then as if she's forcing herself to speak calmly, sighs and adds quietly, "I think it would be best if you didn't see Cyrus for a while."

Ouch.

"This isn't fair, Shannon. He needs me. Maybe if we find him a new school..." My voice cracks slightly.

"Stay out of it, Owen. I'm his mother. Let me do my job."

I slump forward, elbows on my knees, and head in my hands. Arguing is pointless—she's made up her mind.

"At least let me help out financially if you won't let me see him," I plead.

"Absolutely not," she says sharply. "We're doing just fine on our own."

"Come on, it could really help with clothes, after-school activities..."

"I said no! This is exactly why you need to back off. I can handle my son without you throwing your money around."

I sigh heavily. She's way too stubborn and proud to accept any help. Meanwhile, I'm stuck here feeling completely useless.

“Listen, Owen, I need to get off the phone now.”

“So that’s it? Just goodbye forever?”

“No, not forever, Owen. I gotta go.”

With that, she hangs up, and I’m left staring at my phone screen like an idiot. Feeling like I just got sucker punched in the gut, I toss my phone aside and rake my hands through my hair, blowing out a long breath. Well, that was a freaking disaster.

I can't believe she banned me from seeing my own brother. Cyrus needs me, whether she wants to admit it or not. I'm the only positive male role model in his life. If I'm not around, who's going to teach him to throw a spiral or stand up to bullies? Not our deadbeat dad, that's for sure. The thought of Cyrus growing up without me there makes my chest ache.

I push up from the couch and start pacing, too amped up to sit still. I've gotta fix this somehow. Make Shannon see reason, get her to lift this ban.

I wish I could march over there right now and talk some sense into her. But it would only make things worse. Once Shannon gets an idea in her head, there's no changing her mind.

With a heavy sigh, I try to push my swirling thoughts about Cyrus aside. If I let that phone call with Shannon fester in my head, I'm gonna lose it.

The last 24 hours have been a dumpster fire. First Emily's backhanded blog post, then losing the game against Quebec. Then the robbery.

I have to find out who took our trophy. For the team, yeah, but also for myself. I need to feel like I can fix something, anything, after being so helpless with Cyrus.

My mind starts churning through potential suspects. Could it have been that slimeball Georges Lemieux trying to get in our heads before the playoffs? He practically admitted he was going to steal the trophy when he got in my face after the game.

Or maybe their coach, Claude Rousseau? He's had it out for Coach Knight ever since that blowout back in '97. This seems like the kind of petty thing he'd pull just to get revenge.

Then again, Nancy mentioned something weird about Mark being there last night. He's been acting kinda squirrely lately. And he'd have access to the arena after hours.

I shake my head, trying to connect the dots. None of it adds up. But I can't sit here doing nothing. I've gotta start digging and find some real evidence.

For Cyrus's sake, I need this win. I have to prove to myself and to Shannon that I can still protect my baby brother, even if she's slamming doors in my face.

My leg bounces with restless energy as determination courses through me. I'm getting to the bottom of this heist if it kills me. No more sitting around feeling sorry for myself. It's time to take action.

I grab my keys and head for the door, ready to launch my own investigation. Lemieux, Rousseau, Mark—whoever did this—they don't know the storm that's coming for them.

The next night, I pull into the arena parking lot after hours. This mystery has consumed my thoughts all day.

So has Emily's soft, pink lips. But I push that waaay down. I need to find out who stole the Memorial Cup to get justice for the team. And if I can crack this case, it'll prove to Shannon I'm not as irresponsible as she thinks.

I stride towards the employee entrance, trying not to look too conspicuous. Hal's there, a little surprised to see me.

"Hey Hal," I say in greeting. "I forgot to take home my dress suit the other night and if I don't get it to the dry cleaners first thing in the morning... Ya know."

He doesn't need to know I have more than one suit.

"No worries, Cap." he salutes me. "I won't leave my post tonight, not even for a wiz."

"We don't deserve you, Hal," I say, patting him on the back as I enter the arena.

The hallway is empty and eerily quiet without the usual pre-game buzz. I creep along, peering into dark offices and storage rooms as I pass. So far, so creepy.

I'm nearing the area near Mark's office when hushed voices drift out from around the corner. I freeze, pressing myself flat against the wall. Who the hell is in there? I inch closer, straining to make out the words.

"... almost got caught. We need to be more careful," a female voice whispers sharply.

There's a snort, then a second voice—also female—retorts, "Um, we were careful. Janitors have terrible vision. It's fine."

What the...? Is someone planning another heist? My pulse quickens. I have to get visuals on these perps.

Holding my breath, I slowly peer down the hallway. Two figures are silhouetted against an open doorway, tip-toeing like little lemurs. One is petite with a long blonde ponytail—Emily! My eyes narrow. Why is she sneaking around?

The other one has wild, dark hair sticking out in all directions. I don't recognize her at all. The girls continue whispering to each other, oblivious to my presence.

What the heck are they up to? I should confront them, but I need more intel first. I discreetly pull out my phone, ready to snap some evidence.

Just as I'm about to hit record, the brunette whips around. "Hey!" she shouts.

Crap! I flash an awkward smile. "Oh, uh, hey ladies. Fancy seeing you here..."

Emily's eyes widen in alarm before her expression morphs into a scowl. "Seriously, Owen? You're spying on us now?"

"What? No, nope. Just passing through!" I say with faux casualness.

The wild-haired one marches over to me, hands on her hips. She's tiny but somehow manages to look intimidating.

"Listen bud, I don't know who you think you are, but—"

"It's fine, Mags," Emily interrupts, grabbing the girl's arm. She turns to me, eyes narrowed. "We're leaving."

They brush past me, but I step sideways to block their path. "Hang on now. I think you owe me an explanation. What are you two doing sneaking around at this hour?"

The one called Mags fixes me with a death glare and opens her mouth to retort, but Emily speaks first.

"Nothing. Not that it's any of your business. Let us pass." Her tone brokers no argument.

I hold my ground. "Doesn't seem like nothing. Looked an awful lot like you were up to something crafty. So I ask you again. What are you doing here?"

Emily snorts. "I could ask you the same thing." She pokes me hard in the chest.

I'd be lying if I said that little touch didn't burn right through my clothes.

I use one finger to move her hand to the side. "Looking for excuses to touch me, Kitty Cat?"

Yeah, I'm shamelessly having a little fun with Emily with her tiny friend right here. Seriously, do short people have a way of finding each other?

Mags scoffs. She turns to Emily. "Come on, let's just go."

Emily hesitates, holding my gaze. I think I spot a flicker of amusement in her eyes. She bites her lip. "Ya know, for a meathead, you sure think highly of yourself."

"Meathead?!" Now I'm out for blood. "Oh it's on, sister!"

Emily gets all up in my face, her wild hair tickling my chin. I have to fight the urge not to laugh at this pint-sized ball of fury. Or kiss her. Her juicy watermelon scent is getting to me. What is that? Shampoo? Lotion?

Stop thinking about Emily and lotion, Owen. Just stop!

Mags steps between us with a weary sigh. "Enough! We're leaving. Now."

She grabs Emily by the elbow and steers her down the hall. I trail behind them, not about to let them just walk away.

"Hold up! We're not done here."

Emily whirls around, eyes flashing. "The puck's in your court, Jablonski."

What could she possibly mean by that?

With a final witchy grin, she follows Mags around the corner, their footsteps echoing down the empty hallway. I rake a hand through my hair in frustration. Well, that was a bust. I still have no idea what those two were up to.

I'm intrigued despite myself. There's a fiery recklessness simmering under that petite blonde exterior. And I find myself wanting to stoke those flames, to see them rise up and consume us both...

Woah. Where did that thought come from? I shake the image from my head sharply. Focus. I've got a thief to catch. No time for bizarre daydreams about Emily freaking Brooks.

"You miss 100% of the shots
you don't take."
– Wayne Gretzky

MPONI

CHAPTER NINE

Owen

My stall is completely covered in glittery My Little Pony stickers. I blink a few times, wondering if I'm hallucinating. Nope, they're definitely there. All over the shelves. All over the framed action shot of me on the wall.

Sparkly pink, purple and blue ponies grin back at me. Sawyer and Hendrix bust out laughing as soon as they spot it.

"Nice decorating job, Juggernaut. Very badass," Sawyer says, shaking his head.

The rest of the guys turn to look and immediately start cracking up. I feel my face getting hot.

"Aww, I think it's cute," Hendrix says in a mocking baby voice. "Our little Owen is in touch with his feminine side."

I start ripping off the stickers, but there are dozens of them. This is going to take forever.

"Alright, hilarious. Which one of you idiots did this?"

No one fesses up. I scan the room, but all I get are snickers and exaggerated shrugs.

I grumble under my breath, realizing exactly who is behind this childish prank. Emily. That's what she and her crazy friend were doing here late at night. Real mature.

As if the sticker bomb isn't humiliating enough, when I open my locker, a cascade of plastic balls spills out, bouncing everywhere. They're those super bouncy kinds from Chuck E. Cheese's or something. Seriously?! I hear Sawyer and Hendrix cracking up as I scramble to gather them up.

"Having some toy problems there, Owen?" Sawyer smirks.

"Har har," I deadpan, shoving the last few balls back into my locker and slamming it shut.

I'll deal with Emily later. Right now I need to focus on the game. Coach Knight is relying on me to lead the offense against the Hurricanes' tough defense.

As we hit the ice, I feel pumped and ready. The pony stickers and plastic balls were a momentary annoyance, but I won't let anything shake my game mindset.

The puck drops and I'm off, flying across the ice. My legs feel strong and my stick handling is tight. I gain control of the puck near the blue line and see an opening. With a burst of speed, I split the defense and find myself one-on-one with the goalie. I wind up and let a slapshot rip, nailing it top shelf. Goal!

The crowd erupts into cheers as my teammates surround me, giving me fist bumps and helmet taps. But then the goal song starts blasting from the speakers. Instead of our usual classic rock anthem, the arena fills with a synthesized, perky kid's bob song. The only reason I recognize it as "Baby Shark" is because Cyrus wouldn't stop singing it when I would pick him up from summer day camp four years ago. A simpler time when Shannon had no choice but to let me help due to her demanding work schedule. I remember having to bribe him with ice cream to get him to shut up. Full disclosure: I would have bought him ice cream anyway.

The song blares on as I try not to laugh. Emily somehow hacked the music. I've gotta give her credit for creativity with these pranks. But two can play at this game.

I notch two more goals and an assist in the first period. We're dominating the Hurricanes early.

During the intermission, I confer with Coach Knight

about defensive adjustments. He seems pleased with my performance so far.

"Keep it up out there, Juggernaut. I want you leading the charge," he says, clapping me on the shoulder.

As we retake the ice for the second period, I feel locked in. But I can't resist scanning the sidelines for Emily. There she is, bundled up in an oversized hoodie. Even from here, I can see those big hazel eyes fixed on me.

I power through the period, racking up more points for the team. We take a solid lead over Carolina. I keep an eye out for Emily's reactions whenever I score or make a nice play. She's trying hard not to show it, but I can tell she's impressed.

Between periods, I catch her by the Zamboni garage while Joe resurfaces the ice. "Enjoying the show?" I ask with a cocky grin.

She narrows her eyes. "Don't let it go to your head, Juggernaut. Still a long game left."

"Oh don't worry, I'm just getting started," I shoot back.

The final period is a flurry of activity. The Hurricanes rally late, but we manage to fend them off and secure the win.

I'm feeling pumped after the victory. I can't wait to really get Emily back for those pranks now. As annoying as they were, I've gotta admit I like her fiery spirit. No one's challenged me like this in a long time.

I find Emily in the parking lot after the game, leaning against the hood of my car with her arms crossed. She's got on that smug little smile like she's won something, even though her little pranks didn't phase me one bit.

"Well, well, if it isn't Toronto's juiciest beefcake. Nice game tonight, Junk-for-nuts."

I roll my eyes. She just can't resist needling me. "Don't call me that. And move your cute little butt off my car before you scratch the paint."

She hops down, grin growing wider. "So you think my butt is cute?"

"Don't flatter yourself. Now are you gonna tell me what that childish sticker prank was all about?"

Her eyes dance with wicked delight. "I haven't the faintest idea what you're talking about."

"You think you're funny, don't you? That's why you were sneaking around the other night. Do I need to get security on you?"

"Simmer down there, big guy. I was just having a little fun. Don't get your shorts in a bunch."

I take a step toward her, using my height to loom over her petite frame. Her smile falters for a split second before the sass returns.

"This little game of yours stops now."

She stands up taller, refusing to be intimidated. "Or what?"

I clench my jaw, tamping down my frustration. She's

trying to get a rise out of me. I change tactics, softening my tone.

"Look, I already said I wouldn't reveal your identity if you play nice. But pranks like that make me reconsider our arrangement."

She pokes my chest with one dainty finger. "You were lurking around the arena late the other night, too. You can't tell on me without exposing yourself."

She has a point. I grab her hand to stop the poking. It's so small compared to mine. Delicate, but strong at the same time.

Her gaze bores into me. "Now tell me what you were up to."

I hesitate, unsure whether to trust her. But the fierce look in her whiskey eyes crumbles my resolve.

"I was investigating the trophy theft, okay?"

Emily's eyebrows shoot up in surprise. "Wait, you're investigating the robbery?"

"Someone has to get to the bottom of it. I didn't want to just sit around waiting for someone else to solve it."

"Huh," Emily says, clearly intrigued. "So, do you have any suspects?"

I shake my head, reluctantly letting go of her hand. "Not yet. But I have a hunch about someone on the staff. I think he's involved."

"Who is it?"

I blow out a breath. “Mark.” But I quickly add, “This

stays between you and me, okay? If Mark realizes I'm on to him, he might do something desperate."

"Mark the equipment manager? Why do you think he did it?"

I debate how much to reveal. But telling Emily seems less risky than letting her imagination run wild. "He was here. That night. He said he saw the getaway car, but I think he's just covering his tracks. And the more I thought about it, the more it makes sense it's an inside job. Whoever stole that trophy knew exactly how long they had before the generator turned back on in order to evade the security cameras.

"They would have to time it just right," Emily supplied.

"Mmhmm. Plus, his behavior has been... off lately."

"Off how?" Emily presses. Her reporter's instinct is clearly kicking in now.

"He's been staying late a lot, even when there's no reason for him to be here. And he got weirdly defensive earlier today when I asked what he was doing the night of the theft."

Emily taps her chin thoughtfully. "That does seem suspicious. Have you told the cops?"

I let out a derisive laugh. "Like they'd take the hunch of some hockey player seriously. I need more concrete proof first."

"Do... you have a plan?"

"I thought I might find some evidence in Mark's

office. But it would have to be late. Really late, after he goes home for the night."

"I could help you!" she blurts.

"Help me? Yeah right. No way I'm letting you tag along," I scoff. Emily puts her hands on her hips, eyes blazing. "Why not? I could be useful."

"Useful? The only thing you've been useful for is pranking me and writing snarky blog posts."

"Hey! My blog provides valuable insights into the inner workings of the team."

I let out a derisive laugh. "Oh please. Your so-called insights are just veiled attempts to poke fun at us."

Emily shakes her head defiantly, honey-blonde strands escaping her beanie hat. "That's not true. I mean, yes, I take some creative liberties for entertainment value—"

"You mean outright lies?" I interrupt.

"Embellishments," she corrects. "But I also highlight positive things that fans truly appreciate learning about their favorite players."

I snort in disbelief. "Yeah, buried under mountains of sarcasm."

"Look, my readers have really responded to the posts I've written about you lately. Your charity work, mentoring kids...you're more complex than just some arrogant jock."

I blink in surprise. That was almost a compliment coming from her.

Emily goes on, "If I can get an inside look at you

tracking down the stolen trophy, it would make for an amazing story. My readers would eat it up. And it could improve your image too."

I hesitate, mulling it over. She sort of has a point. This could be a chance to reveal a different side of me.

Emily looks up at me with those big *Puss In Boots* eyes. "I promise no snark this time. Just an honest, straightforward account of the investigation."

Ah jeez. I try to ignore how kissable her lips look.

"Alright fine," I concede. Emily's face lights up. "But you follow my lead, got it? No going off on your own."

"Deal!" She sticks out her hand for me to shake. Her grip is surprisingly strong for such a petite thing.

"Tomorrow night. After the game."

"You got it, detective."

She gives me a cheeky salute and starts to walk off, her little hips swaying. I force myself to look away. This arrangement is strictly business.

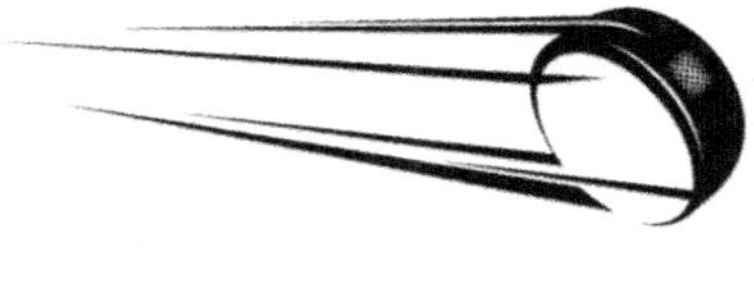

"My sport taught me
what I could do with my talents,
whether in the rink
or in the rest of my life."
- Peggy Fleming

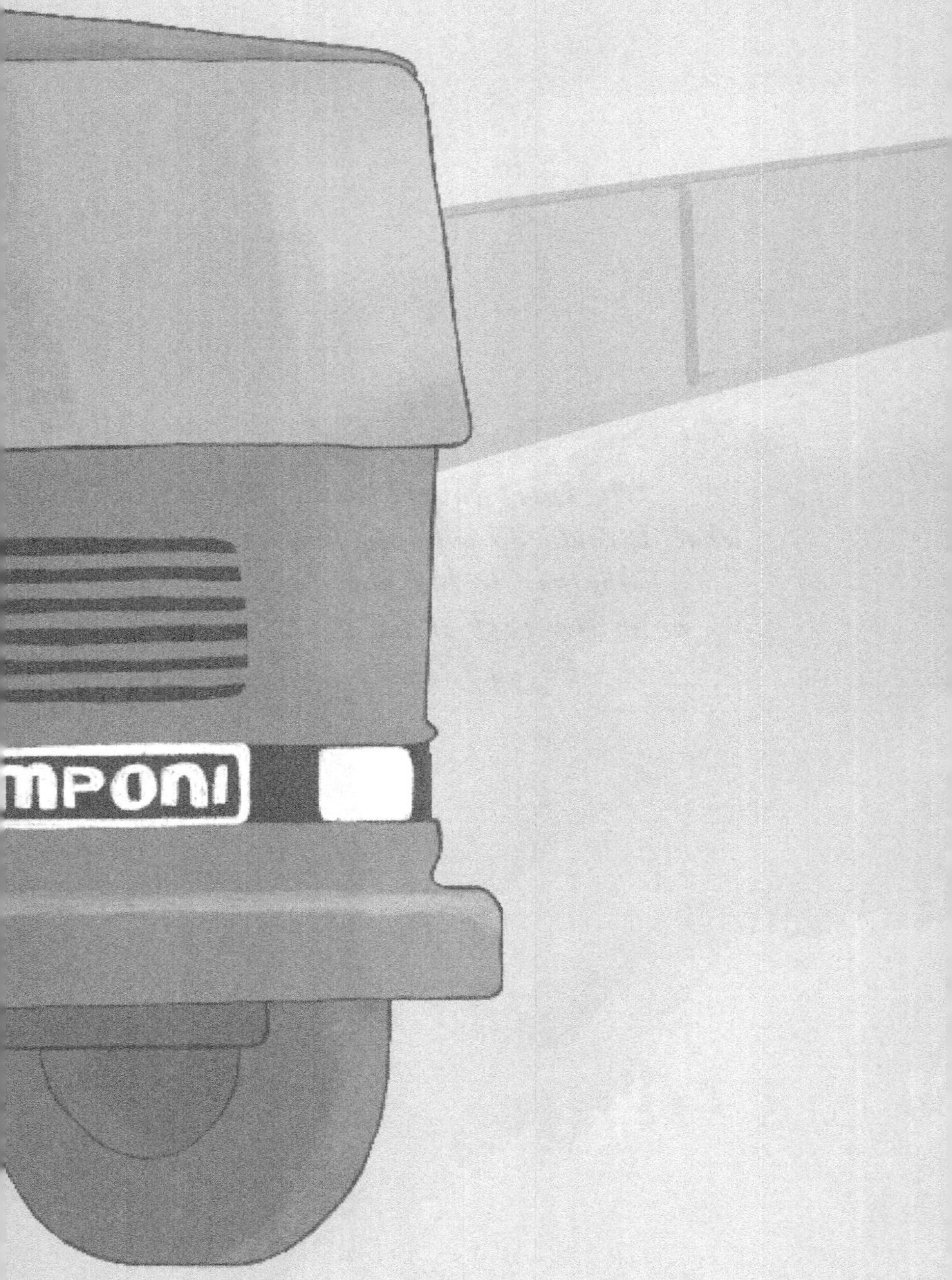
MPONI

CHAPTER TEN

Emily

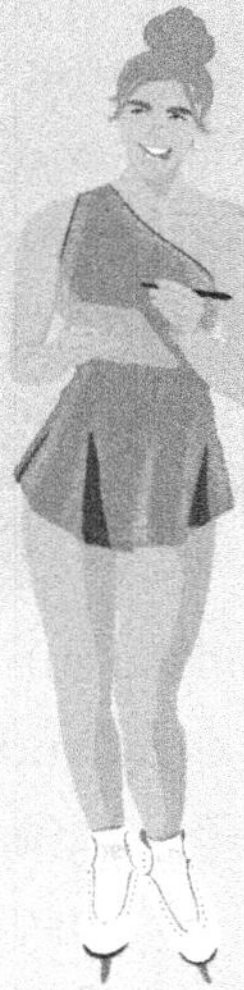

Sneaking around after hours with Owen is the last thing I ever imagined I'd be doing, yet here I am, dressed in all black as I creep through the deserted halls of the Blizzard Dome.

Why did I even volunteer for this ridiculous cloak and dagger investigation? Owen must have used some rakish manipulation to get me to think it was my idea.

"Nice outfit, Catwoman," Owen says with a roguish

grin as he looks me up and down. "Though I gotta say, I didn't take you for the sexy burglar type."

I roll my eyes. “Can it, Jablonski. We’re not on a date, we’re committing a felony here. So keep it in your hockey shorts, okay?”

He just chuckles, clearly enjoying ruffling my feathers. I hate that he looks so at ease, like breaking and entering is just another fun game to him.

We reach Mark’s office and I pull out the key I secretly copied earlier today, turning it slowly in the lock. The tumblers click into place. I glance back at Owen, unable to keep the smugness from my face.

"After you," I say, holding the door open with a flourish.

We slip inside, and I close the door behind us with a soft click. The room is dark and cramped, filled with metal shelves stacked with equipment. Owen brushes up against me as we squeeze past a rack of sticks.

“Cozy,” he murmurs, his breath tickling my ear. I shiver involuntarily.

“Focus, Jablonski,” I hiss. “We’re looking for anything that ties Mark to the robbery.”

I pull a small flashlight from my pocket and begin scanning the cluttered space. Owen sidles up beside me, peering over my shoulder, the fresh pine scent of him attacking my self-restraint.

“Well, well, Brooks, look what we have here.” Owen reaches around me—close, so close—and plucks a receipt off the shelf. "Looks like Mark made a little purchase the day after the trophy went missing."

I snatch the receipt from Owen's hand, my pulse quickening. It's from a pawn shop downtown, time stamped the morning after the break-in.

"This could be it," I breathe. "The proof we need to expose him."

Owen grins, his blue eyes glinting in the dim light. "Ya know, I didn't think we'd be such a good team, but now I'm warming up to the idea."

I fight the urge to smile back. I can't let him think I'm actually enjoying this. But the truth is, it is kind of thrilling, being here with Owen on this secret mission.

We continue searching the small office, bumping into each other repeatedly in the tight space. Owen takes every opportunity to place his hands on me, steadying my waist or catching my arm. Normally I'd shove him away, but I can't afford to make any noise.

"You know, Brooks," he says quietly. "If I didn't know any better, I'd say you orchestrated this whole thing just to get me alone."

I whip around to face him. "You are delusional."

He grins down at me, backing me up against the shelf. "Come on, just admit you have a little crush on me."

My cheeks burn, but I keep my voice steady. "You are the most arrogant man I have ever met."

Owen leans in close, bracing his hands on the shelf

on either side of my head. I'm trapped between him and the cold metal at my back.

"It's just us, Kitty Cat," he whispers. "Why else would you go to such lengths to annoy me?"

My pulse is racing but I refuse to let him fluster me. I slip under his arm and turn the tables, shoving him back against the shelf.

"You listen to me, Owen Jablonski," I say sharply. "The only thing going on between us is this investigation. Understood?"

He looks momentarily surprised and then laughs.

"You're cute when you're flustered. Do you know that?"

"Shhh!"

I go back to searching the office, my flashlight illuminating stacks of paperwork. Owen is close beside me, his muscular frame nearly brushing against mine in the cramped space.

"Hmmm." Owen murmurs, pulling out a stack of papers wedged between two helmets. "I think I found something."

I shine my light over the documents. They appear to be betting slips, pages and pages of them.

"Mark has a gambling problem," I say in surprise. "A pretty serious one, from the looks of this."

Owen flips through the slips, letting out a low whistle. "He's got some hefty bets here. The kind they break legs over."

My mind races, thoughts clicking into place. "So if Mark was desperate for money to pay off debts..."

"He might steal a priceless team trophy to pawn for cash," Owen finishes. He turns to look at me, eyes gleaming. "This is big. The motive we've been looking for."

I nod, pulse quickening. This could be the break in the case we've needed. Wordlessly, I pull out my phone and start snapping pictures of the incriminating evidence.

Owen moves closer, looking over my shoulder. I try to ignore his proximity, the way I can feel his warm breath on my neck as he peers at my phone screen. Focus, I remind myself. "Good thinking, getting photographic proof. Still, I think I'll take a few of these. Just in case."

He stuffs a few receipts in his pocket. I step aside, straightening my clothes with as much dignity as I can muster.

"I think we've got what we came for," I say briskly, stowing my phone away. "Now let's get out of here before we're caught."

My heart pounds as Owen and I slip out of Mark's office. We got what we came for, but now we just have to sneak out.

We ease the office door shut behind us when a noise down the hall makes us both freeze. Footsteps. My pulse skyrockets. Owen's eyes go wide with panic, mirroring my own.

"It's Mark," he hisses. "We've gotta move now!"

We can't go back the way we came, so we take off down the hall—away from the footsteps, but there's nowhere to go. It's a dead end, no other doors or hallways branching off. We're trapped.

The footsteps grow louder, closing in. Owen grabs my arm and pulls me into a dark alcove, pressing my back against the wall. I hold my breath, heart hammering against my ribs. Owen's broad shoulders shield me from view as he peers around the edge of the alcove. We can't let Mark catch us, not when we're this close. Owen shifts, angling his body to block me even more.

"I'm going to do something you probably won't like... but I need you to go with it," he whispers, his face so close to me, I can smell whatever balm he puts in his closely clipped beard. Before I can respond, his mouth descends onto mine in a searing kiss.

For a split second, I freeze up in shock. But as the footsteps echo down the hallway, instinct takes over and I find myself kissing him back, my hands coming up tentatively to grasp his muscular arms.

My head spins, heat flooding through me. I know this is just an act, a cover to avoid getting caught. But as our mouths move together, that fades into the background. All I can focus on is the feeling of his lips on mine, firm and demanding. The scratch of his whiskers against my skin.

Somewhere in the recesses of my mind, alarm bells

sound. This is Owen Jablonski, my enemy. The cocky, womanizing jock who I vowed to ruin. I shouldn't be kissing him like this, shouldn't be arching into him as his lips slide against mine.

But the way he kisses me, like he's pouring every ounce of passion into this moment, makes it impossible to resist him. His lips are firm yet surprisingly soft, molding against my own. My hands grip his broad shoulders and I devour him hungrily, months of pent-up frustration boiling over.

A warmth spreads through my body that has nothing to do with the anger and irritation Owen usually elicits in me. I feel almost limp in his arms, my knees going weak.

How can someone so arrogant and infuriating also be so talented with his mouth? My lips tingle everywhere they meet his. It's like my body has a mind of its own, responding to Owen's kiss even as my rational mind rebels.

One of his hands slides into my hair, angling my head back further, deepening the kiss. I gasp and he takes the opportunity to press me harder against the wall.

I'm in so much trouble here. I need to stop this, I need to push him away... but I can't seem to make myself do it.

He kisses me like he has all the time in the world to explore my mouth. He tastes like mint and something uniquely masculine, a taste I didn't know I craved until now.

My hands clutch at his shoulders, feeling the strength in them. Somewhere in the recesses of my lust-addled brain, I know I should be resisting, that Owen represents everything I stand against. But right now, pinned between his muscular body and the wall, coherent thought is beyond me.

A low groan rumbles in Owen's chest that I feel a shudder through me. The sound sends desire coursing down to my navel, and my fingers give his neck a little scratch of their own volition. He pulls back a fraction, both of us breathless.

"Well, would you look at that. Kitten has claws," he murmurs, voice rough. His eyes are hooded, lips kiss-swollen. He looks as dazed as I feel.

I lick my tingling lips, trying to gather the scraps of my dignity. But I have no quick retort, no witty come-back. Right now, I just want his mouth back on mine.

Owen seems to read my need because he swoops in again, claiming my lips in another drugging kiss. His body pins me in place while his mouth works me into a frenzy I've never experienced before.

I hate that he can make me feel this way with just a kiss. I hate it and I crave it. My hands are in his hair now, gripping the wavy strands. I kiss him back feverishly, taking everything he's giving me.

I'm lost, feeling the sensation of free-falling out of an airplane, when the sharp sound of a throat clearing shatters the moment. We break apart, flushed and breathless. Mark stands there staring at us, eyebrows raised.

"Can I help you two with something?" he asks pointedly.

Owen slips into an easy grin. “Sorry man, we were just, uh...”

Mark tilts his head suspiciously. “Shouldn’t you two have left hours ago?”

“My woman had to work late,” Owen says smoothly, the lie rolling effortlessly off his tongue, “And then... well, my lady likes to roleplay. You understand.”

He smacks my butt and winks at me. I am so going to kill him later. Smiling, Owen jerks his chin at Mark like it’s some kind of bro language I don’t understand. The bro language of philandering d-bags.

Mark nods, eyes volleying between me and Owen.

"We'll get out of your hair." Owen takes my hand and gathers me close to him, and as we hurry past Mark down the hallway, his eyes bore into our backs. As soon as we're out of view, I drop Owen's hand, my lips still tingling from his kiss. What just happened back there? For a moment, I let myself forget who Owen is, the secrets between us.

And suddenly I’m so angry. Humiliated for getting caught, or maybe ashamed at the way I let my guard down.

I round on him with fury in my voice. “My lady likes to *roleplay*? What the heck was that?”

He shrugs. "Just improvising."

"Do you always make a habit of kissing women against their will?"

"Against your will? From where I was standing, you were quite enthusiastic."

"You'd think so, wouldn't you? Typical, arrogant womanizer."

Something like angst flashes in his eyes, just for a second. And then his lip quirks on one side as he scowls at me. "Don't get too excited, Kitty Cat. It was strictly business. You can go back to hating me now."

His arm barely brushes against mine as he walks past me, not giving me another look, leaving me in the hallway with the taste of him still on my lips.

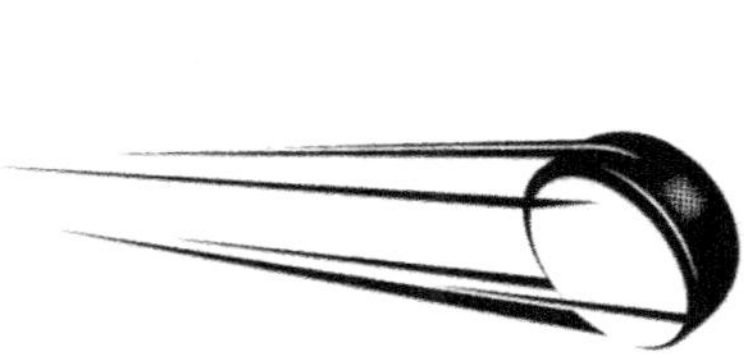

Figure skating
is a mixture of art and sport.
- Katarina Witt

MPONI

CHAPTER ELEVEN

Emily

I am a terrible, terrible person. A terrible, horrible person and an even worse friend.

I can still feel Owen's lips on mine from last night. What was I thinking, letting him kiss me like that? I mean, sure, he's attractive in that cocky, hockey player kind of way. When he's not being a total jerk, I can sort of see the appeal. But he's still Owen freaking Jablonski. Arrogant. Entitled. A player on and off the ice.

I'm such an idiot. I got so caught up in our little Hardy Boys investigation that I let my guard down. And now Owen probably thinks I'm just another puck bunny falling all over him. As if! I was just... going along with it to avoid getting caught. Yeah, that's it. Strictly strategy, nothing more.

Get it together, Emily. You're a mature, independent woman who does not swoon over chiseled cheekbones and bedroom eyes. Even if said bedroom eyes are a gorgeous shade of blue that makes me think of the sky on a brisk, cloudless day...

I give myself a little shake and force myself to think of something else. Anything else.

I decide to give Jaime a call, just wanting to hear her voice and make sure she's doing okay. I ask her what she's doing as I walk down the street toward my apartment building after my morning shift at the arena. I don't mention Owen at all, but the guilt is gnawing away at me.

Jaime sighs dramatically. "Oh, you know me. Moping around, listening to sad songs, staring longingly at old photos of me and Owen together..."

Owen. The man who had his lips on me last night. All over me. I am a poor excuse for a human being.

She pauses, getting choked up. "I just miss him so much, you know? I keep replaying our last fight in my head, wondering if there was anything I could've done differently." Her voice cracks a little. "And now he won't return any of my calls or texts."

I feel a pang in my chest listening to her. "Oh honey, you're not still texting him, are you?"

"The last time we talked, I said some hurtful things I regret. I guess I just want him to know I'm not the jealous type and that I'm sorry."

"Jaime, he cheated on you. He's the one who should be sorry."

I hate myself right now, still feeling the aftershock of kissing the enemy, while Jaime's at home nursing a broken heart. She needs a good friend, not a betrayer.

"You are a beautiful woman, Jaime. You don't need a man to make you feel that way."

"I know." She takes a shaky breath. "I'm trying to stay positive and keep busy, but it's so hard. My heart feels like it's been ripped in two."

I wish I could give her a hug through the phone. "Heartbreak is the worst. But you're so strong, and you'll get through this. I'm here for you, whatever you need."

Jaime lets out another trembling sigh. "Thanks, you're the best. I don't know what I'd do without you right now. Just having someone to talk to helps a little." She blows her nose loudly. "Anyway, enough about me. What have you been up to?"

Other than making out with her cheating ex-boyfriend?

"Oh... nothing."

Lies. I sit on a throne of lies.

I'm about to give her the Owen-free version of my excitement with the stolen trophy, when something catches my eye. Sitting on the curb outside my building is a huge antique grandfather clock. Not just any clock, but an intricately carved oak beauty that looks like it's from the early 1900s. The case is decorated with curved legs, spindles, and carved rosettes. The only thing missing is the pendulum.

"No way," I murmur in awe.

"What's going on?" Jaime asks.

"Someone just left the most gorgeous antique grandfather clock outside my apartment building," I explain. “It's incredible.”

Jaime laughs. "Only you would freak out over trash furniture."

"It's not trash, it's vintage!" I protest. “Although now that I look more closely, this thing is pretty huge and heavy. No way I can get it up to my third-floor walk-up by myself.”

“Do you have anyone who could help you? A neighbor, maybe?”

“No, I don’t want to bother my neighbors. But if you and Maggie want to come over, I think we can manage it between the three of us. I’ll buy you Swiss Chalet and chocolate cake for lunch.”

I can practically hear Jaime’s stomach growling. Swiss Chalet’s mashed potatoes are her favorite.

"Ooh, bummer," Jaime says. "I'd love to come help, but I promised my mom I’d dye her hair."

“Isn’t your mom working right now?”

“Yes... but I need to go to the store for the color before she gets home and I really don’t have time.”

“Well, there’s a Loblaws around the corner from me. You can help me carry this heavy thing up to my place, and then we can go to the store together.”

“I’ll help you.” Cody, of all people, pops next to me so unexpectedly, I almost drop my phone.

"Oh, uh, it's really okay, Cody," I say briskly. “I got this.”

Jaime's voice comes through the phone. “Who’s that?”

“It’s... my neighbor.”

“The creepy guy from the other night?”

“Yup.”

Cody leans his arm against the grandfather clock. "Doesn't look like you can manage it alone. You could use someone... strong and manly."

I cover the phone with my hand. "No thanks, Cody. I'll figure it out."

"Are you sure?"

"Just let him help, Em,” Jaime says. “Otherwise, you'll never get that clock upstairs."

I sigh. She's right. And the clock is so perfect, I'd hate to leave it out here.

"Alright Cody, if you really don't mind," I concede.

"It would be my pleasure!" he says gallantly.

Jaime lets me go, and Cody and I each take one end of the clock.

It's cumbersome and heavy, but together we awkwardly maneuver it into the building and up the three flights of stairs to my apartment. The whole time, Cody is making weird grunting noises and finding excuses to brush against me while changing places on the landings between floors.

Finally, we get it situated in my living room.

I plop down on my couch, admiring my new find.

"Thank you so much for the help," I tell him sincerely. "I really appreciate you taking the time."

"Of course, of course," he says, hovering a little too close. There's that sly grin of his. The thing is, Cody is probably a nice guy. Probably. Maybe he'll meet a girl who doesn't mind bad breath and sweat that smells like pepperoni. That girl is not me.

"Well, I won't keep you any longer," I say pointedly.

But Cody doesn't take the hint. "So, now that I did you a favor, seems like you owe me," he says, raising his eyebrows suggestively. "How about I take you out to dinner tomorrow night so you can... you know, properly thank me?"

"Oh, uh..." I stammer, taken aback by his bluntness. I rack my brain for an excuse. "That sounds... interesting, but I just found out I have a rare condition where I'm allergic to awkward situations, and I fear that might trigger a flare-up."

Cody blinks at me blankly. "Oh sure, I get it. But if you change your mind..."

"Absolutely, I'll let you know," I lie, steering him gently but firmly toward the door.

Cody hangs around awkwardly at the doorway for a few more minutes, even though I keep dropping hints that I need to get going.

“Okay, thanks again,” I say. “But I have to go back to work in a couple hours, so...”

“You work at the Blizzard Dome, right?”

“Yeah. I really should get ready now, though.”

He nods, thoughtful. “I don’t really care for hockey.”

“Oh. Well, it’s not for everyone.” I push the door closed as much as I can with him standing in the way.

“That was some pretty good teamwork, you and me.”

“Yes, it sure was,” I say, still trying to close the door.

He lifts his chin. “I’ll pick you up tomorrow at eight.”

“What?”

“Wear something sexy.”

Before I have a chance to say anything else, he runs away. I slam the door shut behind him and slide the deadbolt for good measure. I really need to be more careful to avoid Cody from now on. The last thing I want is to lead him on any more than I might have just done.

I'm still reeling from the bizarre interaction with Cody as I head into work at the Blizzard Dome later this afternoon. The arena is mostly empty, with just a few staff milling around, getting ready for tonight's game.

Making my way down the hallway towards the Zamboni garage, I hear Owen's voice coming from around the corner. I stop short, pressing myself against the wall. His low baritone is... bringing up *those* feelings again. The late-night caper. The thrill of discovery. The danger. That mind-blowing kiss.

He seems to be on the phone. I probably shouldn't eavesdrop, but curiosity gets the better of me (and also because hearing him talk makes me think about his lips). I inch closer, straining to hear.

"... I just want what's best for him, that's all," Owen is saying, an unfamiliar, gentle tone in his voice. "You know I care about Cyrus."

Cyrus? Who the heck is Cyrus? I wrack my brain, trying to remember if any of the Titan players are named Cyrus. No one comes to mind.

I hear an exasperated female voice, slightly muffled from Owen's phone. "Well, you have a funny way of showing it sometimes."

Owen sighs heavily. "Look, I know it's not ideal, but I'm trying here. It would mean a lot if I could get him for a night next week."

Get him for a night? Is Owen talking about a kid?

My eyes go wide. Does Mr. Bachelor of the Year have a secret love child?!

I lean in closer, hanging on every word.

"I just want to do something special with him,"

Owen is pleading. "Maybe take him to a movie or something. I'll bring him straight home, I promise."

More muffled yelling from the other end of the phone line. I can't make it out, but it sounds like she's playing the single mom angle.

"Shannon, I know you're still upset, but don't take it out on the kid," Owen says, sounding uncharacteristically gentle. "It's not Cyrus's fault."

As I listen in, the pieces start coming together in my mind. Owen Jablonski, star player and legendary ladies man, is actually a deadbeat dad! Why am I not surprised? He's probably got illegitimate kids scattered all across Canada. Cyrus, one of his love children that he abandoned after a one-night stand on the road.

"I'm not trying to undermine you," he continues. "I just miss him. And I know he misses me."

Okay, maybe *abandoned* is a little harsh. But that doesn't change the fact that he's sowing his oats everywhere.

He pauses while the woman on the phone chews him out. I scoff, thinking about Jaime and how she dodged a bullet with him. I thought Owen was just an arrogant jock, but this is next level.

My regret-o-meter just hit an all-time high. I let him kiss me last night. I kissed him back. Actually, let's be real. We full-on made out. And what's worse, it was the hottest, loveliest kiss of my entire life.

And it meant nothing to him.

"Shannon, don't be like that," Owen says, frustration

seeping into his tone. He sounds so desperate, so unlike the cocky superstar I'm used to dealing with.

For a moment, I feel an unexpected pang of sympathy for him. But I quickly remind myself that Owen brought this situation upon himself. This is what happens when you're an arrogant philanderer who can't keep it in his hockey shorts. A knot forms in my stomach. I feel almost... disappointed somehow. I don't know why I care about his personal life. It's not like I have feelings for the guy or anything. Definitely not.

Probably not.

"Alright, fine. But we're not done talking about this." Owen hangs up the phone with a grunt.

Quickly, before he can catch me listening in, I scramble to Joe's office. My heart pounds as his footsteps approach. He's muttering curses under his breath.

My butt barely hits the office chair when Owen appears just outside the office, taking up the entire door frame. He hooks his fingers on the top, leaning his large body in. So casual. Such... swagger. Gone is the desperate, pleading dad on the phone. He's just Owen now. The sultry son of a gun who rocked my world for thirty seconds last night. Or was it thirty minutes? The details are a little fuzzy.

"Hello, Kitty Cat," he drawls, lips curling into a devilish grin.

I hate him.

"What do you want?" I snap, probably more forcefully than I intended.

Play it cool, Em. I cross my legs, trying to look casual, like I hadn't just eavesdropped on Owen's private conversation only to uncover something about him I'd rather not know. My leg slips off my knee on the first try, so I haul it back on there, holding it down with my elbow.

"I just want to apologize," he says softly.

"I didn't lose the gold.
I won the silver."
- Michelle Kwan

MPONI

CHAPTER TWELVE

Emily

Wait. What? Owen, the ultimate preening puck, wants to apologize? To me?

Owen rubs the back of his neck. Is he actually nervous? "Look, I just wanted to say sorry if I crossed a line or anything. I know you're not my biggest fan, and I shouldn't have just kissed you like that without asking. It was inappropriate and I shouldn't have put you in that position."

I stare at him, incredulous. I feel a twinge of disappointment that the kiss meant so little to him, even though I know I should be relieved. Still, it stings a bit that he's so quick to dismiss it.

I'm taken aback. An apology is the last thing I expected from him. I also feel a little salty that he's brushing it off so casually.

"Oh, um, it's fine," I mumble, caught off guard by his sincerity. "We were trying to avoid getting caught. I get it. Don't worry about it."

I tuck a strand of hair behind my ear self-consciously. As much as I hate to admit it, I haven't been able to stop thinking about that kiss. The way his lips felt against mine, his fingers tangled in my hair... it was electric.

Which I should never, *ever* think about, especially now that I know he's a deadbeat dad. And of course, it goes against girl code. I'd die if Jaime ever found out I let her ex kiss me.

Owen shifts his weight, eyes searching my face intently. "Yeah, but still. I stepped out of line." He pauses, rubbing the back of his neck again. "I just wanted to make sure things are cool between us. I know I can be a pain in your side sometimes."

A small smile tugs at my lips. "Sometimes?" I retort with a teasing lilt. Owen chuckles, the sound sending a pleasant shiver through me.

"Alright, more than sometimes," he admits. "I'm

trying to work on it, though. Be less of a... what did you call me before? An egotistical meathead jock?"

I cringe, recalling the blog post from a few weeks ago. "Okay, yeah, I may have gotten a little carried away with the insults."

We share a tentative smile, the lingering awkwardness between us dissipating.

A charged silence fills the tiny office. Owen shuffles his feet.

"So listen, there's something else," he says finally. "Mark's been shooting his mouth off in the locker room about catching us last night. Now the whole team thinks we're hooking up."

My eyes go wide. "What?! Well, that's just great."

Owen shrugs. "The guys have been giving me a hard time about it all day. I denied it at first, but that just made them tease me more. And, I figured it's better they think that than know we were snooping around like Scooby Doo."

I groan internally, already dreading the increased attention from Owen's loud, boisterous teammates. The last thing I need is to be the center of the hockey team's rumor mill. And I certainly don't want it to get to my friends. This is a huge mess.

"So I was thinking," Owen continues, fixing me with those bedroom eyes, "Maybe we should just let them believe we're together?"

I hesitate, chewing my lower lip.

He grins. "No funny business, I promise. You can go back to hating me after we solve the case."

I roll my eyes at his attempt to be charming. But despite myself, I feel a little flutter in my chest.

"Fine," I say, trying to sound nonchalant. "But this is a business arrangement only. No hanky panky."

"Wouldn't dream of it," he replies with a wink.

This is surely a terrible idea. But as Owen saunters back, I have a feeling this could spiral out of control if I don’t do something drastic. We need to find more evidence on Mark so I can get out of this arrangement.

I watch Owen swagger out of the office, no doubt heading to brag to his teammates about our supposed "hookup". Ugh. This is not good. The last thing I need is to become locker room gossip fodder for those Neanderthals.

But I have more pressing issues to deal with right now. Like figuring out who actually stole that trophy. As juicy as it would be for my blog followers, I just can't bring myself to falsely accuse Mark unless I'm 100% certain he's guilty. Which means it's time to do a little sleuthing of my own.

After the game ends, I linger around the arena parking lot, bundled in my warmest winter coat. I'm waiting to see which direction Mark heads after he finishes up his equipment manager duties. Sure enough, after about fifteen minutes, I spot him trudging down Front Street on foot.

I have a hunch where he might be going. Time for

some good old-fashioned tailing. It's much easier in the movies, though.

Just as I suspected, he heads straight for The Crowned Loon. It's the bar where most of the team hangs out after games. And the perfect place to try to get Mark to spill some secrets after a few drinks.

I wait a few minutes after Mark goes inside before following him in.

I slide inside, wrinkling my nose at the stale beer smell permeating the whole place. The bar is packed and noisy. As a woman frequenting a hockey bar alone, I might as well be wearing a sign that says "Puck Bunny Seeking No Strings Attached Fun."

But desperate times call for desperate measures. I need to get Mark talking, and this is his domain.

I spot him bellied up to the bar, beer already in hand. He's chatting with the bartender, but I can't quite make out what they're saying over the din. Even in his civilian clothes he looks uncomfortable, shoulders hunched, leg jiggling nervously.

"Fancy seeing you here," I say brightly, plopping onto the stool next to him.

Mark startles, sloshing some foam over his glass. "Oh, hey Emily." He looks around. "Where's Owen?"

I swat an imaginary fly. "Psshh. Oh, that guy? He's not my boyfriend or anything."

Now Mark is genuinely confused. I can imagine he just sees me as Owen's lovesick girly. Another notch on his hockey stick.

“Yeah,” I say, trying to appear like one of those worldly ladies. “Just felt like checking out the infamous Crowned Loon. I can see why you guys love it here." I force an enthusiastic grin.

Mark eyes me suspiciously. "No offense, but this doesn't really seem like your scene."

The bartender ambles over and I realize I have no idea what to order in a place like this, so I say the first thing I can think of, like they do in movies.

"I'll have what he's having."

The bartender pours me a foaming glass of tap beer. I didn’t think this through very well. I take a sip, wincing from the sour taste. I do not care for this beverage one bit. I should have ordered a Shirley Temple. That’s my regular drink when I go out.

Mark eyes me warily. "Don't take this the wrong way, but what are you doing here talking to me?"

I force out a laugh. "What, can't I enjoy a drink after a long day at work? Boy, what a day, am I right?"

What if I try to burp? Seems like an appropriate thing to do.

“I... guess.”

“How about that stolen trophy? I’ll bet you didn’t expect that to happen.”

Transitions are not my forte, but I’m already feeling the buzz from only two sips of beer, so I kinda don’t care about being subtle.

Mark takes a long, hard look at me, then cracks a

small smile. Apparently, I'm amusing him, or maybe he's feeling tipsy, too.

"No, I sure didn't. Whoever stole it has got big... well, you know."

I reach over the bar for the bowl of mixed nuts. I need to offset this bitter taste in my mouth. Popping one in my mouth, I tilt the bowl to Mark.

"Nuts?"

"No thanks. I'm allergic."

"Oh, sorry." I shove the bowl far away from Mark and take another swig of beer. Nope, still not yummy.

As we chat over the din of the crowded bar, I decide to make up a story about my money woes (not too far from the truth, actually), hoping he'll feel comfortable talking about his financial troubles, too.

It doesn't take long before he opens up about his mounting debts, the years of compulsive gambling, the intimidating loan sharks who keep hounding his phone at all hours of the day and night.

I shake my head sympathetically as he describes how he started betting on sports recreationally in college, but it spiraled out of control after graduation. Now he's desperate for cash, taking risky bets he can't afford to lose.

As the alcohol loosens his tongue, Mark goes into more detail about his gambling addiction, his voice tinged with shame. He tells me how he started small, just placing a few bets on games with his buddies. But once he graduated and was working for the team, he had more access - and more money. He found himself betting bigger and bigger amounts, chasing losses and borrowing from loan sharks.

Before he knew it, Mark was in deep, owing tens of thousands to dangerous people. He skipped rent payments and stopped going out, trying to scrounge up enough to pay just the vig, let alone the principal. But the hole only got deeper. The stress was unbearable.

But the fear in his bloodshot eyes tells me he's running out of options fast, and that's when I realize he didn't steal the trophy. He's too deep in debt - he would have pawned it right away for cash. And he genuinely seems like a good guy who's just made some bad choices.

"Sometimes I just feel so hopeless, you know? Like I'm never gonna get out from under all this," he slurs, getting emotional.

I pat his arm sympathetically. "Hey, it's gonna be okay. You'll figure it out."

After a few more drinks, Mark thanks me for listening and stumbles out of the bar. I watch him go, sighing in frustration. Back to square one on suspects. But at least I'm confident I can cross Mark off the list.

I signal the bartender for my check, lost in thought. I'll have to tell Owen it couldn't have been Mark. Which means Owen and I are back to square one.

I weave through the crowded bar, heading for the exit, mentally exhausted after my chat with Mark. I just want to go home, slip into my comfiest pajamas, and veg out in front of the TV. This whole mystery is turning out to be way more complicated than I anticipated.

Suddenly, a meaty hand clamps down on my shoulder, stopping me in my tracks.

"Hey there, where are you going so fast?" a gruff voice rumbles in my ear.

I whirl around to see the leering face of a mountainous man looming over me. He's got to be at least 6'5" with arms like tree trunks. A bushy beard covers his face and tattoos snake up his neck. Definitely not someone I want to tangle with.

"I was just leaving," I reply evenly, trying not to let my unease show.

"Not yet you're not." He tightens his grip, fingernails digging into my shoulder even through my winter coat. "I've been watching you all night. A pretty little thing like you shouldn't be in a place like this alone."

I try to shrug out of his grasp, but his hand is like a vise, clamping down on my shoulder hard enough that I can feel my bones grinding together. "Let go of me," I say firmly, meeting his beady eyes that are nearly black in the dim lighting of the bar.

He just tightens his grip further in response, his sausage-like fingers digging in deep. I can feel my heart begin to pound, adrenaline flooding my system. This mountain of a man could easily overpower me if I don't get away quickly. I try to subtly shift my weight to my back foot, ready to make a break for it.

He just laughs. "Feisty. I like that."

My heart pounds as he pulls me closer, his massive frame easily enveloping my petite one. I'm desperately scanning the crowded bar for help, but everyone seems oblivious, lost in drunken conversation or focused on the hockey news playing on the TVs. The bartender is chatting up a pair of giggling blondes at the far end of the bar, not even glancing my way. A group of rowdy guys laugh obnoxiously loud, drowning out the music and any chance of someone hearing my cries.

I feel utterly alone as this hulking stranger tightens his grip on me, my bones grinding together painfully under his brute strength. Panic rises in my chest. I have to get away from him now, before this escalates further. I subtly shift my weight to my back foot, ready to make a break for it if I get an opening. Just one distraction is all I need. My eyes dart around the bar again, pleading for anyone to look my way. But the revelry continues on, oblivious.

"I believe the lady asked you to let her go," a familiar voice cuts in sharply.

My head whips around to see Owen coming from out of nowhere, blue eyes blazing. I've never been so happy to see his stupid, handsome face.

The man whirls, surprised to find Owen standing there glowering at him. He's still got one hand firmly clamped on my shoulder, though.

Owen snarls at him. "Let her go before I rearrange your face."

The man's eyes narrow as he sizes Owen up. Even

through the alcoholic haze, he seems to realize he's no match for an angry hockey player in peak physical condition.

"We were just talking," he mumbles unconvincingly, though his grip on me loosens.

"It didn't look like talking to me," Owen says, taking a step closer. His muscular frame seems to expand, radiating menace. "I'm not going to ask you again."

The man wavers, indecision flickering across his face. For a moment, I think he's going to challenge Owen, fueled by drunken idiocy. His eyes dart between Owen and me, cheeks reddening in anger and embarrassment. But then his hand drops from my shoulder and he takes a stumbling step back, nearly losing his balance.

"Whatever, she's not even that hot," he mutters, trying to save face even as he backs down.

But that just triggered something fierce in Owen. He grits his teeth and gets in the guy's face. "What did you say, asswipe?"

"I said she's not that hot."

Rage overcomes Owen's features, for some reason setting him off more than anything.

Within the span of half a second, he lands a punch square in the creep's face. The guy's head snaps back from the force of the blow. Blood immediately starts gushing from his nose. He stumbles backward, hands flying up to cup his injured face.

"What the hell, man?!" he yells, voice muffled.

Owen just shakes out his hand, unfazed like it's just a brawl on the ice with Les Nordiques. His knuckles are already reddening from the impact.

"That's just a warning," he says coldly. "Touch her again, and no one will ever find you."

Wow, that got dark real quick.

Owen takes my hand and swiftly whisks me outside into the cold night air.

"You okay, Kitty Cat?" he asks, anger melting into concern as his eyes search my face. I nod shakily. Now that the adrenaline is fading, I'm left feeling violated and shaken.

"I'm fine," I say, rolling my eyes even as my pounding heart starts to calm. "Just another handsy bar creep."

Owen frowns, his big hand coming up to cup my chin. The gentle brush of his thumb is not lost on me. Surprisingly, it feels so, so nice.

"Are you sure?" he asks gently. His gaze softens, clouded with concern.

A flood of relief washes over me now that Mr. Handsy is gone. "I'm fine," I assure him, offering a grateful smile. "Thank you."

He nods, the tension easing from his broad shoulders. "I'm just glad I got here when I did."

Owen presses a protective hand on my lower back as he guides me down the street.

"Where do you live?"

"The Regency Apartments... on Queen."

"Do you have a car?"

I shake my head. Who needs a car in Toronto?

"And you walk home from the arena every night? All alone?"

"It's not that far."

He shakes his head in disbelief. "I'm walking you home. No arguments."

I don't have it in me to argue. I nod gratefully, and we set off down the street, shoulders hunched against the chill.

As we walk, Owen keeps up a steady stream of mindless chatter, for which I'm thankful. The normalcy of his voice helps calm my frayed nerves. Owen's deep voice rumbles with amusement as he regales me with funny stories from the locker room, like the time the rookie Mason slipped on a puddle and faceplanted right into the buffet table. It's nice to see this softer, sillier side of the usually stoic team captain.

The biting wind seems less harsh with Owen's bulk shielding me. I sneak glances at his chiseled profile when he's not looking, taking in the strong line of his jaw and the way his nose turns up slightly at the end.

By the time we reach my apartment building, I'm feeling much more like myself. We pause outside the front door and I turn to Owen, laughing as I recall what he said to that guy in the bar.

"Touch her again, and no one will ever find you? Where did that come from?"

He shrugs. "I probably got it from a Robert DeNiro movie."

"Thanks again for coming to my rescue tonight," I say sincerely.

He waves me off. "Don't mention it. What are fake boyfriends for?"

My smile fades. "Oh, right. I almost forgot." Then a thought snags. "Were you... following me?"

"No. You left the arena before I had a chance to tell you the news I learned. Luckily, Griffin saw you chasing after Mark. It didn't take much sleuthing to find you."

"You... have news?"

"I overheard Coach talking to someone in his office. They were behind a door—I didn't see who it was. Apparently, there was a gum wrapper found among the broken trophy case glass. A detail we didn't know because we're not the police."

"Then it couldn't be Mark," I say. "He told me he has trouble chewing things because of cracked fillings."

"That's what I wanted to tell you."

"That Mark has dental problems?"

"No. But thank you for that information. I wanted to tell you that I don't think the thief was Mark. The wrapper is from a premium chewing gum called Éclat d'Érable. They only sell it in Quebec."

I gasp. "The Nordiques!"

"It would seem so."

"That's kind of a stretch, though. Pinning a crime on someone based on their chewing gum preferences."

"We're playing in Quebec City next week. Come with me. Maybe you can find clues that I can't."

"Um... hard pass."

"Why? I checked the schedule. There are no events at the Dome next week."

"Okay, I don't want to sound ungrateful for you... almost killing someone for me tonight. But..."

"But? It's okay. Go ahead and spill it."

"I just don't want to... spend too much time with you."

I don't mention that being close to him all the time is confusing my female parts and also conflicting with my morals.

"Can I ask you something?" he asks, tilting his head to the side.

"I guess."

"Why do you hate me?"

"Well, hate is a strong word..."

"You hate me. I can tell by the way you look at me sometimes. The raw contempt. The names you call me. And all those blog posts. For the life of me, I can't figure out why."

"You hurt someone I care about, okay?"

That shut him up quickly. The look of confusion on his face, though.

"I... I..." he stammers.

"A dear friend. You cheated on her."

He shakes his head. "I've never cheated on anyone in my life. I would never do that."

"Oh, you *would* say that. I don't expect you to pour out your confession."

"Who? Who would say that about me?"

"I'm not going to tell you her name. I respect her too much."

He takes a step back and rakes his fingers through that thick mop of hair. It flops into a glorious mess that just makes him more handsome. I hate that it makes me feel all gooey inside.

"Emily, I swear, I'd never cheat on a woman. I haven't even dated in over two years."

"Oh maybe *you* don't call it dating, but the rest of the world does. Guys like you with a different girl in every town—"

He cuts me off with a horrible wheezing noise, like he can't breathe, and he bends over his knees, shaking. He's in that stance for a while, sucking in air through his nose, pushing it out with a feral growl. I'm about to call for help, but then he straightens up. His eyes are closed, but he continues breathing like he's doing Lamaze or something.

"Are you... hyperventilating? Is it asthma?"

"No," he snaps, opening his eyes. "I just don't like being accused of things I didn't do."

I blink a few times, unsure of what to think. Maybe he's one of those guys who doesn't believe sleeping with multiple women is considered cheating?

"Are you sure you're okay?"

"Please," he says between breaths. "Go inside so I

know you're safe and then I can go home." His tone is harsh and primitive. Not gonna lie, he's a little scary looking right now. Maybe he *does* know how to make someone disappear so no one would find them. Like that Robert DeNiro movie.

Without another word, I slip inside the building and go upstairs, utterly dismayed.

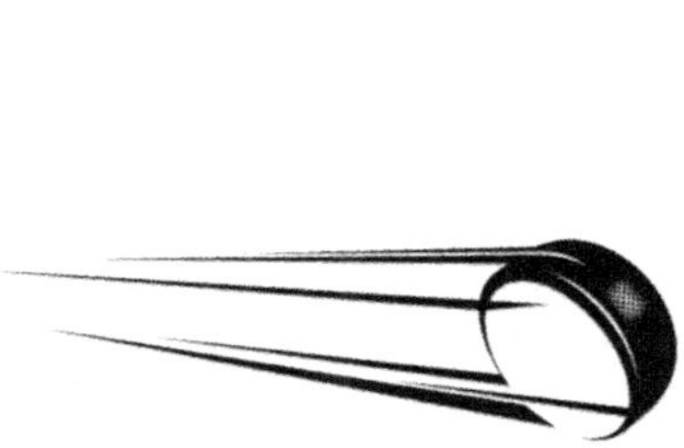

"To win the game is great.
To play the game is greater.
To love the game is greatest of all."
- Bob O'Connor

MPONI

CHAPTER THIRTEEN

Owen

"Is this going to be a regular thing?" Cyrus asks with cheeks covered in chocolate glaze.

"What? Me picking you up from school?"

"You picking me up from school and coming to Tim Hortons."

"Ah. Then no. Sorry bud."

His face falls.

"I reserve the right to mix things up," I add with a

smirk. “Sometimes we might go to Harvey’s. Or ice cream. Or Pizza Pizza.”

Cyrus flashes me a sugary, toothy grin. I should probably instill better snacking habits in the kid. But I suspect he gets enough of that at home.

He takes another bite of his donut and talks with a full mouth.

“I can’t believe Mom’s okay with this.”

“Actually... she doesn’t know, per se.”

"What does purr say mean?"

"Don't worry about it," I wave my hand. "Just don't go blabbing to her about our little excursions. What she doesn't know won't hurt her."

I really don’t want to disrespect Shannon’s wishes, but she’s being unreasonable.

Cyrus nods, his expression serious. "So should I tell her I took the bus?"

"No. I don't want you to lie. But don't offer up the information either. Understand, little man?"

"I think so," he says nodding. "Purr say."

"Good. Now, I wanted to run something by you. How much do you love your school?"

He levels me with a hard stare. "Nobody loves school."

"Right. But in terms of maybe having to go to a different school. Would you miss Simcoe Elementary?"

"No way."

"Okay." I take a sip from my water bottle and think

carefully how to present this idea to Cyrus in a way he'd be interested.

"So, a couple of the guys on the team—the old ones—they've got kids. And they were telling me about this school called Bayview Heights Academy. It's... kind of bougie. The guys were telling me it's got all the bells and whistles. Brand new facilities, huge sports complex, latest tech and gear. I saw some pictures online and it looks legit. I know you don't care much for sports, but they've got a lot of advanced academic programs too. Robotics, coding, 3D printing, all that jazz. I bet you'd like that stuff.

"Robotics sounds fun."

"I mean, there's math and English and Social Studies, don't get me wrong. But they've got some cool after-school programs too - cooking, chess club, drama."

Cyrus perks up at this. "Chess club?"

"Yeah. So if you went there, your mom could pick you up after work since you'd be busy with activities until 5 or 6. No more long bus ride home."

"That'd be awesome!" Cyrus says, nodding enthusiastically.

"I know, right? There is one catch though - you'd have to wear a uniform."

Cyrus scrunches his nose. "Even worse than the bus ride."

We both laugh.

"No way, uniforms aren't so bad!" I say. "Could be kinda cool, actually. Like Hogwarts."

Cyrus grins again, his eyes lighting up. "Maybe. I guess I wouldn't mind a uniform."

"Atta boy," I say, ruffling his hair. "But let me talk to your mom about it first, okay? I need to butter her up."

I have no idea how to do that, exactly, but I'm hoping something comes to mind soon.

Cyrus watches me curiously as I chug the last of my water and crunch the plastic bottle, setting it down next to the other three bottles I've devoured since we've been here.

"How come you don't like donuts and milk?"

I laugh. "I love donuts and milk. Just not during the season. Once we win the championship, I'll celebrate with you and two dozen donuts. How's that?"

"Okay."

"You about done? I gotta get you home. But first..."

"Aww, man."

I'm willing to bet he didn't use the can all day at school, trying to avoid bullies in the restrooms. No way he's getting a urinary tract infection on my watch.

"I gotta go, too," I assure him. "We'll go together."

Cyrus helps me clean up our mess and we head to the back of the shop to use the John. I try not to laugh at the way he's waddling. Kid looks like a penguin. We're almost to the door when who should emerge but Emily. She startles when she sees us, eyes going wide.

"Emily! This is a surprise," I say.

She mumbles a greeting, then picks up speed to slip

past me, but the hallway is narrow and Cyrus is hopping back and forth behind me.

"Actually, I'm glad I ran into you," I say, angling my body so she'll stop and talk to me for a minute. I need to explain my behavior the other night.

I think I freaked her out, first with the Robert DeNiro-esque threat in the bar and then my mini impression of The Beast when she basically accused me of being just like my father. It felt like a sharp object was piercing my lungs. Breaths came short, my vision fading. I didn't want her to see me like that.

"Well, I'm kind of in a hurry," she says, looking back over her shoulder. Her wide hazel eyes dart around as if she's looking for someone. "I'll see you at wor—"

Just then, the women's bathroom door swings open again and another woman steps out. Early twenties, light skin, big doe eyes. Strikingly pretty, even with the alarmed look on her face.

Probably a fan. I knew I should have worn a disguise.

Emily whips her head around, dread flashing across her features.

"Jaime, I..." She falters, at a loss for words. "I'm so, so sorry. I didn't know..."

I give them both a friendly smile. "Jaime, eh? Nice to meet you. I have a cousin named Jaime." I extend my hand. "I'm Owen."

The other girl—Jaime—freezes and does *not* take my outstretched hand. She's gone sheet white.

Cyrus bounces on his toes, now in full emergency

mode. "I'm Cyrus!" he announces, also sticking out his hand.

Emily's eyes tick down to Cyrus. "*You're* Cyrus?"

"I gotta pee," he says.

Jaime's cheeks bloom crimson. Her eyes glisten as they brim with hot tears. Then she shoulders her way between us all and hurries toward the exit.

"Is your friend alright?"

Emily whirls on me, eyes blazing. "What is wrong with you?" she hisses.

"I'm sorry. Was it something I said?"

"I cannot with you right now! Why did you pretend not to know her?"

I hold up both hands. "Whoa, I've never seen that woman before in my life."

"Don't lie!" She's about to tear me a new one, but then glances at Cyrus and presses her lips together.

"I swear I'm not lying. I don't know her."

"Save it, Owen." Emily huffs angrily and stomps off after her friend, leaving me standing there scratching my head. What the hell just happened?

I look down at Cyrus, who is literally crossing his legs now.

"Alright little man, enough drama. Let's hit the can before you explode."

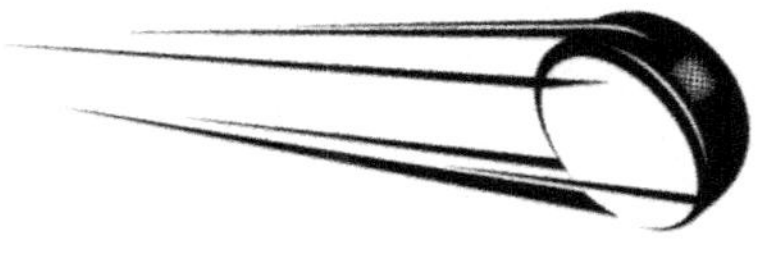

"Think your sport is hard?
Mine is on one of the most
slippery surfaces on earth
and I have knives on my feet."
– Unknown

MPONI

CHAPTER FOURTEEN

Emily

I pace back and forth in my living room, phone glued to my ear as I listen to Jaime's voicemail greeting for the hundredth time.

"Hi! You've reached Jaime. Sorry I can't get to the phone right now..."

I hang up in frustration. I've called and texted at least twenty times since yesterday's run-in with Owen at Tim Horton's. When I chased after her, she was freaking out, sobbing, basically losing her mind, saying all sorts of nonsense. Then she just ran away from me, telling me to leave her alone.

Now, she won't answer my calls or texts. I considered going to her apartment to check on her, but I want to give her space if that's what she really wants.

A knock at the door startles me out of my spiraling thoughts. I peer through the peephole to see Maggie on the other side, holding two large coffees and a bakery bag. I quickly let her in, relieved to have someone to talk to about this whole mess.

"Any word from Jaime?" Maggie asks.

I shake my head. "Nothing. It's like she vanished. I'm really worried, Mags."

Maggie steps inside, plopping her purse on the kitchen counter. "Well, I did some digging of my own. And you're not going to believe what I found out."

She hands me one of the coffees and I take a grateful sip. We sit down on the couch and Maggie pulls two gigantic chocolate chip cookies out of the bag, passing one to me.

"So get this," she says through a mouthful of cookie. "I couldn't reach Jaime so I called her mom. And we had a very enlightening conversation."

My eyes widen in surprise. "You did? What did she say?"

She takes a deep breath before continuing. "So Jaime's mom told me that Jaime has some... issues."

"What kind of issues?" I ask nervously.

"She has a tendency to make up elaborate stories that aren't exactly true. Brace yourself, Em, because basically, Jaime is a pathological liar."

I stare at Maggie, stunned. "What?"

Maggie nods, swallowing hard. "Her mom said Jaime used to tell elaborate fabricated stories since she was a kid. She'll make up these intricate lies and really commit to them, but there's never any truth behind it."

My mind races, slotting memories into this new framework.

"She said Jaime made up those stories about her dad," Maggie goes on. "You know, the ones about him walking out and never contacting her again?"

My stomach drops. Those stories are seared into my brain. "Jaime's told them so many times, usually in tears. And they aren't real?"

"I know, insane, right?" Maggie says. "Apparently he's just an average divorced dad. They have a normal relationship."

My thoughts drift back to yesterday, Jaime's face when she saw Owen. How it drained of color. It clicks now.

I set down my coffee, stunned. "So you're saying that whole story about her hooking up with Owen... none of it was real either?"

"Nope, all fiction," Maggie confirms. "She's made up so many boyfriends, it's not even funny. Her mom said she used to pretend she had a long-lost twin sister. And in middle school she faked running away to join the circus for a week."

My mind is reeling. "That's insane. Why would she lie about dating Owen?"

Maggie shrugs. "Who knows? Her mom said she craves drama and attention. And making up stuff about celebrities probably feels exciting for her."

I shake my head, trying to reconcile this bombshell with the Jaime I thought I knew. Looking back, there were little oddities over the years that make more sense now. Like how she conveniently had an uncle who worked at every cool restaurant she told stories about. Or how she'd disappear for a weekend and claim she was at a friend's lake house that none of us had ever heard of.

I let out an incredulous laugh. "Unreal. I can think of at least three blow-out fights she described having with Owen last year. Venting to us about some argument they supposedly had."

Maggie nods, perched on the edge of the couch. “Yeah, all an act. Remember that one girl’s night, when we were waiting to put on a movie, but then Owen called?”

“Yes! And she sat there and talked to him for like two hours right in front of us.”

“She was on the phone with nobody the entire time.”

“Woah.”

“Somebody give that girl an Oscar.”

I shake my head, memories clicking into place. “And

those expensive gifts she claimed were from Owen. Designer purses, a new iPad... that charm bracelet."

"Oh, that was a cute bracelet," Maggie says.

"I know, right? Did she buy those herself just to lie to us?"

"Where did she even get the money? And those photos on her phone that she claimed were from dates with Owen. They must have been photoshopped! She really put in a lot of effort."

"I know, it's wild," I say. "I mean, she had every detail planned out perfectly."

Maggie nods, looking equally dumbfounded. "When Owen supposedly cheated on her... she sobbed in my car for hours."

How can I forget? Jaime was an emotional wreck, mascara running down her cheeks—she was inconsolable. Maggie and I spent hours comforting her, even canceling our plans that night.

I stare into the middle distance. "It was all... fake.?"

"Aaaalll fake."

"And you're sure about this?"

"One hundred percent. Her mom told me there's no way Jaime was dating Owen. She lives at home. Her mom would know."

"I feel like such an idiot for not noticing the signs," I admit.

Maggie sighs loudly. "I just can't believe we're only finding out the truth now. An entire friendship built on lies."

I meet Maggie's eyes. “Wow. I mean, pathological lying... that's an actual mental health issue.”

Maggie nods, taking a long sip of coffee. My thoughts drift back to our confrontation at Tim Hortons.

"I guess now we know why she freaked out seeing Owen," I say.

Maggie pulls a dramatic face. “Her fake world was colliding with reality.”

“Oh crap! Owen. All those terrible things I wrote about him in my blog.”

“Don’t feel so bad. Maybe he still deserves it after knocking up that chick. What did you say her name was?”

“Shannon, I think.”

But I don’t know anything anymore. Owen wasn’t acting like a deadbeat dad at the donut shop. He seemed to have a pretty good relationship with his son. Then again, I’m basing this assumption off thirty seconds of seeing them together. The world is a house of mirrors. Yeah, I'm pretty much a jaded woman now. Maybe I’ll write angsty poetry from now on instead of a hockey blog.

But I'm determined to do the mature thing and clear the air. I owe Owen an apology, and he deserves to hear it face-to-aggravatingly handsome face.

"A puck is a hard rubber disc
that hockey players strike
when they can't hit one another."
- Jimmy Cannon

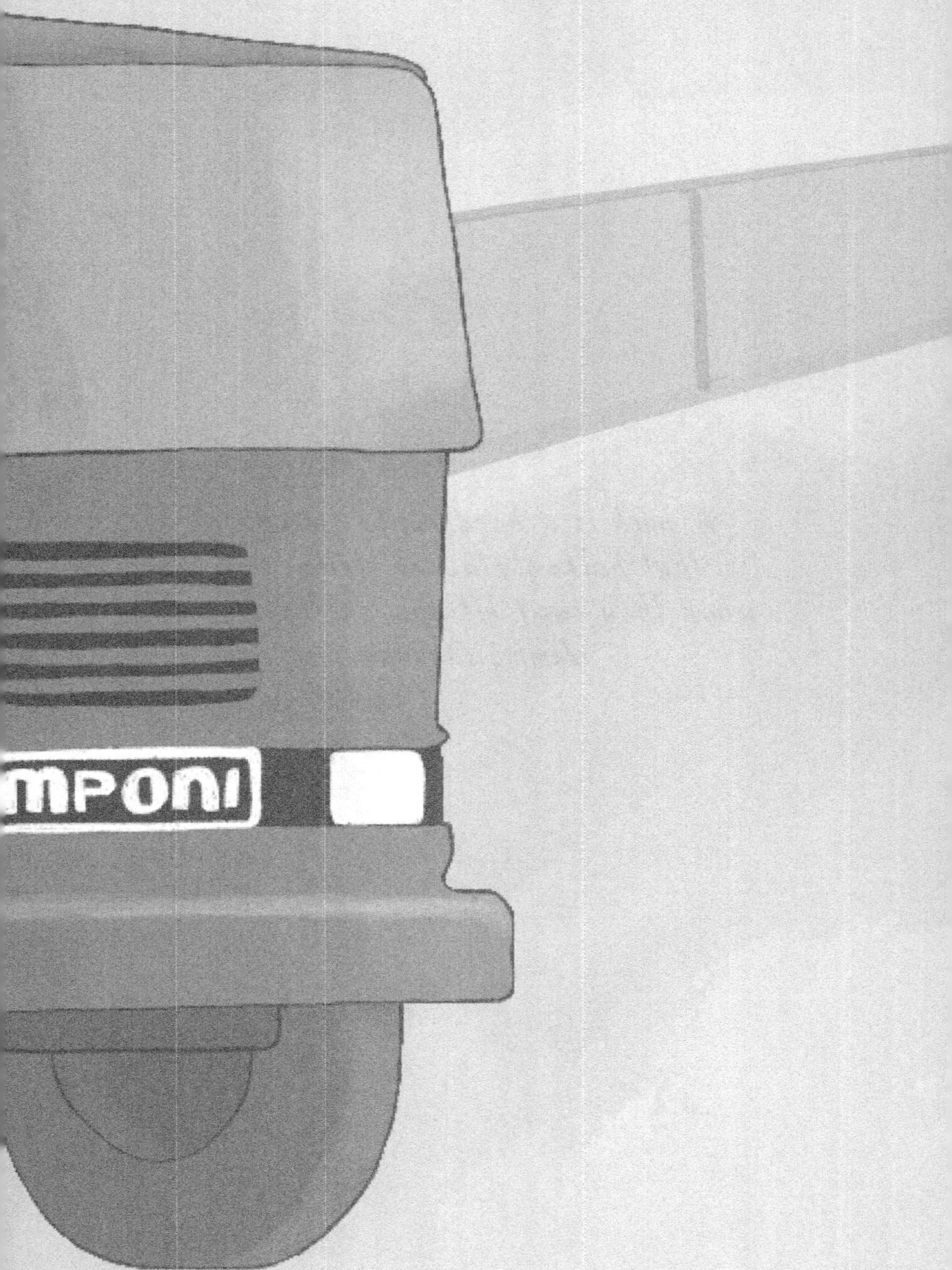
MPONI

CHAPTER FIFTEEN

Owen

As I make my way towards the rink for my usual solo morning skate, I hear the faint sound of blades gliding across the ice. I pause, knowing it's Emily, which I find strange because she's usually done by now so she can avoid me. And considering avoiding me is her favorite hobby, I can't help but wonder if she's changed her tactic to goading me.

Normally, I'd be irritated by the intrusion into my

private skate time. But today, I don't mind at all. I lean against the boards, transfixed, as I watch her dance across the ice.

She's dressed in leggings and a tight leotard, her honey-blonde hair swept into a loose braid. My heart pounds in my chest at the sight of her.

She catches air and her arms extend like wings as she lands—her blades carving delicate patterns into the ice. She takes one jump after the other... spin after spin. A pirouette here, a leap there—each motion seamlessly flows into the next. I'm mesmerized by her fluidity, her poise, the sheer beauty of the shapes she makes with her body. She's ethereal, transcendent... the most graceful creature I've ever seen. Watching her feels strangely intimate, like I'm glimpsing something not meant for my eyes.

Yet I can't look away.

She doesn't notice me at first, lost in her own world. I'm almost hesitant to intrude on this private moment between Emily and the ice. But I can't resist the magnetic pull drawing me towards her. Even when she yells at me in front of a Tim Horton's bathroom.

Finally, she comes to a stop at center ice, catching her breath. Our eyes meet and she gives me one of her witchy grins, nodding in an unspoken acknowledgement before continuing on with her routine. No smart remarks or biting comments. I know she hates me, but the way she's looking at me, it feels like a temporary ceasefire in our ongoing battle of wits and wills. My breath catches in my throat. I need to get out there. To be close to her.

She skates back around and stops right in front of me, a challenge sparkling on her features.

And I do love a challenge.

"Hello. Kitty Cat," I say, fixing my gaze right into her eyes.

Her pretty little lips part ever so slightly, and for the tiniest moment, I swear I see her throat bob. As if trying to gain control of this interaction, she smirks and skates backwards, beckoning me to join her on the ice. Oh, I'll join her, but she is anything but in control.

I step onto the ice, joining Emily, but she's all over the place. Her strong legs carrying her to the opposite side of the rink. She wants to play? Fine.

She's remarkably fast, her strides long and powerful. Her cheeks flush from the chill and exertion, tendrils of hair escaping from her braid and framing her face. She's breathtaking.

I take off, blades carving sharply into the ice. I dig deep, willing my legs to propel me forward. But Emily keeps her pace, laughing as she evades me. She really is a little kitten, wanting to be chased but not caught. Keeping my eyes pinned on her, I glide to center, and send a roguish grin her way. A small smile tugs at the corner of her mouth as she circles around me, her edges crisp and clean.

"You're pretty good," I tease.

She arches an eyebrow, gliding in a larger circle. "Just pretty good?"

I throw my hands up. "Okay, you're incredible."

"HA. You wouldn't know a triple lux from a toe loop."

"You're probably right about that."

Emily glides backwards, regarding me thoughtfully. "Well, you're not so bad yourself, for a hockey player."

"Gee, thanks," I chuckle.

She throws a teasing glance over her shoulder as she glides away, and I follow her with my tongue practically hanging over the side of my mouth.

We do a slow lap around the rink, moving in tandem, the silence between us surprisingly comfortable—just feeling the cut of our blades on the ice.

Eventually, she coasts to the boards, catching her breath. I pull up beside her.

"So..." she begins, not quite meeting my eyes. "I actually have something I need to tell you."

I lift a brow. "Oh?"

She sighs, gathering herself. "I wanted to apologize. For... judging you, when I didn't really know anything about you."

Well, this is unexpected. I fold my arms across my chest, waiting for her to continue.

"I made assumptions that were unfair," she says. "Especially about your... romantic exploits."

I have to bite my tongue to keep from laughing. My

romantic exploits? If she only knew how few and far between those have been lately.

"So," I say. "You're interested in my romantic exploits, eh?"

"No. Not like that." She smacks my arm. "Remember when you asked me why I hated you?"

"Very acutely."

"And I told you—"

"That you think I'm actually a charming devil."

"Only the devil part."

"Touché."

"You see... my friend Jaime..."

"The girl at Tim Horton's?" This is all starting to come together now. At the time, I was too preoccupied with Cyrus to give it much thought. But Emily was mad that day. Mad because she thought I was pretending not to know her friend.

"Yes. For the past year... Jaime had been making up stories." She cringes, but forges through. "Specifically, that she was in a serious relationship with you... and that you'd cheated on her."

I blink, tilting my head as I try to make out whether or not she's joking.

"If this is a prank, it's a pretty crappy one," I say, keeping my tone neutral. I don't take the subject of cheating lightly at all. Not after what my father did. Or, is probably still doing for all I know.

"It's not a joke, I swear."

She goes on to tell me a long, convoluted story about

her unhinged friend, how she'd fabricated a whole history with me, bought herself presents, photoshopped my face in her pictures, and then made up a cheating scenario. Completely fooling Emily and that Maggie girl.

Once Emily finishes telling me the whole drama, I let out a slow whistle. "Wow. That Elvis faking his own death conspiracy has nothing on your girl, Jaime."

"She's not my girl. Not anymore."

"I guess I should feel flattered that someone would go through all that trouble to pretend to date me," I joke.

Emily rolls her eyes, but I can see her trying not to smile. "Don't let it go to your head, Jablonski. She's clearly got more than a few screws loose."

"Maybe I should get a restraining order, just to be safe," I say, nudging Emily's shoulder playfully.

"Anyway... I just wanted to apologize for the whole... judging you thing," Emily says, "And for the nasty stuff I wrote in the blog."

I'm quiet for a moment, letting her apology sink in. This fiery little spitfire just admitted she was wrong about me, which I have to admit, feels pretty damn satisfying.

"Hmmm." I tap my chin, letting her sweat it out for a minute. Her eye twitches, like she's allergic to apologies.

"I said I'm sorry, Jablonski. I swear I will put more stickers on your locker..."

"Okay, okay. If you put it that way... apology accepted."

She sniffs. "Good."

"Great."

"Wonderful."

Several beats pass and I feel like this ceasefire is about to expire. I either want to throw her over my shoulder and spank her, or kiss her stupid until Sunday. All I know is I've never wanted to put my hands on a woman more in my life than I do now. Not in a creepy way. More in a... oh, never mind.

"Just to be clear though," she says, as if reading my thoughts. "This doesn't make us friends." She pokes me in the ribs. "I still don't trust you."

I smirk, grabbing her hand and holding it against my chest. "Duly noted."

We remain like this for a charged moment, eyes locked like we're in a hot staring contest. I don't dare blink or look at anything else, but I still notice as she bites her lower lip. Heaven help me. That alone almost makes me come undone.

I need another taste of those lips. I need to know... does she always taste the way she did that one night? A little bit minty, a little bit sugary. Because that's my new favorite flavor now.

To my chagrin, she breaks whatever spell this is between us and yanks her hand back to turn towards the benches. Leaning on the boards, I watch her every movement as she puts her blade guards on. How she bends and twists to perform such a simple act. How she blows from the side of her mouth when tendrils of her hair fall into her face. She's so small, and yet so strong.

When she makes to leave, I call out, "Hey, Kitty Cat. When you pack your bags for Quebec, bring your skates. Just in case."

She whirls around, giving me one of her sassy looks.

"What makes you think I'm going to Quebec with you?"

A deliciously slow grin spreads its way across my face. "Because. I already bought your ticket."

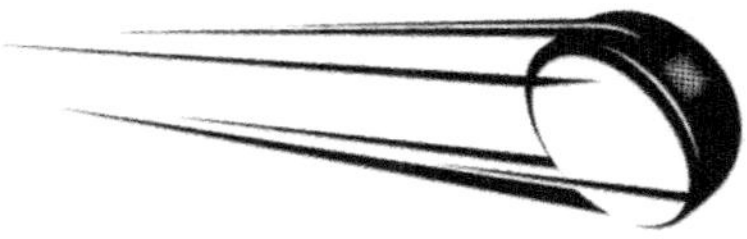

"If you don't have fun,
it's hard to do your best."
- Kimmie Meissner

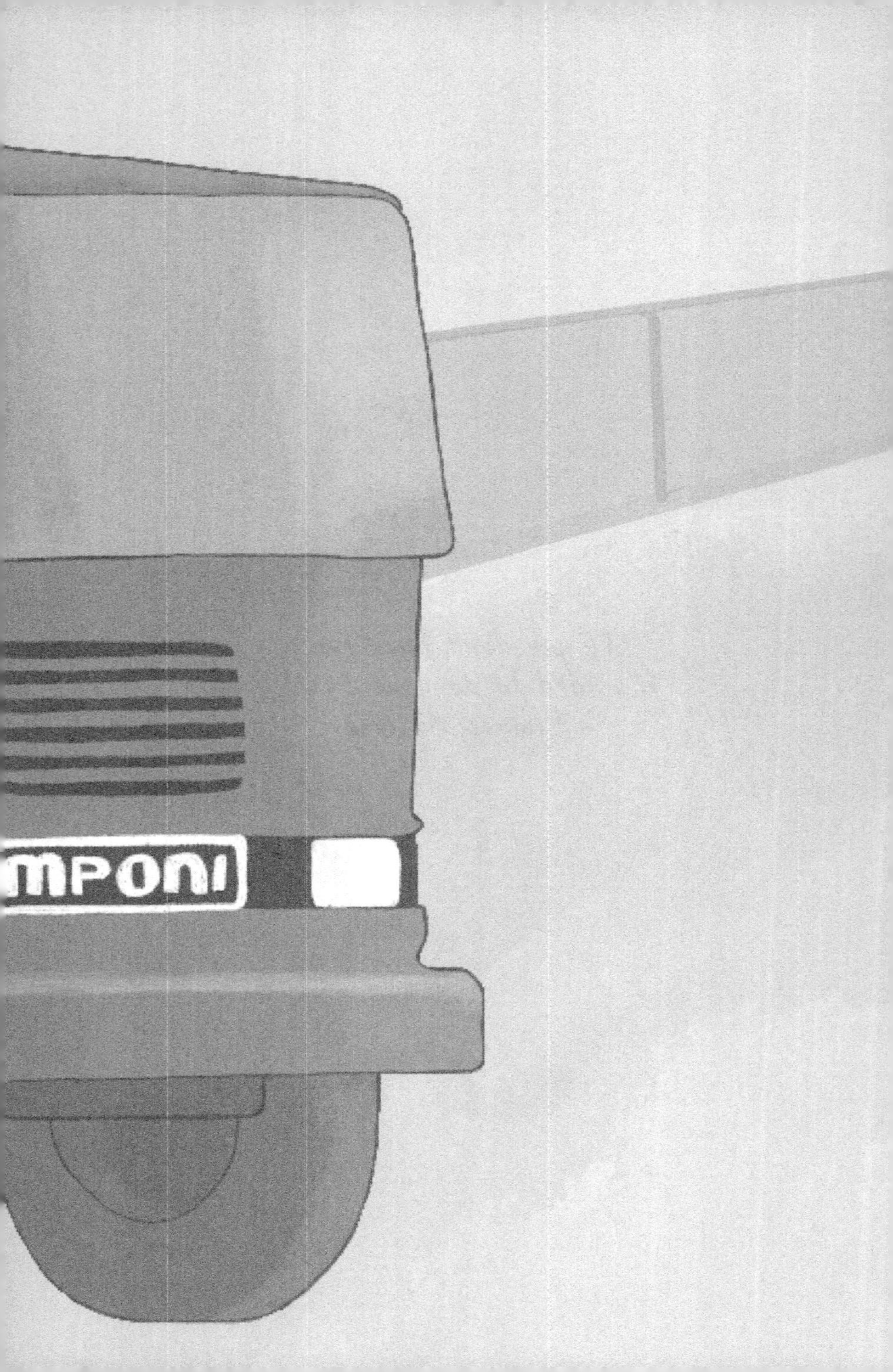
MPONI

CHAPTER SIXTEEN

Emily

I can't believe I let Owen talk me into this little "investigation trip" to Quebec City.

He somehow convinced Coach Knight I was his good luck charm so I can tag along. Truth be told, I think the only reason the powers-that-be let me come is because I work for the team, technically. But here I am, pretending to be the smitten girlfriend.

As we leave the hotel for the Nordiques' arena, Le

Colisée, Owen's typical cocky grin is plastered across his face. I want to slap it right off. Or kiss it off. Either of those options would be extremely satisfying.

"Excited for our romantic getaway, babe?" he asks loudly for his teammates to hear, with an exaggerated wink.

"Romantic getaway?" Griffin McGregor, one of our goaltenders, pulls a face. "Is that what you're calling it? Bro, you need to step it up before Emily comes to her senses."

"If you must know… we're staying in Quebec for some alone time after the game," Owen says. "Just me and my lady."

I roll my eyes and sneer through my teeth. "Let's just find this trophy so I can get back to my normal life."

Owen slings an arm around my shoulder, bending to mumble deeply in my ear. "OhOh, come on, you know you love playing Scooby Doo with me."

"Are you Shaggy? Or the dog?"

"I'm the dog, of course. Kitten. Maybe later you can give me a Scooby Snack."

"Dream on, puck boy. I'm just here for the story."

"Whatever you need to tell yourself."

Owen's hand falls from my shoulder, tracing a slow trail down until it lands on the small of my back so he can guide me toward the waiting SUV. I glare at him, but he just winks. He's clearly enjoying this fake relationship too much.

When we arrive at the arena, a flood of memories

rush back to me. This is where I competed at the National Junior Figure Skating Championships as a teenager, and where I first met Pierre LaMontagne. He was even more arrogant and cocky than Owen, if you can believe it. The coaches fawned over him, praising him as the next big thing in the men's program. He was used to skating solo and being the star. A year or so later, we were paired together, and I was expected to be his equal on the ice. We clashed horribly at first. But over time, I found myself bending to his ridiculously giant ego. I'll never bend for anyone ever again—certainly not Owen. Wait. That didn't come out right.

Moving on...

Eventually, Pierre and I became Team Canada's dynamic duo, hopefuls for Olympic gold. Until it all came crashing down in Beijing.

But that's all in the past now.

As I make my way through the maze of concrete hallways, I feel like a ghost drifting through memories. Sometimes I wonder what Pierre's doing these days. Probably not driving a Zamboni.

Owen somehow managed to get me a backstage pass lanyard so I can snoop around.

"Just act like you belong there and no one will question you," Owen had said with a wink.

Before the game starts, Owen and I have to part ways.

“Your mission,” he whispers. “If you choose to accept, is to infiltrate the enemy’s lair and find that trophy.”

"You know this isn't a spy movie, right?"

He wags his brow and nods. “Don’t get caught.”

Whatever. Weirdo.

There are too many people around for me to snoop, so I decide to wander for a while.

During first period, I befriend the Colisée's Zamboni driver, an elderly man named Alphie. We bond over Zamboni stuff.

If you know, you know.

I casually ask if he's noticed anything strange around the arena lately. He mentions the coaches seem tense and practiced extra late last night. Turns out he’s not a fan of Claude Rousseau, the Nordiques’ head coach. Apparently, Rousseau has a bad temper and screams his head off at the players to the point of his whole face turning red with rage.

“When they lose,” Alphie says. “He throws things. Like skates.”

“He throws skates?” I say, partly entertained, partly aghast.

“Among other things.” He leans in, like it’s some kind of secret. “Last week, he tore up the ice.”

“Ouch!”

He waves it away. “Ach. Nothing we can’t fix. But nobody likes him.”

Hmm. I was going to look for clues in the Nordiques'

locker room, especially that guy Georges Lemieux's locker, who all but admitted he stole the trophy. Or that he wanted to.

I spend the rest of the period watching Owen play. He's all power and precision. So confident on the ice. My heart thrums in my chest, sending tendrils of awareness down to my center... and I hate myself for it.

But the game isn't going well for the Titans. They're down by two goals already, and it's only the beginning of the second period. The Nordiques came out strong and fast, catching the Titans off guard. Owen's been checked hard a few times. I cringe during a particularly brutal hit that slams him into the boards. He shakes it off, but I can tell his frustration is rising.

I meet Owen outside the dressing room during intermission. He's fuming, slamming his hand against the wall.

"I should've had that last one. Lemieux totally blindsided me."

"It's okay," I say, trying to console him. "You're not that far behind. You'll catch up."

He winces, rubbing his shoulder. "Yeah. We'll see."

"Are you hurt?"

"I'll live. Did you find out anything yet?"

"No. I was watching the game."

"Really?"

"Yeah. I mean, I've got time."

"Ah, I see." That flirtatious grin makes an appearance. "You're waiting until after midnight to put on that catsuit again."

"No! I just... never mind." I can already feel myself getting flushed, and I can't let him see it or he'll never shut up about it. "I'll sleuth around next period."

"Are you sure about that? I'm starting to think you like sneaking around with me in the dark." His eyes glimmer at me. "Cramped spaces. The thrill of almost getting discovered..."

"You're such a pig." I smack his arm.

"Ow!"

"Sorry." I forgot about his injured shoulder.

He pouts his lip out, totally faking a frown. "Kiss it better?"

Oh. My. Gosh. Why is he such a flirt?

"In your dreams."

He snakes his arm around my waist and murmurs in my ear. His breath is hot and delicious on my neck, sending tendrils of desire down my spine.

"Come on, Kitten. The guys are watching. Sell this."

His beard brushes against my cheek as he moves to hover his lips over mine. My resolve against him is dissolving quickly.

"Methinks you're enjoying this fake dating ruse a little too much."

His reply is smooth and sultry. "Is that so bad?"

Circling his nose around mine, his gaze flutters to my mouth with unequivocal want.

"Okay, just a tiny one," I say. "But no tongue."

"Just a little bit?"

"Don't push it."

His lips are already on me when he mumbles, "You drive a hard bargain."

Then he overtakes me in a devastatingly glorious kiss. I am officially goo in his arms, and I think I can get addicted to this quite easily. He's a beautiful kisser. There's no other way to describe it. The way he pours his whole being into it. All the charisma and fire. But also with such tenderness, I could literally die in his arms.

Somewhere in the distance, I hear hoots and whistles, and I bristle at the very public show we're putting on.

Owen growls at the intrusion.

Clearing my throat, I say, "Intermission's almost over. Go out there and win this game."

"If you insist." He playfully smacks my butt (the cad) and ambles into the locker room, followed by more teasing. A second later, Sawyer peeks his head out the door.

"Hey Emily."

"Yeah?"

"What do you see in this guy? I mean, look at that ugly face."

Lovely. I'd like to set the record straight, that I, in fact, am not dating Owen. But we dug ourselves into this ruse. The kissing didn't help. I make a mental note to fake break up with him as soon as we get back to Toronto.

Yeah. That's a solid plan, and I'll definitely stick to it.

One hundred percent.

"Like *you're* so hot?" I scoff.

Sawyer is probably the worst flirt of the whole bunch. If anyone on the team is a player, it's him. He could use getting shot down a peg or two.

I hear the oohs of the guys inside, like I just threw down the gauntlet. Hendrix Ellis sneaks up behind Sawyer with a wet towel and smacks it right on Sawyer's butt.

"She got you there, bro."

I don't stick around to find out what happens next, especially since Coach Knight is rounding them up to enforce order. I don't envy his job.

Once the second period starts, I wait a while until most of the staff clear out. When I think it's safe, I creep down the hallways looking for the coach's office. I can hear the dull roar of the crowd filtering down from the stands above me. There are still lots of people walking down the hallways, but not as many while the game's on.

I move away from the main action and get a little lost before I find a stretch of hallway with offices. They look pretty nondescript. I jiggle a few doorknobs, but they're all locked. I'm starting to think this is pointless when a voice startles me from behind. I nearly jump right out of my body, but a gentle hand lands on my shoulder.

"It is I, mon cherie."

Whew. I just got caught jiggling doorknobs by

Alphie, the Zamboni driver and almost peed my pants. What has my life come to?

I press my hand over my chest, sucking in a deep breath. "Alphie! You startled me."

He smiles warmly, giving more definition to the deep lines around his eyes.

"I used to have a different effect on pretty women," he says with a wistful expression. "When I was a young man."

"If you were any more charming than you are now," I say. "You probably broke more than a few hearts."

He laughs and shakes his head, signaling toward the door across the hall. It has Claude Rousseau's name on it. "They lock the doors."

"Oh really?" I swallow hard. "Not that I care."

He winks, producing a huge ring filled with keys. "If someone were to go inside this office, they might find information on how to beat Les Nordiques."

I feign innocence, but Alphie grins at me as he unlocks the door, then presses his finger to his lips. "Shhh. I didn't see a thing."

Rising to my tippy toes, I kiss him on the cheek, and a blush of red sprinkles his face.

"You sure know how to woo a girl."

"My dear," he says. "If I were fifty years younger, you wouldn't stand a chance."

The flirty confidence in his sly smile arouses not-so-unwelcome thoughts of Owen. "I believe you," I say, and as he walks away, I check my feelings.

I am not falling for Owen. Nope.

My heart beats like crazy as I sneak inside the office. I am not built for this. Even when I watch movies where the character breaks into places, I can hardly breathe until the scene is over. The ones where they're downloading evidence on a thumb drive are the worst. I'm always certain someone will catch them. I do not have a thumb drive. Are those even a thing anymore?

I scan the room, looking for anything suspicious. Diagrams and stats cover a whiteboard. Equipment bags litter the floor. After what feels like an eternity of fruitless searching, I'm about to give up when a glint of gold catches my eye. There, in the corner of the room, sits a glimmering bowl of gum. Not just any gum though—Éclat d'Érable, known for its gold foil wrapper.

"Oh you are so guilty," I whisper into the dark.

Suddenly, the doorknob turns. I shove a few pieces of gum in my pocket just as Claude Rousseau walks in. He eyes me suspiciously.

"What are you doing in my office?" he demands in a French accent.

I scramble for an excuse. "I, uh, was looking for the bathroom. Sorry, I got lost!"

He continues staring me down, unconvinced. Why is he back here and not rinkside? Is it second intermission already?

I force a smile and slip past him before he can question me further. My heart is still racing as I go search for Owen. He's not going to believe this.

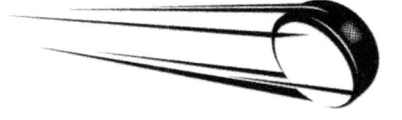

"A good hockey player
plays where the puck is.
A great hockey player plays
where the puck is going to be."
– Wayne Gretzky

MPONI

CHAPTER SEVENTEEN

Owen

"You're right, the poutine is way better here," I say, shoveling another forkful of fries, cheese curds, and gravy into my mouth. Emily wrinkles her nose at me.

"Do you have to eat like such a barbarian?" she asks.

I point my fork at her. "Gotta carb up after the big win tonight."

I still can't believe we actually won. The game was way too close for comfort up until the final period. I really thought we were toast there for a minute.

Emily pulls a face with every bite I take, but I can tell she's fighting back a smile. As we both dig into our late night victory snacks, we fall into a comfortable silence. Every now and then, our legs touch under the table. Can I help it if I'm tall? It's not like I'm doing it on purpose. Not every time, anyway. And since she clearly doesn't pull away, I'm just encouraged to do it more.

After a few minutes, Emily speaks up again. "So about this gum I found in Rousseau's office..."

She pulls the shiny wrapper out of her pocket. Éclat d'Érable, that fancy gum found at the scene of the crime.

"Rousseau's the thief for sure," I declare. Emily gives me a skeptical look.

"Lots of people chew gum, Owen," she points out. "This isn't exactly a smoking gun."

"Maybe not," I admit. "But it's definitely suspicious. We need to investigate this guy more."

Emily grins and leans in conspiratorially. "Funny you should mention that."

She slides a small slip of paper across the table to me. There's an address scribbled on it.

"What's this?" I ask.

"Alphie the Zamboni driver gave it to me," Emily explains. "It's Rousseau's house. Apparently, Rousseau has a mistress he visits every night after home games.

And his wife took their kids on a ski trip this weekend, so the house will be empty."

I let out a low whistle. "Alphie the Zamboni driver is one informative guy. Remind me to send him a gift basket."

Emily laughs. "Don't underestimate the Zamboni driver network. We see everything."

This woman. Devious, but stunning. No one has ever made me feel like this before. I can't explain it other than that safe feeling I get when I'm alone on the ice. Except I don't want to be alone anymore. I want to be with her.

"Well, Kitten, looks like we're back on the case," I say with a smirk. "Ready to go find ourselves a trophy thief?"

Emily's eyes gleam. "I'll grab my cat burglar outfit."

We take a cab across town to the address Alphie provided. It's in a nice neighborhood, and the house is dark and quiet when we arrive. We sneak around to the back. There's a doggy door, but no dog.

"I can fit through there," Emily says.

I give her a look.

"What? It's a big doggy door."

Sure enough, she squeezes her body through the opening, and unlatches the door from inside. Luckily, there's no alarm system.

The house is just as dark and empty as it looked from outside. Emily and I switch on our phone flashlights and start searching the main floor. At first it seems like a dead end. Everything looks normal. But then I notice a door that must lead to the basement.

"Check it out," I whisper to Emily.

She nods, eyes wide, and we quietly make our way over. My heart races as I reach for the door handle and slowly turn it. I just know we're about to find something big. Emily gives me a little shove forward as the door swings open, urging me to go first.

I creep down the stairs, Emily close behind me. She's breathing shakily, as though she's a little afraid. Just the sound of her sweet breath is driving me crazy. At the bottom, I sweep my light around what looks like a combination rec room and office. There's a big TV, a leather couch, shelves full of books and trophies. And at the back, a large wooden desk. She shivers, and I instinctively rub her back to warm her up.

I'm just about to get overly amorous for this situation when Emily turns and grabs my arm.

"Did you hear that?" she whispers.

Now that she mentions it, I can make out footsteps. Someone's home. A door opens and closes on the main floor.

"We need to get out of here, now!" Emily urges.

"How? We're literally on the lowest level. I say we bunk up here until whoever it is goes to sleep. We'll keep each other warm with our body heat."

"Shush! He'll hear us."

"We can pretend we were making out again," I suggest.

"Will you stop?"

There's a hint of a smile on those pretty little lips. She can't help herself. And I don't want her to see me as anything but cool and confident. The opposite of how I feel right now. My heart pounds against my ribs as the footsteps grow louder, sending tremors to my nerve endings. My muscles tense, there's a terrible tightness in my stomach, and I can hardly catch my breath. The only way to fight it, and to make Emily feel safe, is to flirt unabashedly.

"It's so much more fun to get a rise out of you, though," I say.

"Just shut off your flashlight," she hisses, pocketing her own phone.

Whoever's coming, they'll be on us in seconds. I glance around, but there's nowhere to hide in this open basement. Under the desk maybe, but I don't think we'd both fit. Well, after that display of contortionism through the doggy door, maybe we can have fun trying.

Thinking better of it, I tug Emily by the hand, pressing her against the side of the stairwell, and shielding her body with mine in the shadows. Not exactly how I imagined our bodies pressed together this weekend, but hey, I'll take what I can get. Perhaps this at least will give us the element of surprise. What my plan is next, I have no clue.

"Here we are again, Catwoman," I whisper into the shell of her ear. "Are we going to make a habit of this?"

She turns her head slightly toward me, eyes flashing in the dim light. Her breathing is shallow, too. But I suspect it's for different reasons. And for some reason, that relieves some of this suffocating feeling I'm getting. Just the touch of her settles me. And her scent. Watermelon and cucumber. It drives me wild.

The footsteps reach the top of the stairs, then start to descend. I brace myself, ready to strike. A shoe appears, then a leg...

Rousseau pauses on the last step. If he looks around the banister, he'll see us. I hold my breath, waiting for the confrontation.

But Emily is quick. Her little body zips across the room like she's in that Crouching Tiger movie. Just as Rousseau takes the last step down, Emily makes the most graceful leap, spreads her legs into a glorious split, and kicks the daylights out of Rousseau. Right in the face. He drops prostrate like a sack of bricks.

My jaw hits the floor. "You just roundhouse kicked him in the face."

"I panicked! I'm sorry."

"Where did you learn those Kung Fu Panda moves?"

"Years of ballet and figure skating," she says with a shrug, like face-kicking is no big deal.

"Not gonna lie. That's super hot."

"Do you think he saw who I was?"

"No. But we should go before he comes to."

We hear a low groan, and are about to skirt around the body, when I catch a glimpse of his face. It's not Rousseau.

I gasp. "What is he doing here?"

For a moment, we just stand there in stunned silence.

"Did I just... knock out Coach Knight?" Emily squeaks.

"I'm afraid so."

"Craaaap!"

I nod, as if silently echoing her sentiment. Coach Knight is sprawled out on the floor, barely conscious.

"But why would he be snooping around Rousseau's house in the middle of the night?"

I level her with a hard stare. "*We're* snooping around Rousseau's house in the middle of the night."

"Well, we can't just leave him here."

I sigh, kneeling down to check Coach's condition. "Well, you didn't kill him, so that's a plus. Maybe we should get him some ice. He's going to wake up with a huge headache."

I glance around the basement, looking for anything to help.

Coach Knight stirs with a groan and his eyelids start to flutter. As he focuses on us, recognition hits. "What in blazes are you two doing here?"

I open my mouth, but no clever excuse comes out.

"We could ask you the same question," Emily says cooly.

He jerks upright, then winces, gingerly touching his face. "What did you kick me for?"

"I thought you were somebody else," she admits defensively.

"Somebody else? Like the people who live here?"

Emily and I exchange a look.

"Naturally," we say in unison.

"Wow. You two were made for each other. Help me up."

I lend him a hand and haul him to his feet.

He frowns and rubs his jaw where Emily nailed him. "You have ten seconds to tell me what's going on or so help me."

I realize this could get very bad for me. I could get thrown off the team if Coach spills. Then again, so could he.

"I found Éclat d'Érable gum in Rousseau's office," Emily blurts. "We think he stole the Hart Memorial Cup."

"How do you know about the gum?"

"Wasn't there a wrapper found at the scene of the crime?" I ask.

"Nobody knows about that except me and Hal. And now you, I suppose, though I can't imagine how."

"He was eavesdropping," Emily supplies.

"Thank you, my sweet loving girlfriend," I deadpan. "I just love getting thrown under the bus."

“I’m not your girlfriend. We’re coming clean now so we don’t have to pretend anymore.”

She might as well have just roundhoused me, too, because I feel like I’ve been kicked in the gut.

Coach pulls a face. “What are you talking about?”

“Nothing,” I say. “Can we get to the part where you tell us why you’re here too?”

“Not until you tell me what you know about the gum wrapper.”

“Emily’s right. I overheard you talking to Hal. But I wasn’t eavesdropping. You’re kind of loud when you talk.”

Coach nods, seeming to accept this explanation. “When Hal told me about the wrapper, I made him keep it between us. I didn't want to risk tipping off the real thief that we’re on to him. I’ve known Rousseau for years. And when I saw that wrapper, I knew it had to be him. He’s always chewing that disgusting gum.”

Emily hitches one shoulder. “I kind of like it.”

“You tried it?”

She pulls a piece from her pocket. “I’ve always had champagne taste on a beer budget. Want some?”

I cringe. “No thanks.”

Coach scrubs a hand down his face and shakes his head. "For the love of hockey, get out of here. And not a word of this to anyone, understand?"

"Yes sir," I promise, giving him a mock salute.

“And Emily?”

“Yes?”

"I don't know what you're pretending, but this guy's one of the good ones."

She acknowledges him with a nod, and I take her hand, lacing my fingers with hers as Coach follows us out of the house.

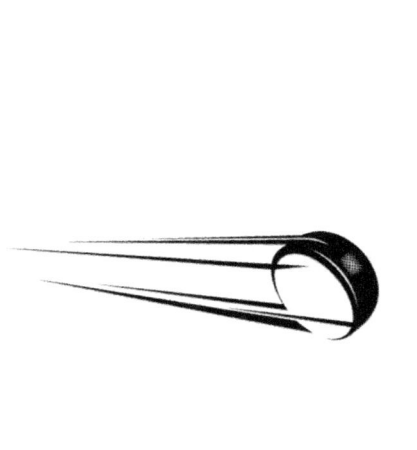

"Winning is not about
how many medals you get
-it's about accomplishing goals
and just being the best you can be!"
- Michelle Kwan

MPONI

CHAPTER NINETEEN

Owen

I glance out the window of the rental car as the landscape whizzes by, fields and farms giving way to dense forest.

"So are you going to tell me where we're going yet?" I ask.

Owen grins, keeping his eyes on the road. "Nope, it's still a surprise."

When he told me he canceled our flights back to

Toronto and wanted to go on an "adventure" instead, I thought he was joking.

“Just sit back and trust me.”

I let out an exaggerated sigh and slump back in my seat. I do trust him, damnit. That’s part of the problem.

The Quebec countryside is beautiful, I have to admit. Snow-covered evergreen trees, the frozen St. Lawrence river coming into view every so often. But the view to my left is the most extraordinary. Owen’s strong profile, his straight nose, those delicious lips I’ve been longing to kiss again. I have to force myself from ogling how the muscles tense in his forearms while he grips the steering wheel. I am not proud of the wanton woman I’ve become around him. I want to climb him like a tree. It’s like he’s unleashed the feral part of me that wants to make out with abandon.

This is not good.

After about an hour and a half, we exit the highway and start winding our way down increasingly narrow roads. Just when I'm about to demand that Owen tell me where we're going, he turns onto a small lane and I see it. Rising up out of the forest, the trees open up to reveal a village with cottages and huts, like something from a storybook.

As we park, I take in the pine trees laden with snow, the trails winding into the woods.

"What is this place?"

"You'll see," Owen says with a smile.

He pops the trunk and takes out our skates with a

wry grin, leading me to an open area where there are a few barn-like buildings, their roofs covered in powder.

"Welcome to Domaine Enchanteur," Owen announces, clearly pleased with himself. "It's supposed to be one of the most beautiful skating trails in the world. I've been wanting to come here for ages."

We go into one of the buildings where Owen pays for the tickets, and after we lace up our skates, he offers me his hand as we head toward the trail entrance.

As we round a bend, the view opens up and I gasp. Before us is a winter wonderland—a huge, winding trail of ice carved through a snow-dusted forest.

It's breathtaking, but Owen is watching me. "What do you think?"

"It's like Narnia," I breathe. I glance at Owen to see him looking at me with such a tender smile, it makes my heart crack. "It's truly amazing," I tell him sincerely.

"I had a feeling you'd like it," he says. "Shall we?"

We step onto the ice and glide forward, still holding hands. The sun filters through the snowy pines above us as we skate leisurely, the chill winter air stinging my cheeks. Beside me, Owen skates with powerful strides, his breath coming out in little puffs of vapor. He's even more handsome out in the elements.

Where is the arrogant hockey star? The lady killer on skates? I feel like I've stepped into an alternate reality where fairy tales are real. There's even a deer in the thicket.

We continue skating in silence through the icy

labyrinth. I'm impressed by how well maintained the sheet is. After about three kilometers, we spot a small hut selling maple toffee. Owen buys us each a small bag and we find a secluded bench further down the trail to rest and eat our treat.

"I'm surprised to see you eating sweets," I say. "Aren't you guys on a strict diet?"

"We are," he admits. "But it's a special day. I'll just do an extra hour of weights when I get home."

"Why is it a special day?"

"Other than spending it with you?" he wags his brows.

"Come on. Cut the casanova act. I can tell there's a sensitive guy under there."

"Don't let it get around. I have a reputation to uphold. I'm supposed to be a preening puck, objectified by all the panty-throwing young women."

"I'm sorry about that," I admit, but laugh when I find an artless grin on his face. "But it was kind of funny."

"Somebody could have tripped on that underwear," he says with a serious expression. "But I guess it's funny in retrospect."

"So... what is so special about today to have you eating toffee in an enchanted forest?"

He hesitates, like he regrets bringing it up. But then he reluctantly says, "It's... my birthday."

"What? Really? Why didn't you say so before? Oh my gosh! Happy birthday."

"Thanks, but I don't like to make a big deal about it. The guys on the team know not to bring it up. And since it's during the season, I usually just get Chinese takeout and watch The Sandlot."

"I love that movie."

"It's a classic."

I watch him take a bite of toffee, feeling a sad pang in my chest. "You don't celebrate with family or anything?"

He lets out a humorless half-laugh. "My family. We're not exactly copasetic."

"I'm sorry."

I can't help but think about Cyrus, how Owen doesn't even celebrate his birthday with his own son. I wonder if that's his choice or the custody arrangement.

Owen wrings the edge of the toffee bag in his thick fingers. "I don't like to celebrate my birthday because... well, a few days before my sixteenth birthday, we found out my dad had been cheating on my mom. He had a whole other family somewhere else. Needless to say, it ruined all our party plans. My mom never truly recovered."

"That's terrible." I don't know what else to say. So I press my hand in his to keep him from destroying the toffee bag.

"I swore I'd never be like him. That's why when you thought I'd cheated on your friend, I got a little crazy. I'd never, *ever* cheat on a woman. When you commit to someone, it should mean something."

I wonder what happened with Cyrus' mom then.

Was the split amicable? Was he trying to reconcile with her?

It hits me here that the things I wrote about in the blog—about him being a player—must have brought back all those feelings.

"And that's why you wanted me to fix your image in my blog. After all the damage I'd done."

"I'm glad you wrote those things." He shifts his hand so our fingers lace together and his eyes find mine in a gentle gaze. "Otherwise, I would have never had the courage to talk to you."

My belly flip flops, and all I can think of is how badly I want this man to kiss me right now. How I want to feel the weight of him, his solid body surrounding me, those strong arms gathering me against him.

Heat creeps up my neck. I know my face must look like a strawberry right now. So I duck my chin into my scarf, biting on my bottom lip.

"You're so beautiful when you do that," he says softly.

GAH! I can't take it. I may not hate Owen anymore, but a relationship with him is way off the table. He has a son. A really cute son, but still. I won't get in the middle like that. Especially if there's a chance he can still make it work with Shannon. Cyrus could have a normal family.

"We should probably keep skating before we get cold." I bid, deflecting the conversation before I change my mind and straddle him right here in front of all the people passing by. It's getting late, and the trails are clearing out, but there are still a few skaters enjoying the magic of golden hour. The last thing I need is to scandalize all of Quebec. Then again, they're French.

We toss our trash in a bin and get back on the ice. Evening is falling, and the fading light casts a magical, soft pink glow over the snowy pines. Owen reaches for my hand again, interlacing our fingers. We left our gloves in the car, so I welcome the warmth of his hand.

The winding trail darkens in the dusk, but as the sun sets, fires light in the distance, and warm fairy lights illuminate in the trees towering over us. Nothing will ever top this.

As we round a bend, Owen lets go of my hand, gaining a few feet on me, and turns to face me, slowly skating backward in front of me. We've reached a more secluded part of the forest. It's just us surrounded by hushed pines.

"When did you know you wanted to be a figure skater?" he asks openly, genuinely.

"I've been practically attached to my skates since I was four. I fell in love with it instantly. I think I've spent more time on the ice than sleeping, eating, and everything else combined."

"You're a natural," he remarks, flashing me that charming grin of his. "I can see why you were an Olympian."

I give a small, rueful smile. "Once upon a time, maybe."

"So what made you give it up?" Owen asks gently. "If you don't mind me asking."

I bite my lip, debating how much to reveal. But something in his expression puts me at ease. He let me see his vulnerable side, after all.

"My partner and I were favored to win gold at the Beijing Olympics," I begin slowly. "But the night before the long program, Pierre trashed his hotel room. He'd been doping. It was a huge scandal, and we were immediately disqualified."

Owen's eyebrows shoot up. "Seriously? What an idiot."

"Yeah, I was completely humiliated. So I left Beijing in disgrace, even though I'd done nothing wrong." My throat tightens. "I guess after that, I just wanted to get as far from the spotlight as possible."

"Wow, that really sucks."

I laugh. "Okay?"

"I mean seriously. It really sucks. If I had a chance to go play hockey at the Olympics, and one of my teammates screwed us over like that? Let's just say he wouldn't have any more teeth and that's saying a lot for hockey players."

"That would suck for sure."

"Sorry. That's probably not the kind of sympathy you need."

"No it's okay. Actually, I hate sympathy. All those looks that I got after it happened. My teammates, my coaches, all those pitying glances... I just wanted to get away."

"Well, then you won't get any sympathy from me."

"Thanks, you're a real pal."

He stops skating and I do too, so I won't crash into him.

"Am I though? A pal? Is that what I am to you?"

"I don't know *what* you are, actually," I admit. "Until recently you were my enemy, so..." I shrug, not knowing how to finish.

Owen skates closer, his blue eyes soft. "Emily..." he starts.

My pulse quickens. He reaches up and brushes a wisp of hair from my cheek, his fingers leaving a trail of heat on my skin.

"You're amazing. Don't let anyone make you feel otherwise."

He takes my hand, pulling me close. My breath catches as he gazes down at me, his eyes burning with intensity. Slowly, gently, he lowers his lips. My heart pounds against my ribs. I need his mouth on mine so badly, it hurts. But...

"WAIT," I cry.

He pauses, but does not back away. His lips hover over mine, barely caressing them with his warm breath. This alone is enough to send me over the edge.

"For how long?" he mumbles, low in his throat. "Because I can stand here like this for a long... *long* time."

I swallow hard. Why is this so difficult?

"Terms." My throat is dry, and I can barely get the word out.

His mouth curls at the corner in a wry grin. He's looking at me so intently, I should be uncomfortable. But I'm not. I love it.

"Terms?" he repeats. "Like, terms and conditions?"

"Yes. Exactly."

His eyes burn into mine, but his expression is so soft, so patient, I almost give in right now, right here. Forget my heart. Forget my reservations. I want to throw caution to the wind. But I know that's not wise. I'm just not ready.

"I'm listening, Kitten."

"I... I..."

"Yes?" His nose brushes against my cheek and his eyelashes flutter down, as if he's taking in my whole essence.

"I don't want to date you."

He freezes, then he lifts his eyes. His look is calculated, like he dare not make one wrong move. Say one wrong word. Lest he scare me away. He licks his lips, tilting his head.

"What do you want, then?" he asks softly.

This. I want this. I want to kiss him. To own him. For him to ravish me.

"Benefits," I blurt. "Former adversaries to...friends. With benefits."

His hands are still on me, but he recoils his chin back. Like he can't wrap his head around what I just said. Was it the friends part? Because that threw me for a loop just now as it was coming out of my mouth.

"You... want to have a physical relationship with me," he says matter-of-factly. "But that's all?"

I nod. "Yes."

"Friends with benefits?"

"Right. But not *benefits*, benefits. If you know what I mean."

He blinks. "Um, you're going to have to be more specific than that."

"You know." I raise my brows, rolling my eyes around. I'm not exactly comfortable saying it.

He chuckles, deep and velvety, and looks at me with amusement. "So, are we talking... first base, second base? Third base?"

My face burns bright red and a giggle escapes me. I feel so ridiculous talking like this.

"What?" He hooks a finger under my chin and nudges it up just a little.

"You're a hockey player and you're talking in baseball metaphors."

He grins, holding back a laugh. "Okay... so we're on the ice. The puck drops..."

"No puck."

"No puck? Okay."

"And no stick."

He pulls a face. "No puck and no stick? That's not even hockey. That's just... skating. That's figure skating, Emily."

"I don't make the rules."

"You are exactly making up the rules right now."

I shrug.

"Okay." He leans away, rubbing his beard between his thumb and fingers. "So... are there lifts and flips and toe loops?"

"Definitely toe loops," I say, already feeling the sensation of my tummy flipping and spinning whenever he's this close to me.

"Anything else?"

"Um... nope. That about covers it."

He's silent for a while, thinking. "But we wouldn't be dating? No feelings? Only... the physical stuff?"

I cringe. He makes it sound so base. Like I only want him for his body. Which I do. Very much. But it's more complicated than that. When I go in, I go *aaalll* in, and I don't know where to stop. The few relationships I've had ended with me giving everything. Risking more. Loving harder. Losing myself in the other person. And none of them *ever* returned a fraction of the love I gave. I've only known heartache and rejection. And so there's this wall around my heart now. It's a nice wall. With flowering vines and lush greenery. I'm happy with my wall.

"Only kisses," I confirm. Don't want all these weird hockey metaphors to confuse him. Even *I'm* confused.

"No commitment?"

I hesitate for a sec. That's a good thing, right? Guys don't like commitment.

"That is correct."

He frowns. Did I say the wrong thing? Why do I self-sabotage like this? I should have just let him kiss me. But I'm afraid of the after. The drive back to the city. The flight home. The working at the same place.

He backs away, looking at me with an expression I can't read. It's not a happy one, I can tell you that.

"Are you interested in another guy, Emily? Is that it?"

"No. I just don't want to complicate things, that's all."

"And dating me would be complicated?"

"Any time expectations are involved it gets complicated. I really want you to kiss me. A lot. But I'm making it simple for you. You don't have to buy me flowers or check in with me all the time. Isn't that what every guy wants?"

A cold shimmer slices in his eyes. "Not this guy. Not me."

My stomach plummets to my skates. I'm messing this up. I'm disappointing him. And on his birthday! Here I am, thinking I was giving him an easy, fun distraction. A girl with no expectations whatsoever. Someone who won't corner him or pin him down. The opposite of the old ball and chain. But all I'm doing is letting him down.

"I'm sorry," I say, looking down at our skates. The ice is well used here. It needs resurfacing soon.

Owen doesn't speak for a long, long while. So long, in fact, that if I weren't staring at his skates, I'd think he was gone. The only sound is my breathing and the thundering of my heart.

At length, I chance a look up at him. His jaw is clenched, and he's looking thoughtfully into the distance. He doesn't even want to look at me now.

The silence is killing me. Forget being friends with benefits. I just need to know we're okay.

"Owen?" I say softly, timidly.

His gaze cuts to mine, his lips pressed together. And he holds my stare—almost to an uncomfortable point. I'm holding my breath, because I won't look away. I dare not even blink, but that's pretty much impossible. Then he lets out a long, hard breath, shaking his head ever so slowly.

Narrowing his eyes, he says, "Oh screw it."

Then he's all over me. His hands. His lips. His hot breath. Strong, calloused hands grip my waist, crushing my body against his, hot and demanding. I open myself to him, wanting more, needing to taste him. He kisses me ravenously, like a man starved, one hand trailing up to cup my jaw while the other splays across my lower back. I feel his fingers pressing into my skin, pulling me impossibly closer to the hard planes of his chest. My hands clutch at his muscular shoulders, feeling the strength coiled within him even as he handles me so gently. His beard scrapes my cheek, a delicious contrast to his soft lips working over mine.

I'm dizzy with desire, my body coming alive under his scorching touch, wound tight with need. Confident fingers drag up the column of my throat, tangling into my hair and giving it a little tug that makes me gasp. He claims my mouth again and again, branding me, staking his claim. I am jello and wildfire and butterflies and I kiss him back with unchecked passion.

When we finally pull apart, Owen rests his forehead against mine. My lips feel raw and tender, and I want more. More. More.

"Wow," he murmurs, caressing my face. He clears his throat.

“Wow,” I echo.

“Terms,” he says, not letting me go.

“I’m listening.”

He kisses me again, softly. On the lips. On the nose. On the apple of each cheek. “We’re doing this. Every. Day.”

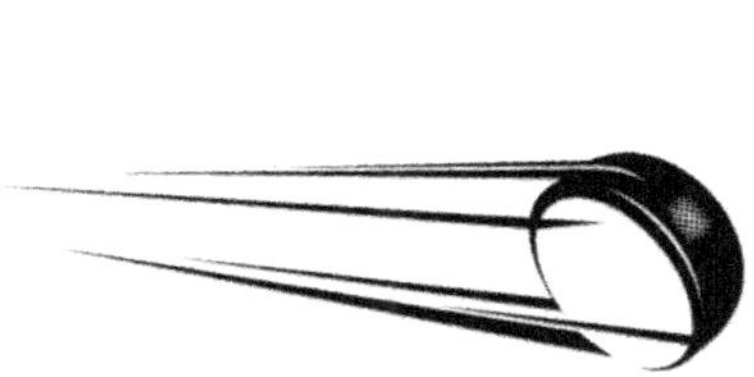

"Canada is hockey."
– Mike Weir

CHAPTER NINETEEN

Owen

Cyrus' face is priceless as he walks next to me into the Blizzard Dome. I'm suited up as usual, and he's wearing the #8 Jablonski jersey I bought him, taking in the sights with pure wonder. I ruffle his crazy mop of hair as some female girls hoot at him in a wholesome way. He loves the attention more than I thought he would.

Shannon finally relented when Cyrus begged her to

let him come to a game, laying the guilt on thick, since he missed my actual birthday.

I take him down the hallways and into the dressing room to show him my stall. The framed photo of me above it still has some sticker residue from Emily's prank. That seems so long ago, like we were different people then. I know at least on my part, I'm a whole new man. It's all because of Emily, even though she's keeping me at arm's length. It's okay. I'll wait for her.

The guys all take Cyrus under their wings. Hendrix shows him the stick room, Griffin gives him a few goal-tender pointers. Even Coach gives him a puck for a souvenir.

The shiner Emily gave him is gone now, by the way. He gave me a long lecture when we returned to practice a few days later. It's all good. We're copasetic.

Once I've geared up, and we're in pre-game mode, it's time for Cyrus to go to the VIP box I reserved for him and some of the players' wives. Paul Nagel and Kevin Tate's wives are both stunning ladies, and each has two kids that go to Bayview Heights—-that bougie school I'm trying to get Cyrus into. Leigh Tate said she'd meet me down here to take Cyrus upstairs, but first I want him to properly meet Emily. Last time, he had a bathroom emergency and probably doesn't remember any of it.

I find Emily in the Zamboni garage, making sure the machine is ready for the game. Cyrus just about loses it. His eyes go wide and his mouth drops to the floor.

"Wow! You get to drive this thing?"

"Yep," Emily says. "Almost every night."

Cyrus looks up at me with such a pure expression of awe. "I want to do this when I grow up."

I smile down at him. "Drive a Zamboni?"

He nods with unflagging jubilation.

"You can be anything you want, little man."

Emily smirks with a triumphant smile on her face and says with mock surprise, "Don't you want to be a star hockey player?"

"Nope."

"I see you've got the jersey already."

He points to his back, which makes him spin around like a dog trying to catch its tail. "It's got my name on it."

"Sure does," she says. "Would you like to ride the Zamboni with me during intermission?"

Cyrus' face. If I could bottle the elation, the disbelief at his good fortune, the almost heartbreaking trembling of his eyebrows, and how he's about to cry from happiness, I'd never be able to keep it in stock. I'd call it Cyrus' Dreams Come True. Seriously, the kid is happier than those who find out they're going to Disney for the first time. You know the ones where the parents decide to film their reactions and plaster the videos all over the internet? Cyrus' reaction blows all those out of the water.

"Can I? Please?"

"I told you. Anything you want."

"Ice cream?"

"They'll deliver ice cream sundaes to your box. After

the chili dog bar and the sushi the ladies will probably order."

"Yay! I love sushi."

"Of course you do." I turn to Emily. "His mom's kind of a health nut."

Emily's smile is tight, but she nods, then says to Cyrus, "Come on down a little early before intermission so we can get you situated, okay?"

He's skipping in circles by now. He hasn't even had any sugar yet. Shannon's going to kill me for dropping him off so hyper later tonight.

"I gotta go take him to meet Tate's wife. I'll talk to you in a bit to go over the details of his ride, okay?"

"Sure."

She seems a little distant. But that's probably because we're back at work now. She told me she felt weird about it. For the record, I don't. But I respect her feelings and won't shove her into a closet to devour her like I want to.

"Is that your girlfriend?" Cyrus asks as we walk away.

"I want her to be."

He makes like he wants to give me a fist bump, so I comply.

"She's a hottie."

"Where did you learn that word?"

He shrugs. "The kids at school say it all the time."

"That's it. I'm sending you to that posh private school."

Leigh and her son Aiden are waiting for us when we get to the elevators. Aiden is just three months older than Cyrus, which in nine-year-old terms, makes him the older, more experienced lad, and the way he's preparing Cyrus for the VIP box, I can tell he takes it quite seriously. By the time I exchange phone numbers with Leigh, the two boys are best friends, and Cyrus can't wait to see the box.

I find Emily about a half hour later, hoping I can convince her into the whole closet kissing scenario I've built up in my mind. She's in Joe's office, logging something on a chart. She's changed her shirt, and instead of the hoodie she had on before, she's in a licenced Toronto Titans jersey. But with her back to me, all I notice is the name stretched across her shoulders. O'Malley.

I've never been a jealous man, but right now, I want to rip that shirt right off her and burn it.

Of course I always want to rip off her clothes, but this is different. Seeing another man's name on her back makes my blood boil.

When she hears my footsteps approaching, she turns to me and offers a half smile, but even that paltry expression falters when she sees I'm not slowing down, and I'm not smiling back. I am in beast mode right now. With dominance in my stride, I march right up to her, crowding her against the desk. Growling into her neck, I grab the hem of her shirt and tug. "You don't wear anyone's jersey but mine, Kitten."

She lets out a shaky breath and nibbles on her

bottom lip, glancing down to where our bodies meet. I'm in full gear already, but the way she's looking at me, I wish I wasn't.

"I'm wearing *my* jersey. I bought it, so it's nobody's but mine."

"It has Sawyer's name on it and you know it."

"Oops. They must have sold out of the inflated ego variety."

"Take it off."

"I beg your finest pardon?"

"Take. It. Off. Before I rip it with my bare hands."

"Ooooh. I thought we've had this conversation, Owen. No pucks."

My eyes sweep down over her figure. So that's what that metaphor means. And for the record, I wouldn't compare them to pucks. I need to find us a closet ASAP.

A sound comes out of me I'm sure I have never made in all my twenty-eight years. I probably sound like a cross between a bear and a dragon and I don't care because Emily's eyes flash big and round as I take the jersey off my own back and shove it at her.

"If you're going to wear a team jersey, Kitty Cat, I don't want to see any name across your back other than mine. And throw that cheap piece of fabric you're wearing in the trash."

As I walk away, I hear her call after me, "I paid a lot for this. Even with my discount."

"Then you wasted your money," I say, and don't look

back as I make my way to the dressing room to put on a replacement jersey.

When I get there, Coach is about to give his "Win one for the Gipper" pep talk. Seems I left them waiting, which is so unlike my character. All eyes are on me when I walk through the door exposing my pads.

Every single guy saw me not ten minutes ago before I went to find Emily, and most of them know where I've been. Coach rolls his eyes, but it's Sawyer who says what everyone is thinking.

"Couldn't keep your clothes on, Jablonski?"

"She undressed him with her eyes," adds Hendrix.

Coach claps his hands. "Okay, settle down. But seriously, Jablonski. Where's your jersey?"

"I gave it to a fan, okay?" I reach into my stall and slip on a new jersey. Then all the guys go silent. I turn around to see Emily standing in the doorway, hip cocked, the concession-bought shirt dangling from one finger. She's wearing my jersey over her tiny frame. She's swimming in it, but pulls it off like it's the latest fashion trend. She is so freaking sexy. I touch my face to make sure my tongue isn't hanging out like in old cartoons.

She looks right at me. "I was told I'd find a trash in here."

Oh, I am going to make her pay for this.

Somebody snickers. I can tell a few of the guys are trying to hold in their laughter.

Coach jerks his chin from me to Emily. "Jablonski," he warns.

I trek over to her with murder in my eyes, but also something else. My whole body is on alert as I take in her figure from head to toe. Suddenly I have fantasies I'll never be able to unsee. Emily in my jersey, walking around my house. Barefoot. Taking over every part of my life.

I could live with that.

She shoves the shirt into my chest and narrows her eyes.

"Just so you know, I'm only wearing this because Cyrus will get a kick out of it. Don't go getting a big head."

The whole room behind me erupts in raucous laughter.

"You earned that one, babe," I tease.

Her cheeks turn pink. It's the loveliest thing I've ever seen.

"Just go do your stretches." With a quirk of her brow, she spins on her heel and walks away.

"Gave it to a fan, eh?" Sawyer goads.

I don't even care about the teasing, because my name is stretched across her shoulders. She's mine.

Intermission rolls around, and instead of heading to the dressing room, I hurry over to the Zamboni gate to see Cyrus get his ride. He's already perched on the machine next to Emily, ready to go out. Leigh had brought him down and left him in Emily's care. Her husband probably told her that Emily's my girlfriend, so she felt comfortable leaving Cyrus with her.

Cyrus turns around to wave at me as he rides onto the ice with Emily. My heart flips at the sight of the two of them, riding side by side, both wearing my name and number.

The booming PA voice announces, "We have a special treat tonight. Getting a ride on the Zamboni is Cyrus Jablonski, wearing the number eight jersey."

Cyrus waves to the crowd as they cheer for him.

"Only time will tell if he wears number eight when he grows up just like the Titans' team captain, Owen Jablonski. And it looks like we have a theme tonight. Our very own Zamboni driver also dons a number eight jersey. Let's hear it for our unsung heroes. Zaaaaaaaamboni."

Music blasts over the speakers. Fans who remained in their seats are cheering. Cyrus is waving like he's in a ticker tape parade. He's having the time of his life. Emily is focused on her job, but every now and then leans in and laughs at something Cyrus says. The sight is like an arrow to the heart, and it hits me. I am falling for Emily Brooks. I'm falling hard. It should scare me. But it doesn't. If I could skate out onto the ice right now and make a fool of myself for her in front of the whole crowd and TV cameras, I would. I'm in love. I'm in love!

The rest of the game flies by. After the final buzzer, I shower and change as fast as I can. When I meet Leigh outside the dressing rooms where she greets her husband sometimes. She's there, but Cyrus is not.

"I dropped him off with Emily," she says when she sees me. "She's such a lovely girl. Cyrus really likes her."

"Oh, he's smitten," I reply. "How did he do upstairs in the box?"

"He's just the sweetest boy. He politely asked for permission any time he wanted something off the buffet. He was respectful and well mannered. Aiden and the other boys loved him. We should schedule a play-date some time."

I tell her I'd have to run it by Shannon but that I'd get back to her. In truth, I'd love to see Shannon making friends with other moms. She works her tail off, is tired all the time, does nothing for herself, and could use a break. It would be great if she had a network she could rely on.

When I find Emily and Cyrus, they're in the nutrition room, of all places. I like my post game snack, so it works out for me. Cyrus is drinking a smoothie Emily had made for him. He's chattering a mile a minute in between sips, still hyped up from the experience. I don't know how that kid can still eat after having chili dogs, sushi, nachos, and ice cream. Where does he put it all?

"There you are," I say, walking by the table to grab a protein bar. "You weren't in your usual places and I got a little worried."

She rolls her eyes. "Don't worry, I'm not corrupting him. I just thought I'd keep him company until you came out."

"It would take an awful lot to corrupt Cyrus," I say, sitting down next to my brother. "Did you have fun, little man?"

"The best! Can I come back next week?"

"We'll have to see if the planets align," I say. "But I'm glad you could come tonight. Made my whole year."

"Me too." He slurps through his straw noisily, getting to the bottom of the smoothie.

"You all done there, sir?" Emily asks. Cyrus nods and lets her take his cup so she can wash it.

"We hung out at the garage for a little while after the game," she says, rinsing out the cup before setting it in the dishwasher. "I got some pictures of Cyrus on the Zamboni posing like a ham. I'll send them to you."

"Can I come visit Emily tomorrow?" Cyrus asks. He's rubbing his eyes, fighting off sleep. Maybe he'll zonk out in the car.

"Tomorrow?" I say. The master of persuasion has upgraded his request from next week for the very next day. Next, he'll be asking to spend the night in the Blizzard Dome. "Tomorrow's a school night, bud."

Emily dries her hands with a towel but doesn't sit down. "But I'm sure your dad was happy you could come tonight to celebrate his birthday. I can't think of a better present."

Cyrus stares at her blankly. "It's not my dad's birthday... I don't think so anyway. I've never met my dad."

Emily's face drains of color, and I can see exactly the moment it sinks in. She thinks Cyrus is my kid. That's kind of hilarious, and then it just explodes out of me. Laughter, deep, freeing laughter. I can't remember the last time I've laughed like this. I can't help myself. All this time, Emily thought I had a son, and I realize that's probably a big reason she's afraid to date me. Oh man. I'm dying.

Emily's bottom lip starts to tremble. "What's so funny? Why are you laughing?"

Oh sweet summer child. I think I'd like to tease her about this for the rest of our lives.

But I don't want to embarrass her in front of the kid, so I slap him on the back and put on my authoritative voice as well as I can through the laughter.

"Do you have to use the bathroom... little brother?" I stress the last two words to drive my point. "There's one through that door right there."

I point to a door on the other side of the room. He needs to go anyway, I'm sure of it.

He hops up and gives Emily a hug, then shuffles his feet the whole way to the bathroom. Once he shuts the door behind him, I turn to Emily with a gloating smirk. "Well well, Kitty Cat. Seems my brother is just as in love with you as I am. Whichever one of us will you choose?"

"He's your brother? Seems like a little detail you could have mentioned."

"Half-brother. And I never would have imagined you'd think he was my son! You sure do jump to a lot of conclusions. Must be a figure skater thing. All that jumping."

"Watch it or I'll drop kick you."

I hold up my hands. "Okay, okay. Truce?"

She sighs. "Yeah, whatever. I feel like such an idiot."

I get up from the table and wrap my arms around her, kissing her on the head. "You're not an idiot. You're just... really dumb."

"What?" she shoves at my chest.

"I'm kidding. I just love it when your face scrunches up like that. You're like a cute little elf."

"You are skating on thin ice, puck boy."

"You're beautiful when you're angry."

She turns bright red. "That's enough, now. Your brother will be coming out any minute. Oh, and before I forget..."

In one graceful motion, she reaches for the hem of the jersey I gave her and flips it over her head. She's wearing a spaghetti strap tank top underneath, but my mouth still goes dry from the sight of all that exposed skin.

She's handing the jersey out to me, trying to get me to take it, but I want her to keep it. I want to see it on her all the damn time.

She shakes it at my chest level. "Here, take it."

But something catches my eye. A smudge on her

bicep. No, not a smudge. A bruise. A grab mark bruise with the pattern of a thumb and fingers.

"How did you get that bruise, Emily?"

Her opposite hand flies to cover it, but I gently peel it away so I can get a better look. Somebody did this to her. Rage curls in my gut.

"Emily," I say with the lowest, most steady growl I can muster. "Who did this to you?"

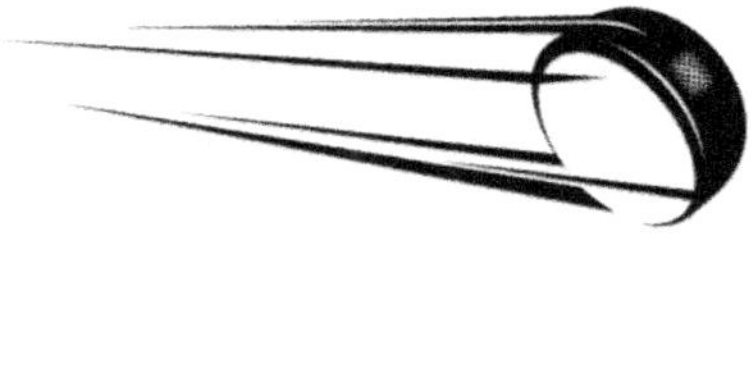

“There are no limits
to what you can achieve.
Dream big, aim high and never give up.”
– Kaetlyn Osmond

MPONI

CHAPTER TWENTY

Emily

I've been home for about twenty-five minutes when a knock comes on the door. My body jolts when I think it might be Cody. I know he didn't mean to hurt me the other day. He's just a lanky, geeky guy. But when he thought I stood him up for our "date" he got angry. I tried to tell him I was in Quebec and that I never even said yes when he asked me out, but none of that registered with him.

He had everything planned that night—flowers, chocolates. And he got all dressed up. When I didn't answer the door, he thought something happened to me at first. But then he let his thoughts fester... scenarios of me standing him up and making a fool of him. He was so upset, confronting me in the hallway. I tried to reason with him. Calm him down. But when I turned to walk to my apartment, he grabbed my arm. Hard.

Honestly, I didn't think much of it. I hadn't realized he'd left a bruise.

I guess he's stronger than he looks.

When I explained all this to Owen, he looked like his head would explode right off his shoulders. He was ready to call in all the guys on the team to teach my slinky neighbor a lesson. Of course I reminded him of the possible assault charges, and that seemed to bring his fury down to a rolling simmer. Plus, he was trying to keep his cool for Cyrus.

Then, he insisted I go home with him. To his house. Yeah. That was a hard no. Lucky for me, he had to drop Cyrus off at Shannon's house with only two seats in his sports car. What kind of person drives a sports car in the winter? Mister show-off. That's who.

So, only after I was safely inside my Uber did he allow me out of his sight and he made me promise to text as soon as I was in my apartment with the door locked.

It's been a long night. I'm tired. I need a shower.

Another knock sounds on the door, this time a little

more urgent. I swear if this is Cody, I am going to blast him with my fire extinguisher. I pick up the small fire extinguisher that I got at Canadian Tire, and stand poised at my front door to either smack him with it or spray him to smithereens with whatever chemical they fill these things with.

I sneak a look through the peephole even though I can only see through it fifty percent of the time.

But it's not Cody standing on the other side of my door. It's Owen. Relief washed through me. Something else washes through me, too. But let's just ignore that.

Setting down the fire extinguisher, I open the door to find that beautiful man taking up my whole doorway. His face is stern. All hard lines. Cheekbones so chiseled, he could cut ice with them. He's leaning on the doorframe with one arm. Head cast down like he'd been listening instead of watching for me to answer. When the door is fully open, he lifts those intense eyes, dark with concern.

"Pack a bag," he says without preamble.

"What?"

"Enough for a couple nights. We'll come back to get the rest later."

"I'm not going anywhere."

"I won't let you stay in this hellhole so your neighbor can come over anytime and manhandle you."

"I told you I'm fine. I can handle it, see?" I show him the fire extinguisher. "Anyway, he's not gonna do that again."

"The hell he isn't. He did it once, he'll do it again. Do you need me to come in there and help you pack a bag? Because I will, and something tells me you won't appreciate me going through your panty drawer."

"And where am I supposed to go?"

I suppose I could crash at Maggie's. But she shares an eight-hundred square foot studio with two other girls. We'd all have to sleep standing up.

Owen cocks his head, but doesn't pass the threshold like he's a vampire waiting to be invited inside. "My house."

"Nah ah. There's no way you're luring me to your seduction palace. Just go home and get some rest. It's late."

"Not without you."

I give him a tender smile because he gets brownie points for worrying about me.

"Goodbye, Owen."

I close the door, making sure to close the deadlock and the chain.

"See, I'm safe inside. I'll see you later this week," I tell him through the door.

He goes silent after that.

After a long shower, I make myself a midnight snack so I can curl up in front of the TV and watch one episode of Full House. My mind is too wound up and I need some light entertainment to settle me.

When I open the trash lid to throw out my apple peels, a stench so rancid reaches my nostrils, it burns my nose hair. How long has it been since I've thrown out the garbage? Since before Quebec? It's bad. Really bad.

I won't be able to enjoy my cheese and apples with that smell lingering in the apartment now that it's out there, wafting around.

So I tie up the trash bag and put on my slides so I can walk to the garbage chute ten feet down the hall.

But when I open the front door, I almost trip on a body on the floor right outside my apartment. Owen's long legs stretch out in front of my doorway. His body is half leaning against the wall and he's scrolling on his phone.

"What are you still doing here? I thought you left an hour ago."

"Nope. I told you I won't leave you alone. Now either you come with me or I guard your hallway all night."

I try to ignore the way my heart tugs at that.

I step over his legs and drag my trash bag down the hallway. But he clasps his large bear-like paws over my small hands and takes the bag from me, tossing it into the chute.

He winces at the smell. "Something die in your trash can?"

"Probably."

We walk the ten steps back to my front door and he settles himself against the wall again, waiting for me to go inside.

"Are you seriously not going to leave? You're gonna stay here on the floor for the entire night?"

"If I have to."

I squeeze my eyes shut and press my fingers over my temples. "You can have the couch, but don't even think about trying anything."

"You really think I'm here to have my way with you?"

"Are you?"

He has to think about that for way too long.

"That depends. Do you want me to have my way with you?"

Yes.

I roll my eyes. "I bought a value pack of toothbrushes at Costco. You can have one."

He follows me inside, watches me bolt up my door, looks around at ev-er-y-thing. He's too big for this small space. Larger than life. I feel almost exposed having him here. Like it's too intimate.

Also, I kind of want to jump his bones, so there's that.

I run my mantra through my head. *No pucks, no sticks, no goals. No pucks, no sticks, no goals.*

He gestures to the plate of cheese and apples on my coffee table. "Don't let me keep you from your... dinner?"

"I like a late-night snack sometimes. I couldn't sleep."

"That makes two of us."

"You really don't have to worry about me. I've lived here for almost a year and have never had a problem."

"You're not even going to ask how easy it was for me

to get in the building? I don't think I'll ever stop worrying as long as you live in this place."

I study him for a minute. Really study him. He's so protective of his brother, anyone would think Cyrus is his son. Not just me jumping to conclusions. And that night at the bar when he got that creep to leave me alone. He was kinda scary. And tonight, standing sentinel outside my apartment. This is just the way Owen is. Carrying other people's burdens on his shoulders. If he's not careful, one day he'll collapse under all that weight... or make me fall for him.

I sit on the lumpy couch, offering him to sit and share my snack. He accepts an apple slice.

"So... for what it's worth," I say. "I think it's chivalrous of you to camp out to make sure I was okay."

He leans back into my lumpy couch, his long legs stretched out in front of him. Even in repose, his body radiates a coiled strength beneath the surface.

"I can't let you get hurt on my watch."

"Why are you so determined to be my protector, anyway? I haven't exactly been nice to you."

Owen's jaw tightens. "Let's just say I know what it's like to feel alone and vulnerable."

He falls quiet, staring down at his hands. I get the sense there's more he wants to say.

"You can talk to me," I offer gently.

He reaches up and scratches his beard. I wish that was my job. Owen's beard scratcher. The Titans can add that to my duties.

"It's just..." Owen starts, then stops himself. He rubs the back of his neck. "I know what it's like... not having someone look out for you."

I wait for him to continue, sensing there's more he wants to say.

"My dad wasn't exactly Father of the Year," he says finally. "Mom must have known he had mistresses. He was never home, always traveling for work. But when Shannon showed up on our doorstep very, very pregnant, the you-know-what hit the fan. And she's not the only one. I know of at least two other ladies in other provinces, and there's probably more. I could have siblings all over Canada and not even know it."

An awkward silence descends. My chest tightens. I never imagined Owen had a childhood like that.

"I'm sorry," I say softly. "That must have been really hard on you and your mom."

Owen shrugs. "I was lucky to have hockey. It gave me something to focus on. But Cyrus... he doesn't even remember our dad."

I have an almost irresistible urge to wrap my arms around those broad shoulders of his. Instead, I reach over and put my hand on top of his, stilling his restless fingers.

"I try to give him some semblance of a normal life. But Shannon works all the time and I'm on the road so much..." Owen trails off, scrubbing a hand down his face. "I feel like I'm just one more adult in his life failing him."

"You're not failing him. He's a great kid."

His eyes light up. "He is, isn't he? It's all Shannon. She's had it rough, raising him on her own. I try to help out financially, but Shannon is too proud. She thinks it ties her to my father. I think she has trouble trusting people, especially men."

"You're a good brother, Owen. Even if you don't get as much time with Cyrus as you'd like."

Owen turns his palm over and laces his fingers through mine. The warmth of his hand sends a shiver up my spine as his thumb absently strokes over my knuckles.

"And what about your mom?"

"I think she was relieved to get rid of my dad, actually. She lives in Vancouver now."

I meet his gaze, my stomach doing a little flip at the tenderness in his eyes.

It's such a sweet moment until...

"So," he says, wagging his brows. "About our friends with benefits deal. When exactly can I cash in on that?"

I throw him a hard stare. "You're not sleeping in my bed tonight."

"It was worth a shot."

It's getting late, and I know I should get up to grab Owen a blanket and that toothbrush. But staring into his handsome face has become my new favorite activity.

His expression grows soft, but I steel my resolve.

No pucks, no sticks...

"Emily..." His voice is deep and liquid. "I want you to know—"

Three hard, consecutive knocks rattle the front door.

Owen checks his watch. "It's two in the morning."

"Emily, are you in there?" The voice is muffled on the other side of the door. "I thought I heard voices."

"That would be Cody," I say.

Owen springs up from the couch. "It's show time."

"It's better if we just ignore him. He'll go away."

"Not before he wakes your neighbors. And then what? He'll come back again tomorrow. And the next day. Guys like that don't know how to take a hint."

"What are you going to do?"

Owen's already unbuttoning his jacket. He tosses it on the floor, then reaches over his shoulder to grab the back of his t-shirt and pulls it over his head one-handed. He tosses that on another spot on the floor. His whole glorious chest is out in the open right here for my eyes to feast on. He's a mountain in my tiny living room. The defined muscles of his arms and shoulders, the gentle slope of his pecs tapering down to the thousand ridges of his abdomen. The dark trail of... oh lawdy. He's unbuttoning his jeans and opening his fly just enough to spark the imagination. Ladies and gentlemen, Owen is a boxers guy.

My whole face is hot. I need to open a window.

But wait. The man has a tattoo above his right hip. A constellation of stars. Before I can get a good look at it, he's bending over, mussing up his hair. When he flips back up, he grins at me and says, "How do I look?"

Once I pick my jaw off the floor, I reply, "Like you've been properly bedded."

"Good. But something's off."

"There is? It doesn't look that way from where I'm standing."

Cody pounds on the door again. "Emily?"

"Aha! I know what's missing." Owen reaches over to me, pulls me into his arms, and kisses me roughly, roaming his hands all over my shirt, grabbing fistfuls of fabric to wrinkle it beyond recognition. Then his hands tangle in my hair, swirling it around—knotting it up. When he pulls his mouth off me, he drags his teeth along my lips, making them feel swollen and raw. He stands back to admire his handiwork.

"That's better. Now you look like you've been properly bedded, too."

I'm in such a state, I don't protest when he saunters over and answers my door, casually leaning an elbow on the frame.

"Can I help you?"

I can see Cody peek inside under Owen's armpit, making sure he has the right apartment. He sees me, then looks back at Owen, taking in his tall figure, the bare chest, the open fly, the bedroom hair. Red splotches appear on Cody's face just as a sour expression overtakes his features.

"What's going on here, Emily? Who's this guy?"

Before I can respond, Owen growls possessively, "I'm her soulmate. And you are interrupting."

"Just go away, Cody," I plead. I don't want this to get ugly.

"Cody?" Owen stands up straight. "You're Cody? The one Emily told me about?"

This seems to give Cody some confidence, as if me talking about him gives him a chance with me. He puffs up his chest. Or at least tries to. There's not much there.

"Yes," he says, lifting his chin. "What of it?"

Owen steps out into the hallway and looms over Cody, crowding his space. "You're the one who manhandled my girlfriend and left your grabby mark on her arm."

Cody stumbles backward, but Owen catches him by the arm in the same place Cody grabbed me. Owen's massive hand wraps all the way around Cody's bicep. His fingers tighten by degrees, each squeeze making Cody squirm.

"How does that feel? Do you think Emily enjoyed being bruised up by you?"

Cody only squeaks.

"Do you?"

"No! No I don't."

"Then why did you do it?"

"I... I don't know."

Owen twists his fingers to bend Cody's arm at a weird angle. He doesn't break it, but I know he's inflicting just enough pain to scare Cody. The whole business is effortless on Owen's part. At most, Cody will have a bruise matching mine.

"You keep your filthy hands off my woman." Owen's growl is deep and scratchy. "Don't look at her. Don't talk to her. Don't knock on her door. Ever. Do I make myself clear?"

"Yes. Yes!" Cody whimpers.

"Say it."

"I... w-won't look at her, or t-talk to her... or knock on her door."

"Good." Owen releases Cody and slaps him on the shoulder. The impact makes Cody wince. "We have an understanding. Now run along."

Owen takes one step back and slams the door on Cody's face. He locks the bolt and the chain, then turns around with a satisfied grin.

Crap, that's hot.

He's just standing there casually, like his state of undress isn't making my legs turn to overcooked spaghetti. I suck in my bottom lip, cataloging every inch of him.

No pucks, no sticks, no goals.

"I think that will do the trick," he says. "What do you think?"

I think you're certifiably gorgeous, good sir.

"I uh..." I stutter. "Did you just call me your soulmate?"

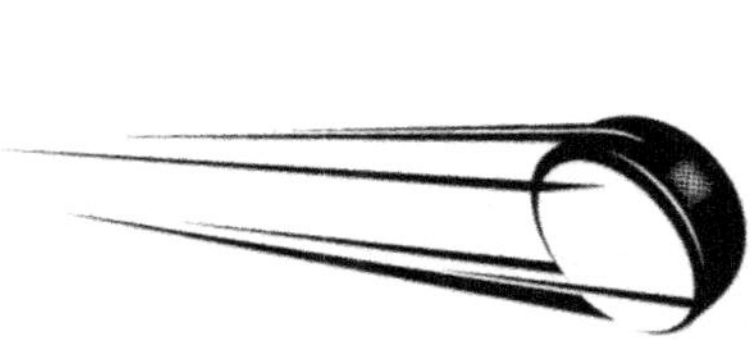

"Hockey is figure skating
in a war zone."
– Unknown

MPONI

CHAPTER TWENTY-ONE

Owen

I'm in the middle of practice when I see him skulk into the rink out of the corner of my eye. What the hell is he doing here? My so-called father. He's not good enough for the title, though. To me he's just Jed.

I try to ignore him and focus on running drills with the team, but I can feel his beady little eyes watching me from the stands. Just the sight of him makes my blood boil.

Coach finally blows the whistle, signaling the end of the drill. It's not time to quit, but I tell Coach I need a break. I throw on my blade guards and make a beeline for the locker room, but Jed runs after me in the hallway. "Owen, my boy!" Jed calls out, shuffling towards me.

That familiar anger rises up inside me. I haven't seen or heard from him in years. Not since the last time I sent him packing.

I keep walking, gritting my teeth. Don't lose it, I tell myself. You're not that scared little kid anymore.

"Owen, wait up!" he pants, struggling to catch up. "Just gimme five minutes, okay? Hear your old man out."

"You've got two," I bite out, turning on him.

His watery eyes light up with relief. "Thanks, kiddo. I knew you'd do right by your dad."

"I'm not your kiddo," I snap. "And you sure as hell aren't my dad. Now what do you want? I'm working."

His smile falters briefly before the salesman mask slips back on. "What, a father can't visit his son at work? I was hoping we could go out, get lunch, catch up."

I snort. "The only time you show up is when you want something. So what is it?"

Jed puts on an exaggerated frown. "Now don't be like that. I'm here because I miss you, that's all."

I have to stop myself from rolling my eyes. He's laying it on thick today. I guess that means he's in real trouble.

"Miss me? That's rich, seeing as you're the one who left."

His easygoing facade falters for a moment before the slick smile is back. "C'mon, that's all water under the bridge now. I'm here to make amends. Start over, you and me."

I shake my head in disgust. This man is unbelievable. "You must be delusional if you think I'd give you a second chance. What do you really want, Jed? Money?"

Bingo. His eyes light up greedily before he rearranges his features into a wounded look. "I just want my family back. Is that so wrong?"

"Cut the act," I snap. "How much are you in the hole for this time?"

His shoulders slump. "Look, I just need a small loan to get myself back on my feet. Five grand. Seven tops. I'll pay you back, I promise."

I let out a harsh laugh. "Let's be honest here. You won't pay me back. In fact, I can pretty much guarantee I won't see you again until you need more money."

"Aw c'mon, Owen," he pleads. "Don't be like that. I know we've had our differences, but family looks out for each other. Right?"

I let out a humorless laugh. "Family? Are you kidding me?" My voice rises to a shout. "You have secret families all across Canada like it's some kind of twisted hobby."

Jed recoils, eyes widening in shock. "Now take it easy, son. No need to cause a scene here."

"Don't you dare call me son," I hiss. "Just go away. Your time's up."

"Come on, Owen," he wheedles. "Don't be stubborn. It's pocket change for you. Help your old man out."

"You're not my old man," I shoot back. "You lost the right to call yourself my father when you walked out and left me and Cyrus. Do you have any idea what that does to a kid?"

Jed's eyes flash with anger. "Don't try to guilt trip me. I did the best I could for Cyrus. It's not my fault the kid's got issues."

My hands curl into fists. How dare he?

"You didn't do a damn thing for him! He's just a little boy, and you abandoned him! What kind of heartless bastard does that?"

"Hey, I never wanted the kid in the first place!" Jed shouts defensively. "His mom tricked me into it. I told her from the start I wasn't signing up to play daddy."

I'm seeing red now, thinking about everything Cyrus has suffered because of this lowlife. The kid can barely tie his own shoelaces but he's expected to take the bus across town after school each day 'cause his mom's working two jobs trying to keep a roof over their heads.

"You don't know how hard it's been for me," he says with a pathetic look.

I step right up to him now, glaring down into his pasty face. "No, you don't get to play the victim here. You did this. You."

He holds up his hands in a conciliatory gesture even as his eyes harden. "I can see you need some time to cool down. But don't go turning your back on your own blood, Owen. you'll regret it."

"The only thing I regret is not telling you to get lost sooner. Now get out of my sight before I have security drag you out."

Jed's face twists into an ugly sneer. "You always were an ungrateful punk. I did my best for you, but you were never satisfied. Ungrateful and selfish, just like your mother."

An icy chill sweeps through me at the mention of my mom.

"Don't you dare talk about my mother," I snarl, hands shaking with barely contained fury.

He sniffs. "I don't know why I bothered coming here."

"I want you to listen to me real clear," I say, my voice low and steady despite the rage coursing through me. "You're dead to me. I don't ever want to see you again. I don't want you going anywhere near Cyrus, either. Or Shannon. Or Mom."

For a second, his eyes flash with the same temper I inherited from him. But then he swallows it back and adjusts his collar. "Making threats now, Owen?"

I shake my head. "Nope. I'm protecting my brother. Because I love him and I will never let him feel unwanted. He's better off without you. That's the one thing I'm grateful for."

Jed just snorts derisively and walks away.

I scrub my face with my hands, trying to get rid of the anxious, sick feeling in my gut.

As soon as he's out of sight, the rage leaves me in a rush, replaced by bone-deep exhaustion. I slip away on unsteady legs to find some place quiet, ending up in the media room. But the silence only makes me feel worse. I can feel my breath coming shorter, my heart starting to race. Slumping down on the floor, I squeeze my eyes shut. My chest feels tight, like a steel band is wrapped around it. I try taking deep breaths, but I can't seem to get enough air. I need to take my gear off, but I can't. A wave of dizziness and nausea washes over me. The walls are closing in, suffocating me. No. No. I can't do this, not here, not now. Spots swim before my eyes. I claw at my chest, willing my lungs to work. But it's no use. My vision starts to go dark around the edges. I'm losing control.

I'm not sure how much time passes. It feels like an eternity of struggling to breathe, struggling to stay conscious, feeling like I might die. I may have momentarily passed out. I'm not sure. But there's a voice, soft and distant, like someone calling for me in a dense forest. I can't see her. Only the voice shrouded in mist.

"Owen," she calls. "Owen..."

And then, a gentle hand on my shoulder, an anchor pulling me back.

"Owen. It's okay. Just breathe with me." Her voice is calm but firm.

I cling to her voice, using it to drag myself back from the edge. My breathing starts to slow, the tightness in my chest loosening its grip. I see a blur of honey-blonde hair and Emily's face comes into focus. She's on the floor with me, stroking my hair.

"I need you to do something for me, okay?"

I nod. She moves her hands down my body, down my legs. She starts unlacing my skates.

"I need you to name three things you can see. Owen, trust me. Three things."

I watch her, making quick work of my laces. The pressure begins to ease.

"I... see you. Unlacing my skates."

"Good. Two more."

My eyes dart around the room. "I see the big TV."

She has one of my skates off by now. "One more. You can do this."

I look up. "Lights. Lights on the ceiling."

My other skate comes off. "Now name three things you can hear." She pulls down a big sock. Then unfastens a shin guard, moving to the next leg to repeat the process.

"I can hear your voice. And the Velcro."

Gradually, inch by inch, the panic starts to loosen its talons.

"You're doing such a good job, Owen. What else do you hear?"

"Uh... the hum of the air conditioner."

She bends over to place a soft kiss on each of my knees. "Now I need you to move three different body parts. Can you do that?"

"Yes."

I clench and unclench my fingers, then with my legs free from the armor, I bend my knee.

"I'm going to pull you up to a sitting position so we can take off your padding. But you're heavy, so you need to help me out, Owen."

"I... think I can sit up on my own."

"Okay good. That will be number three."

I hoist myself up and Emily helps me out of my jersey and padding. I feel much better now. I can breathe. She sits with me, stroking my legs, my arms, my shoulders. Her hands are the most soothing things ever to touch my body.

After a long while, she asks, "How often do you get these?"

"Not since I was seventeen or eighteen."

"Are you seeing a therapist?"

"No."

"Okay." She strokes my beard, combing it with her fingernails. She can ask anything she wants of me right now and it's hers. Jewelry, designer clothes... a house. She just continues to soothe me, then gently adds, "But can we talk about what happened another day? When you're feeling up to it?"

I cast my gaze on her beautiful face. "Sure."

Cupping my hands under her jaw, I lean over to kiss her softly. Her lips are warm and pliant, and although I could completely lose myself in her, she grounds me. She's an anchor to all that is good. I lift her by the waist and settle her on my lap, roaming my hands up her back.

As my mouth moves over hers, I vaguely register several sets of hard footsteps marching down the hallway. There's excited chatter, people rushing by, mild commotion somewhere in the building.

Then Griffin pokes his head in the room, looks at Emily straddling me, then glances at my clothes and gear spread all over the floor.

"What are you guys doing in here? Actually, I don't wanna know. Just get up to check this out. The Hart Memorial Cup was found."

"If figure skating were easy,
they'd call it hockey."
– Unknown

MPONI

CHAPTER TWENTY-TWO

Emily

Malcolm Chase, the owner of the Toronto Titans, steps into the conference room, dress loafers clicking authoritatively against the polished wood floor. The space is packed with reporters, all talking at once. He sits behind a long table, clears his throat and leans towards the microphone, reading from an iPad.

"Thank you all for coming on such short notice. I have an important update regarding the recent robbery of the Hart Memorial Cup from the Blizzard Dome arena. Early this morning, our office administrator, Nancy Lambert, uncovered the missing trophy in an equipment closet belonging to Mark Walsh, the team's equipment manager."

Murmurs ripple through the crowd. He raises his hand for silence before continuing.

"The trophy was found wrapped in towels and hidden underneath some spare goalie gear. Ms. Lambert discovered it when searching for social media props. She immediately notified security and myself. Mr. Walsh was called in for questioning."

A hand shoots up in the sea of reporters. "Was he arrested?" a female voice calls out.

He nods. "Mr. Walsh has been taken into police custody for further investigation. He has been suspended indefinitely from his position with the team, pending the results of the ongoing investigation."

More hands fly up, voices clamoring over each other.

He points to a lanky man in glasses near the front. "This question is for Coach Knight. Did you suspect Mark Walsh before today?"

All eyes turn to Coach Knight, who sits stiffly behind the table next to Nancy and a few other key executives. He’s giving silver fox vibes in his sharp gray suit. He leans forward to speak into the mic. "I was as shocked as anyone to learn of Mark's alleged involvement. He was a trusted member of our staff for many years. My focus now is supporting my team and ensuring this doesn't become a distraction during playoffs."

A female reporter in the front row stands up. "Ms. Lambert. What was going through your mind when you came upon the trophy in Mr. Walsh's office?"

Nancy, her blond hair in a neat updo, wearing a stylish navy dress, leans into her microphone. "Only a sense of loyalty to our team and all the dedicated people working hard behind the scenes. This situation has rallied us together like never before, and has only proven what our esteemed owner, Malcolm Chase, has instilled in this treasured organization: each staff member is worth their weight in gold. Equality is the Titans' way."

She kinda went off subject there, but okay.

"Is there any other evidence that the equipment manager took the trophy?" another reporter asks.

Nancy nods. "Yes, we have reason to believe Mr. Walsh is the one responsible, but we are uncertain if the trophy was taken as part of a prank gone wrong."

"What was the purpose of this supposed prank?"

"Mr. Walsh has not provided a clear explanation," Nancy says smoothly. "However, we believe it was intended as a practical joke that got out of hand. Rest assured, he will be disciplined accordingly."

A prank? This is the first I've heard of this. I glance at Owen standing next to me with a questioning look.

"The suits must be trying to protect the club's image," he whispers in my ear. "Making it seem like an innocent prank is better publicity than admitting someone stole your trophy."

“Not a heck of a lot better,” I say.

Reporters start shouting more questions, but Nancy raises a hand. "Please, I know you are all eager for more details. Rest assured, we are cooperating fully with the police. But we do not wish to impede their work by sharing sensitive information at this early stage."

A few reporters shout questions about how this will impact the team's performance next season. Coach Knight shoots them an icy glare.

"We don't dwell on excuses or setbacks. The Titans are winners, through and through. This changes nothing. The Titans will come back stronger than ever. This incident, while regrettable, will only make us more united and determined heading into playoffs. Our eyes are fixed firmly on bringing home the Cup again this year."

The sound of camera shutters clicking echo inside the small press room. Reporters are all shouting their questions at once. One guy going on about aliens, another saying something about a conspiracy.

Malcolm Chase speaks up. "Any accusations of a wider conspiracy within the organization are patently false. This was the isolated action of one misguided individual. Let me be crystal clear: the Titans do NOT tolerate criminal acts from anyone associated with our club. We hold ourselves to the highest ethical standards at all levels."

I still can't believe it was Mark all along. He's a bit eccentric, but fundamentally kind underneath his quirks. My spidey senses are tingling. Something about this doesn't sit right. It all feels too tidy. Too staged. I glance over at Owen and can tell from his furrowed brow that he's just as skeptical as I am.

Owen and I linger in the hallway after the press conference ends. "This is such baloney," I whisper angrily. "There's no way Nancy just randomly found the trophy under some equipment. It wasn't in there that night we snooped around."

"Are you sure we didn't overlook it?"

I pause, feeling my cheeks flush at the memory of our heated kiss. "Umm... ninety percent sure. You... were kind of distracting me."

He wags his brows. "But it was a fun distraction, though. Maybe we should go back and investigate again"

"Stow it, Lothario."

The way he's flirting tells me he's back to his regular self. He really scared me earlier.

"Besides," I go on. "Mark's back teeth are shot. He wouldn't chew Éclat d'Érable even if he could afford it."

"Maybe he chews with his front teeth?" Owen suggests.

"He's also allergic to nuts. One of the ingredients of Éclat d'Érable is almond extract."

"I still can't figure out why you like it."

"It's not bad. Kind of a cross between Almond Joy, maple candy, and licorice."

"You lost me at licorice."

"Why would Mark steal the trophy only to just bring it back and hide it in his own office?" I add, getting back on the subject. "That's idiotic. Almost like someone planted it there to frame him."

"Someone who wants to make the team look sloppy and disorganized." Owen muses. "Like Rousseau."

My mind starts spinning. "Do you still think it could've been him? Trying to ruin our reputation before playoffs?"

"I'm not ruling him out yet. I do think we would have found the trophy at his house if Coach Knight hadn't interrupted us."

"What about your dad?" I say carefully. "The timing of the trophy suddenly reappearing right after he left the arena is a little sus. Maybe he's blackmailing Mark."

Clearly, I've watched too much Murder She Wrote reruns.

Owen lets out a harsh laugh. "I wouldn't put it past him, but he doesn't have the brains to pull off something like this."

"We should talk to Coach Knight," I say. That old grump might have more info.

"Talk to Coach Knight about what?"

We turn to see Coach emerging from a nearby doorway. He crosses his arms over his broad chest and stares us down. "You two aren't still playing cloak and dagger, I hope. I thought I told you I'd handle it."

I crane my neck to look him in the eye. "You don't actually believe Mark stole the trophy, do you? The gum—"

"Nobody knows about the gum but us. And no, I don't believe he stole it. But I can't have my star center playing Hardy Boys all over Canada. So drop it." He jerks his chin at Owen. "Emergency team meeting in five."

He shakes his head while walking away. With all the excitement over the Hart Memorial Cup, I wonder if he knows what Owen went through earlier. The panic attack. Perhaps Owen wouldn't want him to know. Small mercy for Owen that tonight's not a game night.

"I am SO not dropping it," I say.

"Me neither." He kisses me briefly. "I need to get to that meeting. Will you wait for me?"

My heart twists in my chest. I would wait for him forever. The thought scares me like crazy. But it's the good kind. The thrilling kind. Like that final clicking ascent up a roller coaster right before the steep drop kind.

"If I say no, you'll skip the meeting and follow me home."

"Correctamundo."

I shake my head, trying to hide a smile. "Then I'll wait."

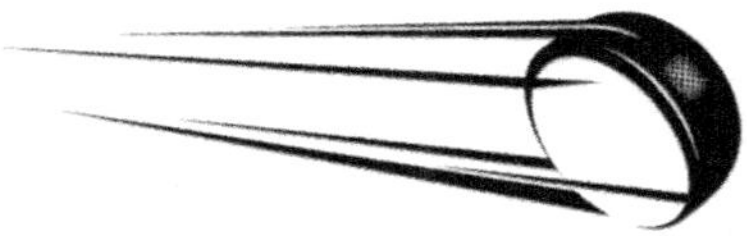

"Only one thing is ever guaranteed,
that is that you will definitely
not achieve the goal
if you don't take the shot."
- Wayne Gretzky.

mPOnI

CHAPTER TWENTY-THREE

Owen

I drag myself into the Blizzard Dome gym on my day off, dreading this lame touchy-feely team building nonsense the coaches have cooked up. I'd rather spend the day loving on Emily, buying her things, taking her anywhere she wants to eat. We haven't had a real date, well, ever. Instead, I gotta sit in a circle with the guys, sharing our feelings, or whatever hippie bonding rituals the coaches have planned. They insisted it was necessary after the whole trophy scandal, to "reunite" and "be in agreement" or some crap like that. As if holding hands singing Kumbaya is going to magically bring us all together.

The only bright spot is that Emily came with me this morning, since I've put my foot down about letting her stay at her apartment alone while Creepy Cody is still lurking around.

I glance at Emily sitting in the PT room, watching us through the glass, laptop open, probably working on a new blog post for Blades After Dark. She glances up and gives me a little wave and a smirk that says she knows exactly how much I don't wanna be here. I roll my eyes and mouth "save me" dramatically. She just laughs and goes back to typing.

At one point, the assistant coach suggests we all say one nice thing about the person to our left. I get stuck complimenting O'Malley's calf muscles.

After an excruciating hour of trust falls and leading each other around in blindfolds, Coach finally sets us free. I make a beeline for Emily, who's now packing up her stuff to leave.

"How was the lovefest?" Emily asks as I approach.

"Oh, it was delightful. We braided each other's hair and made friendship bracelets," I deadpan. "Hendrix even let me borrow his scrunchy."

Emily laughs. I love her laugh.

"So, what should we do on our day off?" I ask. Emily bites her lip as she thinks about it, the simple action driving me crazy. I want to kiss her so badly, but the rest of the team is filtering out of the gym right now.

She scrunches her nose adorably in thought. "Hmm, not sure yet. Maybe we could catch a movie? Or there's that new exhibit at the ROM I've been wanting to see."

She wants to go to a museum on her day off? I press a hand on her lower back and try to get away from the stampede of the guys bolting through the PT room to get the heck away from each other. As we walk far enough down the hallway away from prying eyes, I gently grab her wrist and pull her in close. "I missed you today," I murmur before kissing her softly. Emily laughs between each caress of my lips on hers.

“I’ve been less than fifty feet from you the whole morning.”

“I missed you just the same. After an hour of dudes falling into my arms, I’m gonna need some physical decompression. Preferably involving your lips.

I lean down and capture her mouth again. She sighs into the kiss, sending tendrils of awareness down my spine. Her lips are so soft and she tastes like sugar.

“Mmm. Delicious. What have you been eating?”

“Somebody brought in a box of Tim Bits.”

Heaven. I can’t remember the last time I ate a donut. I take another taste before trailing my way down the column of her neck, sprinkling hot kisses all over her skin. One hand cradles the back of her head while the other presses against the small of her back, drawing her closer.

"I have an idea," I say, nibbling at her earlobe. "And I'm just spitballing here... we can go back to my place and practice some of the bonding activities I learned today. But with fewer clothes."

Her whole body shivers, and I think for a moment she might slide into a puddle on the floor, but then she playfully shoves my chest. "How about somewhere very, very public where we'll be forced to behave? Like... the Distillery District. I haven't been in a while."

That sounds a thousand hundred percent less exciting than having Emily all to myself. But in all honesty, I'd go anywhere as long as she's with me and I can call her mine.

"What's in the Distillery District?" I ask.

"Cute shops, galleries, restaurants," Emily lists off excitedly. "There's an old whiskey distillery you can tour, too."

I like whiskey. But I can't drink until after we win championships. Plus, I try to avoid places where the fans might recognize me, especially after the Memorial Cup fiasco.

"Hmmm. Sounds touristy."

She perks up with a new idea. "Oh I know! What time does Cyrus get off school? We can take him to the Science Center."

"He would love that." And I love Emily for suggesting it. As much as I'd love Cyrus to take after me and play hockey, I'm over the moon proud to have a brainiac brother. Science is his jam. Who cares about getting recognized? I'll wear an ugly hat or something.

I take the opportunity to steal another kiss, cupping my hands behind her jaw, brushing my thumb across her cheek... slow and tender.

I love you. The words are practically dripping from my lips as I kiss her. I want to tell her out loud. I want to sweep her in my arms and wife her up right now. But I'm afraid I might spook her so early in our relationship.

Once I part from her, I brush a loose strand of hair from her face. "Question. Are we still doing the *friends-with-benefits-that-aren't-really-benefits* thing?" I ask. "Because this feels an awful lot like we're dating now. Just sayin'."

She opens that beautiful mouth to respond, but then, Nancy Lambert power walks by and spots us.

"Owen, Emily! Just the two I wanted to see. Got a minute to pop into my office? I have something I'd love your thoughts on."

Emily and I share a curious look but follow Nancy to her office. This woman is like a steamroller on steroids.

"Have a seat, you two," Nancy says, settling behind her large mahogany desk. "I have an exciting proposition for you both."

Emily perches on the edge of the leather chair, back ramrod straight like a cautious cat ready to bolt. I lean back more casually, trying to set her at ease with my body language.

She goes on to explain that the team is looking for

ways to repair public relations after the trophy scandal, especially among the younger demographic.

"That's why I was looking for props. I know I'm not the social media manager, but I wanted to try out some ideas before presenting them to her. But then... well, you know what happened next."

Yeah, I know exactly what happened next. Finding the trophy gave Nancy instant status as a hero while Mark took the fall. I don't trust this woman.

"Anyway," she goes on brightly. "Then I thought you could help us with your blog, Emily."

Emily makes a face, feigning innocence.

"Don't be coy. I know it's you. I know a lot of things, in fact. How you two have been snooping around like a couple of home-grown sleuths."

"We... uh..." I start. But she waves me off.

"It's cute, really. Adorable even."

I glace sidelong at Emily. She's clearly uncomfortable. I hope my expression conveys that she only needs to say the word and we're gone.

"Anyway, about the blog. Just think it over," Nancy says. "We'd love your help, but no pressure."

Emily nods slowly, like she's calculating her next words. "What kinds of posts are we talking about here?"

"Oh, mostly feel-good stuff. Interviews with the players and staff. Every now and then you could write a story with a little more meat. The... political underbelly of pro hockey. That sort of thing."

She opens her desk drawer and reaches inside for a

pad of sticky notes and writes down a number. "Of course, you'd be compensated handsomely."

She slides the paper across the desk and leaves it there casually. Neither Emily or I dare to touch it, but bending over to take a peek, I can say there were a few more zeros than I'm sure Emily gets in ad revenue from her blog.

"Would either of you two like a mint? Or gum?" She reaches back into her desk and takes out a small dish filled with golden wrapped pieces of Éclat d'Érable. I swallow hard. It's all coming together now. I'm ready to jump out of my chair. But Emily is calm, cool, and collected.

"Don't mind if I do," she says, plucking a few pieces from the dish. She unwraps one and pops it in her mouth. "I just love this brand."

"It's good, isn't it?" Nancy agrees. "Owen?"

I wave my hand. "I'll pass, thank you."

It's times like these I wish I could communicate with Emily through telepathy.

Red alert! Nancy's the bad guy.

But Emily's happily chewing the gum, chatting away about the maple flavor and wondering if it's locally sourced.

"Does this arrangement sound like something you would be amenable to?" Nancy asks.

"Hypothetically speaking," Emily says slowly, "These meatier stories you're talking about... if someone felt undervalued and underpaid compared to their male coworkers... I could understand if they wanted to send a message to management about addressing pay equity."

"Perhaps we could work together to expose certain... deficiencies around here, yes," Nancy says carefully. "I may know some secrets."

Emily leans forward eagerly. "And hypothetically, if someone had taken the trophy to make a statement, it would have been for the greater good. To fight for equality."

I brace myself, ready to shield Emily if things escalate. But Nancy simply arches one perfectly groomed eyebrow. "I'm not entirely sure I follow your meaning."

"That was an interesting speech you made at the press conference yesterday about each staff member being worth their weight in gold." Emily says, casually leaning back in her chair. "All I'm saying is that if a certain female executive in this room felt undervalued, she might do something drastic."

For a long, pregnant pause, Nancy glares at Emily, eyes narrowing into slits. Then, with one smooth motion, ticks her head to the side, gets up, and walks to the door, locking it with an ominous click before returning to her seat.

"That's quite an accusation, Emily," Nancy finally says.

I meet Emily's gaze, feeling the tension rise in Nancy's office. She gives me a subtle nod before addressing Nancy again.

"Do you know I'm the lowest paid Zamboni driver in

the league? In fact, I'm willing to bet the vast majority of women working for this organization are getting seventy cents on the dollar compared to men in the same positions. I don't care if you stole the trophy or not. I want to expose Malcolm Chase and his bro club in my blog, and I'll need your help."

Emily straight up just accused Nancy of stealing the Memorial Cup right to her face. Dang, my girl has guts. I'm just over here trying not to soil my sweats, even as my heart pounds out of my chest.

Nancy's mouth tightens into a thin line.

"We won't say anything," Emily says gently and takes my hand in hers. "Owen's with me on this."

I am? Oh right. I am. "One hundred percent," I say.

"With your insider knowledge, you could be a great source to take down the men ruining this club," Emily goes on. "What do you say? Are you in?"

Nancy stares at Emily pensively before sighing. "It's true. As one of the few women in upper management, I'm extremely underpaid compared to my male colleagues."

I resist a triumphant fist pump. Emily's plan worked - she got Nancy to admit her motive.

"Hypothetically speaking," Nancy goes on, "If one were to steal the trophy as a form of protest, it would be to shed light on the rampant inequality in this organization."

Emily nods along encouragingly. "I'd be happy to

share those secrets anonymously. The public deserves to know the truth."

The two women share a look of understanding.

"Well, you've given me some interesting food for thought," Nancy replies. She stands abruptly, tugging down the hem of her blazer. "Now, if you'll excuse me, I'm late for a meeting. I'll be in touch about—"

An authoritative pounding on the door interrupts her dismissal of us, followed by a forceful rattling of the doorknob.

"Nancy? Open up."

It's Coach Knight, but I hear the murmurs of a few others with him.

Nancy rolls her eyes. "What is it now?"

Coach Knight continues banging on the locked office door.

"Open up, Nancy!" Coach yells, his fist making the door rattle.

I glance at Emily, eyebrows raised. She gives me a subtle nod and quickly pockets her phone. Smart girl must have hit record as soon as Nancy locked the door.

I stand up and stride over to the door, ignoring Nancy's frantic hand gestures telling me not to open it. I turn the lock and pull it open.

Coach Knight immediately bursts in, face redder than a stop sign, with a small army of cops on his heels.

"What's going on here?" Nancy demands.

"I'll tell you what's going on," Coach growls. "You set

up my equipment manager to take the fall for your little stunt."

He slaps a piece of paper down on Nancy's pristine desk. "I have a signed statement here from Mark saying you paid him off to confess to stealing the trophy when really it was you all along."

Nancy scoffs. "That's preposterous. Mark is just trying to save his own skin."

Coach Knight shakes his head. "I don't think so. See, Mark has a bit of a gambling problem. Ran up quite a debt he can't pay back. When you offered to clear his debts in exchange for taking the fall as the thief, he agreed. But when I went to visit him today, I convinced him otherwise."

"Mark has no proof of these outrageous allegations." Despite her confident words, her face has gone pale. "It's his word against mine."

"Not quite," Emily pipes up. She holds up her phone. "I just recorded you admitting that you stole the trophy to protest gender inequality at the Titans."

She presses play and Nancy's incriminating words fill the small office.

"As one of the few women in upper management, I'm extremely underpaid compared to my male colleagues... if one were to steal the trophy as a form of protest, it would be to shed light on the rampant inequality in this organization."

You could hear a pin drop in the loaded silence that follows.

Nancy opens and closes her mouth wordlessly before

finally sputtering, "That... that's not admissible. You didn't have my consent to record me!"

Emily just smiles sweetly. "Actually, only one party has to consent to a recording. And that would be me."

"Now just a minute," Nancy sputters. "That was all hypothetical, I never actually confessed to—"

“Ma’am,” One of the cops steps toward her, “It would be wise to stop talking now. Anything you say or do may be used against you in court.”

Nancy sinks down in her plush leather chair, all the fight gone out of her. The officer cuffs her wrists while reading her rights.

Emily winks at me, her eyes dancing with mischief and triumph. I've never been more attracted to this woman. The second we're alone, I'm gonna kiss that smirk right off her face.

"You little minx," I whisper into her ear.

As the officers prepare to take Nancy out of the room, Coach shakes his head at us.

“Why am I not surprised to find you two in the middle of this? I thought I told you I would handle it.”

“You did,” I say. “We were just minding our business when she all but dragged us in here.”

He glares at me. “Really?”

“It’s true,” says Emily. “We were on our way to pick up his brother from school. I must have accidentally hit record on my phone.”

I nod. “Actually, he’ll be out of class soon...”

One of the police officers approaches us with a

notepad in hand. “We’re going to need your statements. Don’t go anywhere.”

Emily frowns.

“Not so fun after all, is it?” Coach gloats. “Now let’s put this unpleasant business behind us and focus on hockey.”

I flop down on the bench outside the police station, exhausted after hours of questioning. Emily plops down next to me, equally drained.

"Well, that was an ordeal," I say. “Why make us come all the way down to the station?”

Emily nods. "No kidding. I'm glad it's over."

I turn to look at her, still in awe. "You are brilliant," I tell her, stroking her chin.

Emily bites her lip, glancing down shyly. "Really?"

"Really," I say earnestly. "Watching you in action was a massive turn-on, not gonna lie."

She snorts. “It doesn’t take much to turn you on.”

“So, wanna get outta here?” I waggle my eyebrows suggestively. “I believe we have some trust falls to practice.”

Emily laughs and smacks my chest. “You’re ridiculous.”

“Ridiculous...ly crazy about you, Kitty Cat.” I lean in slowly. Emily meets me halfway, her lips pressing softly against mine.

Kissing her feels like coming home. Like she's the family I've been searching for my whole life.

Before we get carried away outside of a police station, I end the kiss by giving her a sweet peck on her nose. "You do realize this gives you a juicy story for your blog now, right?"

Emily's eyes light up. "Oh my gosh, you're so right! This is gonna be epic." She whips out her phone, fingers flying as she starts taking notes, completely in the zone.

Just then, Coach Knight exits the station and spots us on the bench. He ambles over, hands on his hips.

"Well, we got Mark his job back on the condition he attend Gambler's Anonymous meetings and get on a debt repayment plan with help from the club. So I suppose some good has come out of this mess after all."

I nod, relieved to hear Mark won't face any criminal charges.

"As for you two," Coach says gruffly, "it seems I can't turn my back for two seconds without you stirring up trouble. But... I suppose things worked out in the end this time."

Emily and I exchange a grin. Coming from Coach, that's high praise.

"Now, if you'll excuse me, I have a team to whip into shape for our game on Friday. I expect you bright and early for practice, Jablonski."

He gives us one last stern look before lumbering off towards his car. Emily turns to me, eyes dancing with excitement.

"So, I guess it's too late to go to the Science Center?"

I smile and wrap an arm around her shoulders, pulling her close. "I think Cyrus probably took the bus home by now. But I can call Shannon and ask her if it's okay to pick him up there."

"Look at you. Asking permission."

"I'm trying to be a better man."

For her. Because of her.

"But first, let's eat. I'm starving after all that drama. What do you say we grab a bite at St. Lawrence Market?"

Emily nods eagerly. "I'd love that."

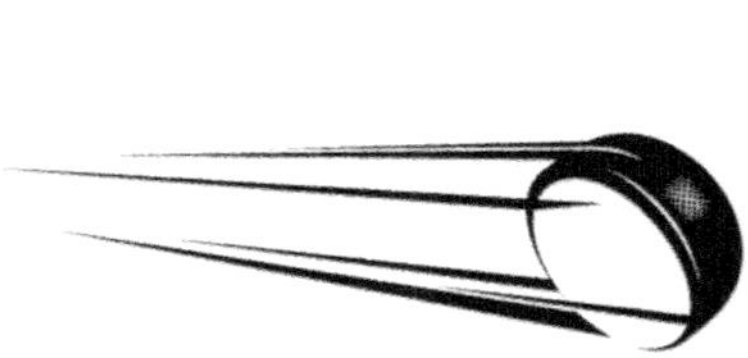

"Hockey is the only job I know
where you get paid to have a nap
on the day of the game."
- Chico Resch

MPONI

CHAPTER TWENTY-FOUR

Owen

Emily dances around my kitchen wearing one of my old Titans jerseys, the oversized fabric swallowing her petite frame. The hem skims the tops of her toned thighs, and I find myself wishing it would ride up just a little more to reveal those cut-off jean shorts I know are hidden underneath. She bops along to the pop song playing from her phone, using a spatula as a microphone while she flips the grilled cheese sandwiches in the pan. I will never tire of this.

Seeing her happy and relaxed in my home, it does something to me. It just feels right having her here, even if she refuses to move in. I know better than to push. For now, I'm content with our current arrangement—her days spent here cooking up a storm in my gourmet kitchen while I sleep on her lumpy couch at night, keeping guard like a faithful watchdog.

Emily loves having full access to my big kitchen and quality cookware to experiment with new recipes. She says it helps spark her creativity or something artsy like that. And I'm certainly not complaining about the amazing meals I get out of this little arrangement. Once I finally convince her to let me buy us a house in a better neighborhood, I'm going to marry this woman. I know asking now will spook her, though, so I'm biding my time. I can be a patient man when I want to.

As she plates up the sandwiches, Emily catches me staring and grins. "You know, you could help instead of just standing there looking pretty," she teases.

I shake my head, moving into the kitchen to wrap my arms around her from behind. "Nah, I like the view too much." I nuzzle into her neck, placing a kiss below her ear.

She swats me away with the spatula, but I can see a faint blush on her cheeks. "Behave yourself and grab the chips."

"Yes, dear," I say in my most polite voice, dodging another swat as I grab the bag of chips.

We settle in at the kitchen island, Emily perched on one of the stools while I stand and lean against the counter. The grilled cheese is perfection, gooey and buttery, with crispy fried cheese on the edges... just how I like it.

“What are you going to do during my hour with Gwyn?” I ask around a mouthful of crunchy sandwich.

Gwyn is the team resident therapist. After about a thousand denials that I suffer from anxiety, Emily gently coaxed me into trying it. She went to my first session with me. But now, Gwyn prefers it if I go alone. Usually Emily shops at Borders Books while she waits.

“Actually,” she says hesitantly. “I’m going to visit Nancy at the jail today to talk about the whole Malcolm Chase issue.”

I pause with my sandwich halfway to my mouth, frowning. Nancy may have had good intentions with the trophy theft, but I don't fully trust her.

"Em, is that really necessary?" I ask. "She committed a crime, after all."

"I know, but she was fighting for a good cause," Emily argues. "The women staff at the arena do deserve equal pay. Nancy just... went about it the wrong way. I still think it's important to show her some support."

I'm about to suggest that visiting a felon in jail is a ludicrous idea when there's a sharp knock at the front door.

Emily's head perks up.

"Are you expecting someone?" she asks.

I shake my head. "No, not that I can think of."

The knock sounds again, more insistent this time. I get up from the kitchen table and head over to the front door, peering out the peephole. I'm surprised to see Shannon standing there on my front step, an impatient look on her face. What is she doing here? She's been to my house exactly once in the past five years, and that was to return the new iPhone I'd bought for his fifth birthday. I suppose it was an extravagant gift for a five-year-old. She still won't let me get him one. I have to wait until he's sixteen, apparently.

I take a deep breath before opening the door. Shannon's standing there, an unimpressed look on her face as she holds up an official letter bearing the crest of Bayview Heights Academy.

"Care to explain this?" she asks sharply, shaking the letter.

"Oops." I make a face, paired with an exaggerated shrug. "Surprise?"

"You went behind my back, Owen."

"You *what*?" Emily's bare feet pad on the hardwood floor behind me. "You said you weren't going to do that anymore."

Lovely. I have two women mad at me now.

"In my defense, this was set in motion before I said that. So technically—"

Emily lands her angry feet right next to me, looking

every bit the snack I wanted for lunch before she started grating the cheese.

"I'm sorry," Shannon says, eyes scanning Emily's bare legs. "I didn't know you had company."

I realize it probably looks like my lady friend isn't wearing any pants. Maybe that will convince Shannon to leave.

I hook a thumb over my shoulder. "This is Emily."

"Hi!" Emily waves.

"Oh you're Emily? The Zamboni driver? Cyrus doesn't stop talking about you."

"He's an amazing kid," Emily says.

"I think so," Shannon agrees. "Then again, I'm biased."

"I love your earrings."

Shannon's hand flies to her ears. "Thanks. Cyrus used his allowance money at the school holiday fair so he could give me a Christmas gift. I made sure the tooth fairy left extra cash the next time she visited."

"They're gorgeous. Cyrus had great taste."

Shannon walks right by me to shake Emily's hand, telling her how Cyrus likes to draw pictures of himself riding a Zamboni. The girls continue to chat as I close the door, mumbling under my breath, "Um, okay. Come in I guess?"

"Would you like something to eat?" Emily offers. "I make a mean grilled cheese. White English cheddar and brie."

“Thanks, but I just ate. I only came to chew this guy out.”

Emily waves her hand in my direction. “Chew away.”

Shannon turns to me, holding up the envelope. "Apparently, Cyrus has been accepted into a school I knew nothing about. A very expensive school. Then I turn the page and what do I find? His tuition and fees for the next three years have already been paid in full by an anonymous benefactor. You wouldn't happen to know anything about that, would you, Owen?"

I rub the back of my neck, avoiding her accusatory gaze. "I may have pulled some strings to get him a spot..." I admit. "And taken care of the finances. But Shannon, it's a great opportunity for him! That school has so many advantages - small classes, excellent facilities, top-notch teachers. Cyrus will thrive there."

Shannon sighs, her posture drooping slightly. "I appreciate you looking out for him, Owen. But you should have talked to me first before going behind my back like this."

“She’s right, you know,” Emily chirps.

“Thank you, my wonderfully supportive buttercup.” I say through my teeth.

She shrugs one shoulder adorably.

"Listen, Shannon. You're absolutely right, I'm sorry," I say earnestly. "But please, put aside your pride on this one. Let Cyrus go to this school. He already made friends that go there. Titans kids he met at the game.”

I see her expression soften just a fraction. As much as she wants to resist, even Shannon can't deny what an amazing chance this is for Cyrus.

Finally, she sighs, shaking her head. "Alright. I'll allow Cyrus to attend on one condition—I pay half of the tuition."

I start to protest, but she silences me with a look. "Those are my terms. Take them or leave them."

“But... it’s already paid for.”

“Then I’ll pay you back.”

“Quit while you’re ahead, big guy,” Emily warns.

“Okay,” I concede. “You can pay me back.”

And I’ll set aside that money for his college education. Maybe put it in stocks so it will grow. I’m a genius.

Before I know it, Emily is packing Shannon a tupperware full of the chocolate chip cookies she made yesterday. And I mean that plastic container is filled to bursting. I know I’m not supposed to have sweets, but I get a little possessive about the treats Emily bakes for me. When I look in the cookie jar, there are only two left.

I’m pretty much invisible as the ladies chatter about things I don’t understand. Emily gives Shannon a paper bag for her goodies. Not only the cookies. The last of the pasta salad I love so much with feta and artichoke hearts, the buttermilk biscuits she made from scratch, and a bottle of my best wine.

As Shannon heads out, I see her and Emily exchanging phone numbers.

"We should get coffee sometime," Emily says

brightly. "We can do that buddy-read. And hey, if you ever need a break, I'm happy to babysit."

Shannon smiles warmly. "I'd like that. Thank you, Emily."

"Wait, what?" I cry. You just met and already you're BFFs? I'm Cyrus' flesh and blood and I have to bend over backwards to have him for an afternoon!"

They ignore my rant and hug, and I have to admit, it makes me happy to see them bonding. Shannon has always been so guarded, keeping people at arm's length. But Emily's natural warmth seems to have broken through some of those walls.

After Shannon leaves, Emily turns to me with a pleased smile. "So... that was unexpected."

I wrap my arms around her waist, drawing her in close. "*You're* unexpected."

I kiss her neck, working my fingers down the jersey and slip them under the hem. I lift it up so her denim shorts are exposed. She moans, tilting her head to the side to give me better access. I run my lips down to her collarbone, nibbling at the skin along her shoulder where the jersey hangs low. My hand reaches around to her backside. I feel for the soft edge of the fabric where it meets her skin and... give her a smart swat.

"Ouch!"

"You love it."

"Maybe... But what was that for?"

Pressing soothing circles on the tender spot, I say. "My cookies. My pasta salad. My homemade biscuits..."

"I thought Cyrus would like them. I can always make you more."

"Promise?"

She smiles as I press my mouth on hers, my lips grazing against her teeth. "I'll get back to you on that."

Reluctantly, I pull away, but only because my stomach is growling.

"Let's eat before we're late. I want you to wait for me at Borders, then I'll go with you to the jail. Okay?"

"To protect me?" She gives me an exaggerated eye roll.

"No," I say gently. "To support you. I know you can protect yourself."

She blinks, surprised and gratified. "Thank you. That means a lot. But I'm afraid waiting for you to visit Nancy will run into my other appointment."

"Other appointment?" My mind races. What kind of appointment? The doctor? Is she sick? Or... Do women, by chance, visit the doctor when they're ready to start having babies? No. Don't be ridiculous. That's just wishful thinking.

Emily smiles shyly, like she's got a little secret, but is too embarrassed to say. "Well, I was going to wait to tell you just in case things fell through..."

I hold my breath. She wants babies. I know it.

"But... I'm going to see my old coach this afternoon."

What? Her coach?

I try to keep my face neutral. "Oh?"

"We're going to discuss if I'm too old to compete in

the singles program. I never stopped training on my own, so I'm not out of shape but..." She looks to the floor.

I cup her chin and lift her head. "Look at me, Kitten. You're twenty-four. That's not old."

"Olympic skaters are teenagers. I'm ancient by comparison. I dunno. There's always curling."

Her eyes well up, but I press my lips on each of her cheeks to catch the tears. "Your coach wouldn't want to see you if he didn't think you had a chance. Let's just see how your meeting goes today. That's all you have to do right now."

"Thank you."

"And if it comes down to it, I know you'd be the best curling champion there ever was. Also the sexiest."

She gives me a sarcastic stare. "Okay, what do you want?"

"What? Nothing!"

"You call me sexy when you want something. Is it the biscuits?"

I pause, putting on my thinking face. "Are biscuits a euphemism for something else? If so, then yes."

"Dork." She shakes her head and marches briskly back to the kitchen, but my hand catches hers and I spin her back around, dipping her body halfway to the floor. Yeah, I've been watching figure skating videos. Sue me.

"Only because I love you," I say cheekily and plant a kiss squarely on the lips.

She stiffens, then blinks at me, open-mouthed.

"What did you just say?"

Oops. I just spooked her. Backtrack!

I smirk crookedly, then lower her to the floor, leaving her stunned as I stand over her body. She lifts herself to her elbows, and for a moment, I think I should just postpone my appointment with Gywn and have a little therapy at home with Emily. But I am a dork. She's right about that. So I step over her, ready to walk away. I take one step, then her legs sweep under me, tripping me from behind. My ass hits the floor, and then she's on top of me, poking me in the ribs.

"Say it again."

"No."

She yanks my shirt up, exposing my chest.

"If you think this is torture, think aga— OW!"

Her fingers pinch each of my nipples and then she twists!

"Say. It. Again."

"Your biscuits are sexy."

She twists harder. "Say it."

"Okay! I love you."

I'm breathing hard by now, partly because of the nipple pain, partly because she just takes my breath away.

She lets go, even though her body still pins me down. And I say it again, this time in a soft, reverent whisper. "I love you."

The most radiant smile breaks across her features as

she looks down at me. Her golden hair dangling, framing her face like a curtain.

"You are the most infuriating human being on the planet, you know that? You're over-confident, opinionated, hot-headed, overprotective..."

"Well, you, *lady*, are impulsive, brassy, unpredictable... and the most maddeningly stubborn woman I've ever known." I stroke my thumb over her cheek. "You're also strong and smart. And I love you."

It's as simple as that. I don't know how to say it more plainly.

She tosses her head back and laughs. "Why? Why do you do that?"

"Do what?" I trace my fingers in circles over her knees. "Love you?"

"Make me fall deeply in love with you."

Something like a supernova explodes in my chest. It's wild and crazy and achingly beautiful. Just like Emily. Unexpected, surprising, astonishingly wonderful. More than I ever hoped for but just what I needed. And I will spend the rest of my life striving to deserve her. But that doesn't mean I'll let her win every time.

I drag the palms of my hands along her waist, grab hold, and flip her onto her back, pinning her to the floor.

"Because, Kitten," I growl. "Like attracts like. Love attracts love. And however much it feels like a blindside hit, we were always meant to collide. You are the other half of me."

Her eyes grow soft and she smiles up at me tenderly.

It's such a beautiful sight; the rise and fall of her chest, her arms bent over her head, her hair spread out on the floor. I lean down and kiss her and she breathes in, then out, full and sated.

"So... pairs?" she hums.

"Yes," I repeat, kissing her once more. "Pairs."

THE END

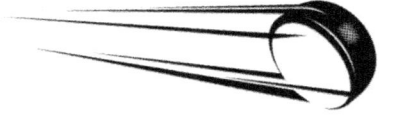

"If at first, you don't succeed,
you get back up, and you try ...
and you try ... and you try it again ...
except ice skating,
I hate this crap, I quit!"
– Little Richard

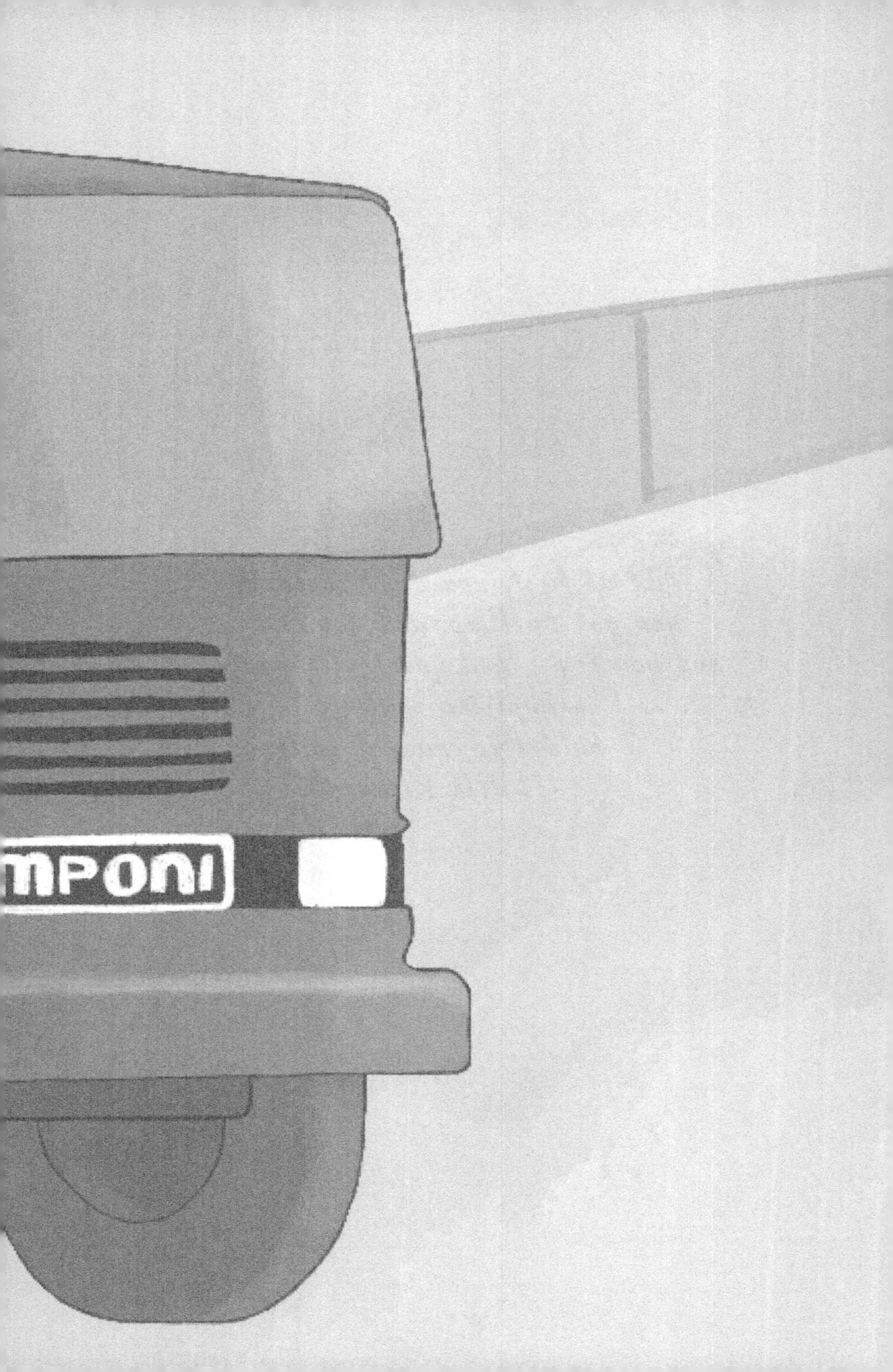
MPONI

CHAPTER EPILOGUE

Emily

"Alright, ladies! Who's ready to get splatted?" Maggie shouts, pumping her paintball gun into the air.

That crazy nut has really gone all out for my bachelorette party.

There are strategically placed barriers and trenches at the outdoor paintball place she rented out, creating an epic battle zone that looks straight out of a war movie.

Bunkers and barricades are scattered throughout the place, providing the perfect spots for ambushes and sneak attacks. A thick layer of vibrant, splattered paint already coats portions of the ground.

"Emily! Over here!" Shannon calls out, waving me over behind a barricade. I scurry over, dodging a few stray pellets on the way.

"Having fun?" I ask with a grin as Leigh Tate loads up her gun next to us.

"Are you kidding? This is the most excitement I've had in years!"

Leigh chuckles, “So you don’t feel guilty we didn’t bring the boys?”

Leigh and Shannon have become close friends ever since Cyrus started play dates with Leigh’s son, Aiden. The boys go to school together along with Titans defenseman Paul Nagel’s son. The three boys are insepa-rable, and are currently having a pool party at Paul’s house while us ladies pummel each other with paint balls.

“Heck, no!” Shannon replies.

Leigh high-fives her. “Amen sister. I’m usually the one setting up pizza and cake while they have all the fun.”

A big glob of teal paint splats near us.

I look over to see Maggie doing her best Rambo

impression, screaming at the top of her lungs, "I'm comin' for ya, suckaaas!"

Where did all this aggression come from? Oh yeah. It's just Maggie being wild as usual.

"I'm on your team!" I cry from across the way. "Don't shoot."

"Why are you over there conspiring with the enemy, then?"

I yell back. "We're just talking."

"This is no time to talk, soldier."

I'm starting to think Maggie's taking this a little too seriously.

Suddenly, the gate from the armor room bursts open. In stride a group of rowdy hockey players, led by none other than Sawyer and Hendrix, all of them geared up with paint guns poised and ready. I spot Owen immediately, looking as handsome as ever, despite his mischievous smirk.

"What are you guys doing here?" I demand, trying and failing to hide my amusement.

"Crashing the party, obviously!" Sawyer hollers back. "You didn't think we'd let you ladies have all the fun, did you?"

Griffin, usually the level-headed one of the guys, lets out a battle cry and runs past his buddies, shooting paint everywhere. I honestly don't think he even cares about teams. He's shooting everyone.

With that, chaos erupts. Bright splatters of paint start flying in every direction. I duck behind the barrier, laughing uncontrollably as Maggie gets nailed square in the chest by a vibrant red splatter from Sawyer's paint grenade. She lets out a dramatic gasp, clutching at her heart like she's been mortally wounded.

"You'll pay for that, playboy!" Maggie hollers, her eyes sparkling with mischief. She scoops up a handful of neon green goop and flings it back at him with impressive aim.

This is going to be an all-out war zone, paint splattering every surface. For a few wild moments, we're all kids again, carefree and living in the moment without a care in the world.

"Quick, we need a plan of attack!" Shannon urges Leigh, eyes alight with competitive fire. I meet Owen's gaze from across the room, his beautiful blue eyes locking onto mine with an intensity that makes my breath catch in my throat. A roguish grin tugs at the corners of his mouth as he winks, the simple gesture sending a flutter through my chest. For a fleeting moment, the rest of the world fades away, and it's just the two of us, just like in the movies.

The paintball battle rages on around us and it might as well be in slow motion. How can I even pay attention with Owen's gaze burning into me like that? He arches an eyebrow at me, a silent invitation. Before I can overthink it, I'm on my feet, dodging a few stray paint pellets as I make my way over to him.

"Come here often?" Owen murmurs as I approach, his voice low and sexy.

"Only when I'm about to get married," I quip back. "Aren't you afraid of ruining that pretty face?"

He lets out a low chuckle that sends a shiver down my spine. "You're worth it."

Before I can respond, Owen's hand finds my wrist, giving a gentle tug as he leads me away from the chaos. My breath catches in my throat as we duck around a corner, suddenly shielded from view behind a barricade. He crowds me back against the wall, that roguish grin of his sending my heart into a frenzy.

"I missed you, Kitten," he growls in my ear.

"Since this morning?"

Owen leans in, his lips brushing the sensitive skin just below my ear. I shiver, every nerve ending feeling electrified by his touch. His breath is warm against my neck, sending delicious tingles racing along my skin.

My pulse quickens as Owen's nose grazes my cheek, his lips hovering tantalizingly close to mine. I can feel the heat radiating from his body, the solid strength of him pinning me against the wall. Slowly, torturously, Owen pulls back just enough to meet my gaze. His eyes are the darkest blue now, smoldering with an intensity that steals my breath away. After a year and a half with him, he still has the same effect on me.

My heart pounds against my ribs as I drink in the rugged angles of Owen's face, the sensual curve of his lips. I can almost taste the intoxicating blend of his cologne and the faint pine scent that is uniquely him.

His fingers tangle in my hair, cradling the back of my head as he devours my mouth.

"You're intoxicating," he murmurs against my lips, his voice low and gravelly with desire. I pull him flush against me, kissing him back, getting lost in everything Owen.

He pulls back slightly, his eyes dark and smoldering as they roam over my features. A roguish grin tugs at the corners of his mouth. "I can't wait any longer. Let's just say our vows right here, right now."

I laugh at his playful impatience, even as I'm tempted to find a preacher to do the job right here, right now.

"I think we can hold out seven more days." I wind my arms around his neck, playing with the soft hair at his nape. "Then you can have me all to yourself, and we don't even have to go out for a whole month if you want."

The impish gleam in Owen's eyes tells me he likes the sound of that idea very much. He leans in, capturing my lips in another hot kiss that has my toes curling in my shoes. I melt against him, lost in the dizzying sensation of his solid warmth surrounding me.

Suddenly, a bright splatter of neon pink explodes against the wall beside us. We break apart with twin gasps of surprise, only to find ourselves surrounded by a ring of our friends—each brandishing their paintball guns at us and wearing matching mischievous grins.

"Attack!" Maggie crows, her gun aimed squarely at us.

Before I can react, a volley of vibrant splatters rains down around us. I shriek with surprised laughter as streaks of red, blue and purple explode across my shirt and face. Owen lets out a playful growl, immediately shifting to shield me with his larger frame.

"They've gone rogue!" he hollers over the chaos, raining a hellfire of paint bullets aimlessly at our friends. We're back-to-back, shooting like gangbusters as everyone starts to scatter. Brilliant blue splatters coat the ground around Sawyer and Hendrix as they duck for cover.

I cling to Owen's back, peering over his shoulder to take aim at Shannon. A well-aimed shot nails her on the back with a neon yellow splatter. She lets out a dramatic groan, falling onto the ground in an overly theatrical display.

The battlefield erupts into absolute chaos. Nobody seems to care about teams or rules anymore—it's an all-out war. Paint splatters fly in every direction as the guys let out raucous battle cries.

"Every man for himself!" Sawyer hollers, ducking behind a barrier before popping back up to rapid fire a round of red pellets at Griffin.

I duck instinctively as a streak of pink whizzes past my head. Owen's arm encircles my waist, pulling me flush against his solid warmth as he shields me from the onslaught.

Sawyer lets out a mischievous whoop before breaking away from his bunker, sprinting full force towards Maggie with his gun raised. She doesn't even have time to react before he launches himself at her, tackling her to the ground in a tangle of flailing limbs.

For a split second, he just looks at her. Then the moment passes. Sawyer blinks rapidly, rolling off of Maggie as a grin stretches across his face. He aims his paint gun and splatters a vibrant red streak across Maggie's shirt with a triumphant crow.

It's absolute pandemonium. The guys are shouting and hollering, dodging paint pellets as they careen around the arena like a bunch of overgrown kids.

No one seems to be working as teams anymore. Well, except for Owen and me. He pulls me behind the safety of a nearby bunker, his eyes gleaming.

"Hey future Mrs. Jablonski. Wanna get outta here and recreate that chapter in your favorite book?"

"*That* chapter?"

He glances down at my paint-covered body. "You know the one."

"Won't they miss us?"

"Miss us? We could be halfway to Niagara before they realize we're gone."

"Why aren't you at your bachelor party, anyway?"

"Don't change the subject. Come on. I'll take you out to Shawarma on the way home."

"Shawarma? You could have led with that."

"I thought I'd pull out the heavy artillery last."

"Hmmm. When you put it that way."

"So, is that a yes?" His fingers brush away a floppy strand of hair from my face.

"Just promise me one thing," I say.

"What's that?"

"You'll never stop looking at me the way you're looking at me right now." I reach up to touch his face, loving the scratchy texture of his beard. He leans into my touch, pressing my palm into his cheek with his big, strong hand. Then his lips find my fingers, kissing them tenderly.

"That would be impossible, Kitten," he says. "This is the only way I know how to look at you."

I immediately drop my paint gun, which falls with a clank to the ground, and plant a big, fat kiss on his face. He swoops me up into his arms, gathering me close to his chest, and carries me to safety like he's some war hero. Meanwhile, the raging battle continues in full force behind his back.

I never thought I needed anyone to protect me. Turns out I do, and there's no one but Owen who could possibly fit in those skates.

WANT MORE?

I hope you enjoyed reading **Head Over Skates**. I had a blast spending time in the hockey world with Owen and Emily. Now I have a surprise for you... Scan the **QR** code to get access to **Head Over Skates Bonus Stuff**, including an exclusive scene I wrote for my newsletter subscribers, and a delicious art print you'll drool over.

Start Reading

If you loved what you read and want all the laughs, banter, and sizzling kisses, visit gigiblume.com for more titles to binge.

TITLES BY GIGI BLUME

BACKSTAGE ROMANCE SERIES

Confessions of a Hollywood Matchmaker

Love and Loathing

Secrets of a Hollywood Matchmaker

Driving Miss Darcy

The Friend Act

Backstage Romance Box Set

PRECIO BROTHERS SERIES

Messy Love

The Hate Zone

Nacho Boyfriend

Just Amigos

STANDALONES

Bewitching the Ghost

Head Over Skates

ACKNOWLEDGMENTS

I couldn't have gotten past the first chapter without help and encouragement from the following boss ladies:

Carina Taylor
I can always count on you to keep me feeling sane even though I'm clearly not. 🩶 YOU!
Kristyn Fortner
I'd be lost without you. Thanks for making sense of my chaos, and for being my best cheerleader.
Ellie Hall
How am I so lucky to have a writing buddy 100% smarter than me? Don't tell the others.
Savannah Scott
For the gentle advice all the times I message you with my hair on fire. Thanks for holding the bucket of water.

Thank you, ladies, for being my support system. LOVE XOXO

GET TO KNOW GIGI

Gigi is a USA TODAY bestselling author and hopeless musical theatre nerd who has perfected the art of lolly-gagging.

Former professional wedding singer, Gigi lives in Southern California with her personal chef (AKA husband) and two weird and awesome teenagers who take after her more than she's comfortable with. Quoting movies and pop culture with her kids is one of her favorite pastimes. A Hufflepuff and die-hard Whovian, she's convinced magic is really a thing, still believes in Santa Claus, and finds miracles everywhere.

When Gigi's not writing about swoony book boyfriends and the women that bring them to their knees, she likes to belt out showtunes, embarrass her kids, and get distracted by her dogs.

instagram.com/gigiblume

Printed in Great Britain
by Amazon

44542616R00212